Death in High Provence

George Bellairs (1902–1982). He was, by day, a Manchester bank manager with close connections to the University of Manchester. He is often referred to as the English Simenon, as his detective stories combine wicked crimes and classic police procedurals, set in quaint villages.

He was born in Lancashire and married Gladys Mabel Roberts in 1930. He was a devoted Francophile and travelled there frequently, writing for English newspapers and magazines and weaving French towns into his fiction.

Bellairs' first mystery, *Littlejohn on Leave* (1941) introduced his series detective, Detective Inspector Thomas Littlejohn. Full of scandal and intrigue, the series peeks inside small towns in the mid twentieth century and Littlejohn is injected with humour, intelligence and compassion.

He died on the Isle of Man in April 1982 just before his eightieth birthday.

ALSO BY GEORGE BELLAIRS

The Case of the Famished Parson
The Case of the Demented Spiv
Corpses in Enderby
Death in High Provence
Death Sends for the Doctor
Murder Makes Mistakes
Bones in the Wilderness
Toll the Bell for Murder
Death in the Fearful Night
Death in the Wasteland
Death of a Shadow
Intruder in the Dark
Death in Desolation
The Night They Killed Joss Varran

Death in High Provence

An Inspector Littlejohn Mystery

George Bellairs

ipso books

This edition published in 2016 by Ipso Books

First published in 1957 in Great Britain by John Gifford Ltd. and in the Unites States, by Penguin (1963).

Ipso Books is a division of Peters Fraser + Dunlop Ltd

Drury House, 34–43 Russell Street, London WC2B 5HA

To

Fred and Lottie Faragher

Contents

Chapter One
Visit From a V.I.P.

As was his custom on arriving outside his flat in Hampstead, Littlejohn knocked out his pipe against the street-lamp by the door. It was a mild evening in early summer, and he paused to sniff the fresh air of the Heath, which smelled good after the petrol-laden atmosphere of London itself. He was a bit late home and the church clock at the end of the road struck seven as he started to climb the stairs to the first floor.

He knew right away that something unusual was going on in the flat. Meg, his bobtail sheep-dog, which usually greeted him joyfully in the vestibule, began to bark apologetically from the kitchen at the sound of his steps, which meant there was somebody there who found her *de trop*.

As he took his key from his pocket, the door opened and his wife met him. Instead of the usual cheerful smile, she gave him a grave, almost comic look which signified that callers had interrupted their evening meal.

"There's a V.I.P. here...."

She even forgot to ask the usual question about what he'd had for lunch.

Inside the dining-room a man was standing examining the Toulouse-Lautrec which hung over the fireplace and which Littlejohn's friends of the Paris Police Judiciaire had given him as a memento of their war-time association. He turned to face the Chief Inspector as he entered.

A tall, athletic man, with a strong nose and chin, heavy determined lips, dark pouched eyes, and a fine head of dark brown hair. He was apparently in his mid-fifties. He wore a loose-fitting suit of fine grey worsted with elegance and, as he turned to greet Littlejohn, he removed the black horn spectacles and gave him the half-haughty, half-surprised look which the caricaturists captured almost every day. It was Spencer Lovell, the Minister of Commerce.

The dog barked again, and Littlejohn understood why. Lovell, a bachelor, owned half-a-dozen cats and had written a book about them. He had openly confessed his contempt for dogs.

"I'm sorry to disturb you so late and in your leisure, Littlejohn."

"That's all right, sir. Sit down, please."

Mrs. Littlejohn entered with the sherry. She wore her hat and coat.

"Don't let me drive you out, Mrs. Littlejohn."

"You're not doing, Mr. Lovell. I've a call to make."

Littlejohn gave his wife a grateful look, rose, and let in the dog. He had, in the past, visited the Minister in his own flat in connection with a burglary, and had emerged covered in cat hairs. Lovell's cats hadn't been locked up on that occasion! Meg entered, altogether ignored the V.I.P., and, after greeting her master with a friendly butt in the knees, stretched quietly by his side and started to snore.

Lovell lolled in his chair, sipping his sherry.

"Cigarette, sir?"

"I prefer my pipe, if I may."

They both started to smoke.

"You're a bit surprised to see me here?"

They smiled at one another. They were the same build and about the same age, and they got on comfortably together.

"Listen, Littlejohn. No use beating about the bush. We've only met casually before, and all I know of you is through the newspapers and from what I hear of you."

"The same applies to me, sir."

The Minister raised his eyebrows in surprise for a minute and then smiled.

"We understand one another, then. I want your help, and I couldn't very well ask you over to the Ministry. All the world knows what goes on there, and this is personal and private. Your wife was good enough to telephone Scotland Yard to enquire about you and they said you'd left. So I waited."

He puffed his pipe and turned his head to see how Littlejohn was taking it.

"I've not put in an official request about you. The Commissioner, however, knows I'm calling and what it's about. But you are quite free to say yes or no after I've told you my story."

Littlejohn refilled the glasses.

"Your very good health."

"And yours, sir."

"It's very difficult to begin."

Littlejohn felt a bit surprised. Lovell's reputation as a parliamentarian and politician was high and he had a name for quick thinking. A former barrister in the Northern Circuit, he had been born within twenty miles of Littlejohn's native town, and had risen rapidly after his election to parliament.

"Did you ever hear of my brother, Christopher?"

Who hadn't? The death of Christopher Lovell and his wife in a motor accident during holidays in the south of

France had been one of the sensations of the year. It had happened in February and had cut short a distinguished career in the Foreign Office.

"Yes. I read about his untimely death in the newspapers."

Lovell nodded his head.

"That's why I've called to see you. I'm not satisfied about the way my brother and his wife died."

There was a pause and complete silence, punctuated by the snores of the dog. Lovell's eyes were fixed on the picture over the fireplace, as though he'd forgotten what he'd been talking about.

"You think there was foul play, sir?"

"I don't know. I just don't know. Did you follow the affair in the papers?"

"Superficially, that's all."

Lovell rose and paced the rug uneasily.

"I'm so afraid of starting a mare's nest, Littlejohn. It might be that Chris and his wife just met their deaths through speeding along dangerous roads. In such an event, it would only be wasting your good time asking you to look into it. I can only, therefore, leave the decision to you. He was my only brother and we were very close. There were only three years between us in ages and I was the elder."

He paused, obviously trying to keep sentiment out of it and seeking words to express his thoughts reasonably.

"Candidly, I don't like it at all. The accident occurred at St. Marcellin.... The Commissioner tells me you know Provence."

"I was there with a friend, an Inspector in the Sûreté at Nice, studying the Dominici affair last autumn."

"Ah.... Then you may know the place. It's a village between Aix-en-Provence and Manosque, just off the main road, near the southern tip of the Forest of Cadarache. The nearest town, Manosque, is twenty miles away. Know it?"

"Not exactly, but I visited the neighbourhood. We spent a night in Manosque."

Already Littlejohn felt a vague sense of uneasiness. He and his colleague, Dorange, of Nice, had made their unofficial tour of those parts, and they were decidedly grim. The natives, a secret and clannish lot, had proved most unhelpful. How another unofficial enquiry, this time on his own, would fare, he'd no idea, but he could guess.

"I see you're already vaguely aware of what you're up against, Littlejohn. I've tried it myself, without success."

"You've been there already, sir?"

"To bring home my brother's and his wife's bodies. In the brief time at my disposal I tried to get precise details of how it occurred. Nobody seemed to know. It was like beating my head against a stone wall. You have methods of your own, and a professional knows what to look for and how to do it. I'm no good as an amateur detective."

Littlejohn could well understand it. He still remembered the hard eyes, the secret exchange of queer looks between one man and another, the dreadful feeling of being an utter stranger among strange folk.... He caressed the soft ears of his dog and thought it nice to be home among his own people, people he understood.

"Why do you think there was foul play?"

The Minister sat down again and stretched his legs and re-lit his pipe.

"The place, to begin with. Chris used to visit the identical village before the war. He began his career in the army and was a military attaché at the British Embassy in Paris. Whilst there, he made a bosom friend of the Marquis de St. Marcellin, and spent a lot of time at his château. St.

Marcellin was in the French army and they'd much in common. Whilst staying with him one time at the château, Chris met Elise de Barge, who later became his wife."

"And the Marquis is still at St. Marcellin?"

"No. He died just before the war. A shooting accident. Chris was there at the time and it upset him frightfully. So much so, that he never went again. He and Elise were married in Paris, he came home shortly afterwards, the war broke out, and that ended Chris's relations with the St. Marcellin family. Then, they both met their death in the very village.... I don't know what they were doing there or why they went."

"Do the family still occupy the château?"

"Arnaud de St. Marcellin succeeded his brother, Bernard, after the accident. I met Arnaud when I was there. A very decent chap and frightfully cut-up about it all. He couldn't help."

Lovell was on his feet again, pacing the room nervously.

"There was a proper official enquiry into Chris's accident and it was found to be due to a skid on a greasy road. The police were quite satisfied. The car hit a tree at high speed. There were no witnesses, but all the experts concurred. They seemed quite surprised that I should continue asking questions."

"They would be!"

"I see you know all about those parts and the French officials. It was a complete dead end."

Lovell continued his pacing, smoking a cigarette now, seeking words to express his feelings.

"I'm a lawyer, Littlejohn, and used to evidence. On the face of it, the thing was obvious. A plain, straightforward accident. I ought to accept it as such. All my training says it's logical to do so and reasonable to accept the verdict."

He threw out his arms in almost a gesture of despair.

"I've never believed in the supernatural, or whatever you like to call it. Two and two make four to a lawyer like me. But the thought of Chris won't let me rest. I can't sleep for it. *I want to know.* Did he die with his wife, both of them smashed to pieces in a fast car, or did somebody kill them both?"

He poured himself another glass of sherry and drank it off without even asking Littlejohn or looking for the Chief Inspector's glass.

"What were they doing at St. Marcellin at all, and why, of all places in the world, should they die there?"

"Did your brother's wife come from those parts?"

"No. She came of a family at Cap Ferrat, near Nice, and they still live there. She happened to be a guest of the St. Marcellins at the time Chris met her."

"Do you know anything of her background, sir?"

"I met her people at the time of the accident. Her father is a retired banker and she was their only child. They were at the wedding, too, but never visited England. Very nice people indeed."

"And after Bernard's death and his own marriage to Elise, your brother never visited his old haunts again?"

"No. They went to stay with the de Barges at Cap Ferrat regularly, but they always went by air to Nice until this year. Then they decided to take the car and go through High Provence and return by the Rhône Valley."

Dusk had fallen and the two men in the firelight could hardly see one another. Littlejohn didn't want to put on the lights; the dimness of the room was conducive to conversation.

"Did you go through your brother's papers after his death?"

"Yes."

"You found no hint or reason for their breaking the journey at St. Marcellin?"

"No. Nor did I find any diary or record of his connections with the Marquis in times past."

"It might appear that your brother wished to forget them?"

There was a significant pause.

"What do you mean?"

"Don't you think it strange that your brother, after the death of his friend, Bernard, and his marriage, should suddenly shun St. Marcellin and his friend's family? It looks as if they and the place had become distasteful to him. For example, did his wife break some previous romance when she met your brother?"

There was another silence, as though the Minister had either fallen asleep in the twilight or else had been struck by some truth too dreadful to comment upon. The dog snored softly, now and then crying in joy at her dreams, and the electric clock hummed like a fly exploring the room.

"I never thought of that. And I was never aware that any such thing occurred. They were a happy couple... very happy. And yet..."

Lovell paused as though exploring in the archives of memory for some record, some sign which might give him a clue about his brother's thoughts and habits before he died.

"Come to think of it, something must have happened before he left St. Marcellin for the last time. He was always a bit of a harum-scarum in his youth and rather wild as a young man. His escapades were almost legendary in his days at Cambridge, and even in the army.... I thought when he met and married Elise that he had simply settled down. He was fond of women before he married and his name was coupled with quite a few. Just wild oats... nothing more. He calmed down after he married. But looking back..."

Again a pause, with the hiss of the gas fire and the regular breathing of the dog alone disturbing it.

"Looking back, there did seem to be a kind of sadness in him, as though he'd suddenly become disillusioned. You'd find him thinking about something else as you talked, and he wasn't listening to you at all. And his wife, if she was there, would gently touch the back of his hand and give him a kind of secret smile, as though she knew what held him and wanted him to know she was with him and understood."

The Minister struck a match and held it to his cold pipe, puffing softly, his cheeks moving like a pair of bellows.

"You're a good listener, Littlejohn, and thanks for your patience and for sparing me the time to tell you all about it. It's most unusual for me to grow imaginative or sentimental. I think we'd perhaps better have the light on. This firelight and the half-darkness around make me almost feel that Chris is here listening to us."

Littlejohn switched on the table-lamp at his elbow. The spell was broken. There were the old familiar pieces of furniture, the Toulouse-Lautrec on the wall, the portrait of Letty, his wife, on the mantelpiece, and an unframed snapshot of himself tucked behind the clock. It showed him smiling and walking along the promenade at Cannes, dressed in flannels and an open-necked shirt. A tout had photographed him on his way to see a dead body, and his wife said it was the best and happiest photograph he'd ever had taken.

"So you see what I'm asking of you?"

Littlejohn awoke from his own reveries with a jerk.

"If you'll undertake it, I'd like you to go to St. Marcellin, find out what you can, and try to put my mind at rest. If you return and say you're as much in the dark as I am, I'll let it go at that. We'll at least have tried and my conscience will be easier. If you find it was an accident pure and simple, that will close the affair. If on the other hand ... "

Littlejohn looked up.

"Yes?"

"If it proves not to be an accident, I shall have to see about re-opening the case with the information you provide."

"Haven't you pursued it further through the Foreign Office and the embassy, sir?"

"I have. But what can they do? The French police are fully satisfied. We can't send anybody official to re-open the matter in the face of official reports that it was accidental. I can't just go and say to the Foreign Office, I've got a presentiment that there's something fishy about the whole business. After all, I've my reputation for levelheadedness to maintain. No, this has to be done privately and the Commissioner has gone very far in agreeing to release you for a week or two to look into it for me. As I said, he told me it would all depend on your views. What do you say?"

Littlejohn knocked out his pipe and slowly refilled it.

"I'll be quite candid, sir. I don't look forward to such an investigation with any pleasure at all. I know that part of the South and I don't fancy conducting an enquiry there, especially as it's to be unofficial. In other words, I'm going purely as a civilian holiday-maker and while I'm there I shall have to undertake what amounts to a full-blown case from scratch."

The Minister rose and took up his hat and gloves.

"That's it, Littlejohn. I'm sorry I've taken your time. Your own views are exactly those of the Foreign Secretary and the Commissioner at Scotland Yard. It seems I'll have to let the matter drop and ease my conscience as best I can."

He held out his hand in farewell. Littlejohn ignored it.

"But, sir, the thought that an Englishman and his wife, alone save for each other, in that part of the world, might have been murdered and the matter hushed up, also gives *me* a conscience. You see, last year, I was unofficially involved in the Dominici affair. Nobody will ever know the truth about that. Now, you suspect a repetition. ... I can't let it pass. I've got to go, now."

The Minister's handshake was not of farewell this time, but of emotional thanks.

"I'll not forget this, Littlejohn."

"You must not say that. I'm anxious to get to the truth now, just as much as you are. I'd like to take my colleague, Cromwell, as I don't fancy that neighbourhood on my own. Too overwhelming without good company. But two of us would look too much like policemen. I'd better take my wife, sir."

Half an hour later his wife, returning, found him packing his bag and both their passports were on the table.

Chapter Two
Hôtel Pascal

The Littlejohns arrived at St. Marcellin late in the afternoon.

They had flown from London to Marseilles, and there Littlejohn had rented a hire-and-drive car from the railway offices. It had been raining in London when they left and so it had continued to Lyons. There, quite suddenly, they had run out of clouds into clear southern skies and merciless sunshine.

Summer had been late and uncertain at home; here it was at its height. In Hampstead, the buds of the almond and cherry trees had been struggling to burst into flower; here summer fruit was being sold cheaply before it became overripe and rotten.

They took the route from Marseilles to Aix after lunch, left the sea behind, and passed into the well-cultivated countryside flanked by parched terraces which gently rose to hills covered in pines and oaks. They ran through Aix without stopping, across a stretch of arid uplands to the north, and then they struck the valley of the Durance, with its olive slopes. Beyond, the Alps of Provence rising on the skyline.

The sun was overwhelming and held the countryside in a crushing grip. Littlejohn, as yet unacclimatized, was stunned and suffocated by the sweltering heat. Even with all the windows of the car open and the rush of their speed, it was like driving through a tunnel of hot, stifling air, and the waves of it wrapped around them and made them gasp for breath.

"It's like going through an immense hair-dryer," said Mrs. Littlejohn. They took turns at driving; the white, dazzling road, on which the sun created mirages of shimmering heat, exhausted them.

Now and then they would stop to smoke a cigarette. Littlejohn even neglected his pipe, which tasted foul and strange. He bought cherries, lush and large, from a woman who seemed to be the last inhabitant of a deserted village they passed on the way. In the fields, the corn was ripe and the vines flourishing and promising a good harvest. A few large olive trees struggled for life near the roadside, their twisted roots seeming to explore the hard, caked soil in search of a little water. There was a scent of dry grass in the air and the pines and fir trees gave off a pungent aroma of resin. Brown tiled roofs, rotting and covered in lichen, a tumbledown church tower, and nobody but the peasant woman in sight. Littlejohn spoke to her in French and found she didn't understand what he was saying. Continuing, they passed more prosperous holdings, fresh and green, irrigated by a skillful network of ditches, which, in spite of the drought of summer, still held water.

"I'm almost sorry I took this on," grumbled the Chief Inspector. "We'll need a holiday to recover."

His wife smiled and pushed a cherry in his mouth. She looked fresh and cool in spite of it all and he felt ashamed of his bad temper.

They had driven through Meyrargues and Peyrolles and at the defile of Mirabeau the landscape changed again.

There, the waters of the Verdon, joining the Durance, seemed to bring with them a kinder breeze from the uplands of High Provence, which now came in view. There was a faint scent of lavender and thyme on the air, and the planes, oaks and poplars on the roadside gave them welcome shade. They turned right at a by-road for which they had been watching. A new signpost marked the way. Behind them, *Peyrolles;* ahead, *St. Marcellin, Ginasservis.* They climbed gently through the groves of lemons, olives and almonds, and skirted the deep-rooted trees of the Forest of Cadarache.

Another deserted village perched high on the rocks to the left, and then a descent by a steep, winding road. The village of St. Marcellin came upon them suddenly, set in a background of hills, with mountains beyond. Behind, they had left the sun-tortured river valleys with their clear brazen skies; ahead lay the distant peaks, over which hung great clouds like burning walls, the sun lowering in the west illuminating them like the reflection of a vast fire.

A compact village of medium size. The secondary road, fringed with trees, ran right through it, widened to hold a main street of about twenty houses, and then narrowed again. Another by-road crossed the main highway in the middle of the village. Thence a number of narrow alleys, like the strands of a great spider's web, radiated uphill on either side, and to these clung ancient cottages, roofed in old, golden, moss-covered tiles. They seemed to cling with precarious tenacity to the stony earth, huddled and lurching close together for protection. And one of the side lanes on the left suddenly broke away like a long thread, to climb uphill to an eyrie on which a citadel of ruined stone thrust itself skyward from the living rock. To the right, near the crossroads, a church with a squat tower hid in a thick mass of trees and beside it, a vicarage, badly in need of repair, like most of the other property in the place.

The Littlejohns halted at the church. A few people about the village and a group of children apparently just out of school, sporting in the road with shrill cries. On a seat in the vicarage garden the priest was asleep, a handkerchief over his face, his breviary on his knee, one finger marking the place between the closed leaves.

"If there isn't a decent inn here, it means going back to Mirabeau."

But Mrs. Littlejohn's eyes were already fixed across the road. Beneath an avenue of plane trees stood a fountain, a tall column of stone rising from a plinth, with four jets emerging from copper pipes and splashing into a large basin set in the earth below. Behind the fountain were two iron tables with iron chairs and, visible through the trees, an inn. *Restaurant Pascal. Marie Alivon.* The door stood open and a screen of beads hung in the doorway. Advertisement plaques on either side. *Byrrh... Bière D'Alsace... Tabac...* A tall, narrow, three-storeyed building with a cream-washed frontage, green-painted iron balconies on the first floor, drawn green shutters keeping the sun from the upper rooms. To the right of the door on the ground floor, a broad, shallow window with a window-box full of red and pink geraniums so strong and thriving that they formed a screen masking the interior.

They parked the car under the tall cypress trees of the churchyard and crossed to the hotel.

"We'll have a drink and, if we like the place, we can enquire about a room."

Littlejohn was prepared to leave it all to his wife. He was used to sleeping in odd places when on duty.

Time seemed to stand still in St. Marcellin. The children had dispersed, the streets were empty, and nobody seemed interested in the arrival of strangers. A dog crossed the sundrenched road and the curé slept on in his garden. The only other signs of life were the sounds coming from unseen places. Rhythmic blows of a hammer on an anvil in a smithy somewhere, the sound of a flail on a threshing-floor, the hum of a motor-cycle on a distant road, the fresh splash of the water-jets at the fountain. The air smelt of stables, hay, and apples stored in lofts. The church clock struck four on a cracked bell. Nobody about, and yet you felt that, from behind the closed shutters of the houses, you were being watched.

Littlejohn and Letty sat down at one of the iron tables and sighed simultaneously. The shade of the trees and the cool sound generated by the fountain were a relief in themselves. Merely to be there in each other's company, relaxed and unspeaking, was a joy. From where they were sitting they could see the school, a single-storeyed, robust little stone affair, side by side with a well-kept red-tiled house, fresh with paint and with a flagstaff rising from the small gravelled enclosure in front. It was perhaps the town hall or, in such a modest village, the mayor's house. The gable-end of the latter gave on another narrow street, a cul-de-sac, arcaded on each side with ancient pillars supporting the tumbledown arches of close-shuttered, apparently deserted houses. The paint had peeled from them and the lintels were out of square. The street terminated in a shallow tunnel, closed by a rotting, nail-studded door, above which an iron crucifix was clamped on the wall.

The Chief Inspector became aware that someone was watching them from inside the inn, and before he could look closely, the beads of the curtain which covered the door moved, and a woman materialized like a ghost from behind them. A tall, dark woman with jet-black hair drawn tightly back and resting in a bun in the nape of her strong neck. She seemed about forty, judging from her figure, which was well developed to the verge of plumpness. She had the oval face and straight nose often found in those parts, a clear sunburned complexion, and red lips. Her eyes were of an unusual clear grey, quite out of keeping with her hair and general colouring, and added to her beauty. A placid, patient look.... She did not seem surprised to find foreigners sitting on her chairs, but stood gravely beside them, smiling faintly.

"Good day.... Can I get you anything?"

The voice was clear and pleasantly monotonous.

"Two beers, please."

She was wearing a sober print dress and white shoes with high heels. She nodded, smiled and disappeared, and shortly returned with the drinks, a carafe of water, and a plate of black olives. As she arranged the table, Littlejohn noticed the wedding-ring on her finger and the long, slender hands with their grace of movement.

"Are you passing through St. Marcellin?"

She seemed to be seeking something civil to say before leaving them.

The Littlejohns had arranged their programme beforehand, like actors in a charade who must, for the success of their adventure, keep their identities and even their very thoughts secret.

"My husband is writing a travel-book on Provence. We are motoring about, seeing things, and I am making some sketches."

"There is not much to see in St. Marcellin."

The tone was sad and the woman looked round her at the deserted street and the shabby property lining it as though to confirm her words.

"All the same, it is shady and cool here after the heat of the highroads. It's getting late, too."

The woman nodded.

"We have a spare room. It is plain and simple. It is there."

She pointed to the shuttered window on the first floor, but made no further effort to persuade them. Two old men emerged from a side street and tottered, almost bent double, to a seat under the cypresses, sat down, and peered across at the strangers. A bare-legged child appeared driving a small flock of goats down the road, and halted to milk one of them for a woman who handed out a dish from one of the cottages.

The woman had apparently been thinking of further hospitality.

"I could give you a nice dinner, too. A well-fed capon, and there are truffles from the plateau of Riez.... They are very well-known and are good.... And there are mountain strawberries."

They followed her indoors and the bead curtain rustled and clicked behind them. A cool room beyond it, with cream-washed walls and the red honeycomb tiles of Provence forming the floor. Tables and chairs set out in front of a small zinc counter behind which stood a row of bottles. The splash of the fountain pervaded the whole place.

"The room is above this one."

They went with her through a door behind the bar into another room with a French window at the far end and a vine rambling over it.

"You could dine here."

Throughout she gave them the choice, without presuming the place would suit them. This room, too, had a red-tiled floor and was cool and airy. The view between the tendrils of the vine was a short one; a small patch of grass, a row of vines, some olive trees, and then the wall of what looked like a farm. Over the roofs the mountains were visible.

The scents of the place were too numerous to identify. The oily smell of sardines in some hidden hors d'œuvre, herbs, lavender, tobacco.

Littlejohn became aware of another door, just ajar, leading he knew not where, perhaps into a kitchen behind. It was thence the fumes of tobacco were emerging, and a closer look revealed the thin curl of smoke gently wafting in the room they were inspecting. A man was standing behind the other door listening to all that was going on.

"You own this place?"

Mrs. Littlejohn was obviously charmed by the bright room, the old, well-polished furniture, the atmosphere of decency and cleanliness. The solitary round table was set ready for a meal, with a snow-white cloth and glistening glasses.

"Yes.... My husband died in the war. His name was Gaston Thomasini. I keep my maiden name because it goes with the business. They shot him as a hostage."

She said it in a matter-of-fact tone, as though her sorrow had grown bearable with the years and had been lived through.

"My name is Marie Alivon.... I was born here. This inn belonged to my mother.... You wish to see the room?"

There was a third door leading to the stairs, which were also tiled in red honeycomb. At the landing, three doors, one each for the front rooms and another for the back.

"The arrangements are simple.... We have no running water and, if you require a bath, I will bring up hot water and the hip-bath left by an English gentleman who once stayed here painting. He insisted on the bath and bought it in Marseilles."

She smiled. Littlejohn wondered where the family bathed, and in his mind's eye saw an elderly-looking amateur painter, a retired colonel, in fact, lugging a bath all the way to St. Marcellin because he couldn't exist without his daily tub.

The room was large and clean, with the usual tiled floor, and overlooked the fountain and the cypress trees. Marie Alivon threw back the shutters to show them the view.

"The fountain runs all night. It never ceases. We are used to it. I hope you will find it all right."

"It will lull us to sleep."

The woman smiled sadly and nodded again.

"I will leave you to look over the room and perhaps you will think about it. I will be in the bar."

She spoke French in a monotonous, soothing singsong, with none of the exciting inflexions. Now and then, she paused for a word, not for lack of it, but considerately, choosing simple words as to a child whose vocabulary is limited.

"You speak good French."

She said it to Mrs. Littlejohn and smiled again.

"Here most of the people speak the dialect. Many of them know very little French.... I went to school in Manosque, you see."

She was gone, silently, as she had appeared, leaving a vague feeling of mystery, as though behind her calm exterior lay some strange history.

"Well?"

"Well?"

Littlejohn and his wife smiled at one another. It seemed to be an afternoon of quiet smiling, as though, somehow, the placid atmosphere had made everyone good-tempered and placid, too.

There was a chest of drawers lined with clean white paper and emitting the slightly bitter smell of box. A linen chest which neither of them cared to open, but left for exploration later. It seemed too massive and formidable for the heat of the day. A large double bed, with a huge red feather quilt and large square pillows. The Littlejohns tested its resilience with their hands. It emitted the scent of lavender and straw and clean linen. There was a dressing-table, too, with a dim mirror, and a marble-topped wash-stand with an ewer and basin and clean towels, as though the newcomers had been expected before they even showed themselves. The furniture was antiquated and of old polished walnut, and the rest of it consisted of a large wardrobe and a red velvet armchair, its seat deformed by a broken spring. Long white curtains with a pattern of faded roses hung at the windows. In one corner another door gave into a clean, empty boxroom, which, in days gone by, might have been a powder-closet. The fountain splashed its water, the quartet of jets granting no respite at all. One grew used to it and it added a soothing atmosphere to the room. Then came the sound of horses being led to stables somewhere, and even the noise of chains being rubbed against tether-posts, presumably in the farm behind.

"It will do very nicely."

They both said it together and, in childish delight, each linked the little finger of the right hand with that of the other and shook them, as they'd done in childhood whenever two people had said exactly the same thing at the same time.

Littlejohn lit his pipe. It was the first time since London.

"That's better."

They seemed to have forgotten the purpose of their visit and it now began to nag at their minds again.

"You'll have the usual form to fill-in if we stay here. What will you put?"

"You've answered that already, Letty. I'm an author and you're an artist. I shall put that down on the official slip."

At Marseilles, when they landed, it had been a different matter. On his passport, Littlejohn was a Chief Inspector and had registered himself as such. It had caused a slight commotion and not a little bowing and scraping, for his reputation had soared in France since he'd solved the murder of Sammy, the bar-keeper, at Cannes. "We're on holidays and haven't yet decided where we're going," he had told the police after they'd given him and his wife a splendid lunch at the airport. He was sure that already the Marseilles police had advised his friend Dorange, of the Nice Sûreté, of his arrival, and that, before he returned home, he would have to call at Nice and offer his excuses. Meanwhile ... it was difficult travelling incog., and no mistake about it. ...

Marie Alivon was waiting for them in the bar.

"You like the room?"

"Yes. We'll stay, Madame Alivon."

She did not ask for how long. Hers seemed to be a slow, grave wisdom which took things as they came.

"We may be here a day or two. We like it."

"I will bring across your luggage, then."

She didn't call the man who Littlejohn was sure was somewhere about the place, but made for the door, and Littlejohn went with her, handed the bags from the car, and took the bulk of them himself. She protested, but he insisted, and together they carried them to the room. His wife followed, and he took out his keys and unlocked the two suit-cases and the wardrobe trunk. He left Letty unpacking a few things and went below to sign the register and fill in the police forms for visitors. He grimly put himself down as an author, added the rest of the details, and handed them back. The forms were new ones, as though, again, guests had been expected and a fresh supply had been obtained.

Another visitor had arrived in the meantime. A little fat man with a round red face, chubby white hands, and a black upturned moustache like the Kaiser Bill caricatures of the first world war. He was dressed incongruously for such a place. A black suit, white linen, and patent leather shoes which he dusted with his handkerchief as he sat at one of the tables. Marie Alivon answered his greeting, filled a glass at the bar with *Dubonnet,* and placed it before him. He eyed Littlejohn up and down and then addressed him in French.

"A visitor ... English, too?"

Littlejohn greeted him.

"Just here for a day or two to gather local colour for a travel book I'm writing.'

"You speak good French."

"My neighbour in the next flat in London is French and we are good friends. He has taught me."

"I know several people in London."

The red light went up for Littlejohn. Here he was, pretending to be an author seeking inspiration, and if he wasn't careful he would find himself on the track to betraying himself.

"I think I'll have a drink, Madame Alivon."

The little man jumped to his feet like an India rubber ball.

"Forgive me ... Monsieur. What did you say the name was? You must drink with me to a happy stay in our village. It is my native place, I left it and entered business in Grenoble, and now I am retired and home again. I am the mayor of the commune and that is my house over there with the flagstaff ... Another *Dubonnet?* Two more, Marie. ... *Encore deux. ...*"

"You are here alone?"

"My wife is upstairs unpacking."

"She must join us.... No, no, I insist. You must both drink to a happy holiday. Not many people come here to stay. I don't know why you are staying, but we must make it a happy one. I insist on Mrs.... What did you say your name was...? Littlejohn? It is unusual, if I may say so.... *Petit Jean,* in French, like a little boy's Christian name, eh?"

He cackled, straightened his tie, and again dusted his shoes.

"Marie.... Please tell Mrs. Littlejohn we await her to drink with us to a happy holiday."

Marie Alivon hurried upstairs obediently. The mayor straightened his tie again, and then took out a pocket mirror and a comb, and with their help combed his moustache and smoothed his black hair, which was thin and strategically plastered about his head to hide certain bald spots. When Mrs. Littlejohn entered, he proved himself a complete masher, and kissed her hand.

"My name is Anselme Savini, madame. I am mayor of this commune and I bid you welcome."

His large dark eyes, with their prominent whites and protruding eyeballs, rolled as he bowed her to a chair.

They spent a boring three-quarters of an hour whilst Monsieur Savini chattered mainly to Mrs. Littlejohn about the village, its history and claim to fame, his own business successes in Grenoble, and his own claim to fame as well. In the end, intoxicated by his own eminence and his financial acumen, Monsieur Savini began to talk of nothing else. Mrs. Littlejohn, though middle-aged by now, was still good-looking and well turned-out. Good-looking, sophisticated women were rare in St. Marcellin and Monsieur Savini was making the most of his chances.

"You must come to my house, taste my wine, and see my pictures. I have some Utrillos and I was a friend of Picasso. ... You will be interested. Bring your husband, too, if you like. ... And now, *au 'voir,* my friends, and again welcome to St. Marcellin. And, by the way, whilst you are here, you must not miss visiting the château. The Marquis is a friend of mine. I will introduce you. It is not so spruce as it was. Money is scarce for keeping up such places. However, we will meet to-morrow."

He bowed himself out, tripped over the step, and hurried off to hide his discomfiture. Mrs. Littlejohn left to finish her unpacking and to change for dinner, and Littlejohn finished his drink. His wife was soon back.

"Can you come upstairs a minute?"

He followed her, wondering why she seemed a little more excited than usual.

She had unpacked one case and the wardrobe trunk. The other lay closed on the bed.

"I left that case on the bed, open, when I came down for my *apéritif.* Now it's been closed whilst I've been away."

"Madame Alivon must have been up."

Mrs. Littlejohn tightened her lips and shook her head.

"She was in the room all the time that little bore was trying to flirt with me. No, it was someone else. Besides, the drawers have been opened and the contents of the bag I was unpacking turned over. I'm sure of it ... *I'm sure of it.*"

"I believe you, my dear. You know best how you left things."

"Someone came up here when I was below, and it wasn't Marie Alivon. Do you think they're suspicious about us?"

"I don't know. ... Wait ..."

He sniffed the air. Tobacco smoke again. Littlejohn had left his own pipe in the ash-tray, below, and the open windows should have dispelled any of the smoke he'd made an hour ago. He went to the door quickly and flung it open.

There was nobody there, but the smell of tobacco smoke was heavier than ever. Somebody smoking a pipe had been listening at the door!

Chapter Three
The Talkative Baker

Dusk came suddenly, manifest by the long shadows of the trees and a refreshing breeze from the hills, which blew down the road and made the leaves rustle gently. The Angelus sounded on the cracked church-bell and, as though it were a signal, the village began to bestir itself.

The old men on the seat beneath the church cypresses rose and shambled away after shaking hands. A number of old women dressed in black began to make their ways to church for prayers. They were peasant types, thin, bent and shrivelled. The bus from Manosque arrived and emptied its passengers opposite the mayor's house.

There were a mere half-dozen people on the bus. Mainly girls, who seemed to be coming home from jobs in the town. They were dressed in what they considered to be the latest town styles. Smart costumes, fashionable cheap print frocks, with bare arms. High heels, nylon stockings. They were giggling noisily, and one detached herself from the rest and made for the *Hôtel Pascal.*

Littlejohn, smoking on the balcony of the bedroom, saw it all happening, and followed with his eyes the course of the solitary girl as she crossed the road to the inn. Tall, dark and vivid, with a full figure and sturdy arms and legs, she tottered across the cobblestones of the rough footpath on her high-heeled red shoes. She wore a print flowered frock and little beneath it. Her face was oval and her dark hair gathered from her face and tied in a horse-tail behind. Her make-up was put on inexpertly. She was so obviously of the strong peasant build and stock that her efforts to look a city girl were almost pathetic, with a flavour of a caricature. In England, she might have been taken for twenty-three or four; here, in the south, she was probably sixteen or thereabouts. She thrust aside the bead curtain and almost immediately after, Littlejohn heard her steps on the stairs and the door of the room opposite their own slammed as she entered.

The village was still busy. Men cycling home, a postman in uniform and *képi* left the shop opposite, in front of which hung a letterbox, and crossed to the inn for a drink. It was a sign for other men to make in the same direction and soon the hum of voices rose from below. The *garde champêtre,* the mayor's runabout, mainly concerned with duties as game and forest warden, appeared and joined the rest. There seemed to be no official police station in St. Marcellin and the headquarters were apparently at the mayor's house.

Littlejohn watched the men as they arrived. Two out of every three were smoking pipes. It was going to be like hunting for a needle in a haystack finding out who was the mysterious smoker who listened at keyholes at the *Hôtel Pascal.*

More footsteps on the stairs and a tap on the door. It was Marie Alivon again.

"Dinner will be in half an hour... Perhaps one of you would like a bath?"

The Littlejohns looked at one another.

"Shall we toss for it, Letty?"

"We can only heat enough water for one, and it will take an hour or more in the boiler. Perhaps it will do after dinner?"

"About two hours after then, please, Madame Alivon."

Marie Alivon nodded and to show where the bath would be sited, opened the box-room, took out a large rush mat from the linen chest, and placed it in the middle of the tiled floor. Then she put clean towels on an old-fashioned wooden towel-rail behind the door.

"We will bring up the bath when my brother returns."

The door opposite opened and the girl from the Manosque bus appeared. She had changed her shoes and frock and put on more powder and rouge.

"This is my daughter, Blanche. She works at a wine merchant's in Manosque."

The girl hesitated and then offered her hand to Littlejohn and his wife. She seemed shy and well-mannered and spoke in the same quiet, refined way as her mother.

"I hope you have a happy stay in St. Marcellin."

"You prefer work in the town, Mademoiselle Blanche?"

"Yes. It is too quiet here. I would like to stay in town all the time, but my mother won't agree. When I am a bit older and can keep myself, I shall try to get a job in Paris or Lyons."

Below, the men had had their drinks and were now moving away in small knots, chattering twenty to the dozen, mainly in patois. Soon Littlejohn heard the metallic crashes of bowls... There must have been a bowling pitch round the corner of the inn.

On the way down to dinner the Littlejohns met the bath coming up. It hid the head and shoulders of the man carrying it; his abdomen and legs could be seen blindly climbing the stairs. He halted, raised the bath above his head, and made way for them to pass. A tall, thin man with a short brown beard. A peasant, again, knotty and strong of frame, with the same grey eyes as his sister, Marie. Only whereas they added to her appearance, in her brother they made the face look weak. There was a curved pipe between his teeth in spite of the bath.

"Good evening.... Here is the bath. I am César Alivon, brother of Marie."

Having introduced himself and given his credentials, César then lowered the bath over his head and shoulders and stumbled upwards with it again. They could hear him fumbling with the door of their room and, after staggering his way to the box room, dump his burden and leave.

The meal already described by Marie Alivon was waiting for the Littlejohns in the private room.

An appetizing *hors d'œuvre* of tomatoes, sardines, fillets of herring, black olives and sausages, served with a tempting flavour of oil and garlic. The chicken and the truffles from Riez were cooked to perfection, and followed by mountain strawberries in red wine, with whipped cream in a dish. Then goat's-milk cheese, flavoured with thyme, appeared. They drank red wine from a carafe which had been placed there without ordering. A full, kindly wine, whose potency soon made itself felt.

Marie Alivon attended to them quietly.

"I hope you will like the wine. It is our own. We have a vineyard on the slopes just behind the inn.

"We do not take cream with strawberries here, but I know the English like it. And the cheese is made in the village and is known as Banon."

The window was open and they could hear the noise of bowls as the men played outside and their shouts of praise and advice to one or another. Frogs began to croak intermittently. Darkness was at hand, and Marie Alivon closed the window to keep out the flying insects and switched on the light, a single bulb with a large bead shade in the centre of the ceiling.

Littlejohn made conversation between the courses.

"Does your brother live here with you, Madame Alivon?"

"You met him carrying up the bath? Yes; he is one of the gamekeepers on the estate and acts as under-bailiff as well."

"The estate ... ?"

"There is a château a league outside the village on the Ginasservis side. It belongs to the Marquis de St. Marcellin."

"I see. Your brother had just arrived home when you asked him to bring up the bath?"

"No. He came back early in the afternoon. He had business in the village. The traveller for the chemicals for the vines had come and there were orders to give. You like our wine?"

After dinner they sat a long time, sipping the remainder of the wine, drinking coffee and enjoying the lethargic pleasure of feeling well-fed. In the quarters behind the inn, there was much ado about heating bath-water. Finally Marie Alivon appeared.

"Madame is ready for her bath?"

As soon as Mrs. Littlejohn agreed, there began a procession of carrying cans of hot water to the floor above. Littlejohn wondered what would happen when the bath was finished with and the water had to come all the way down again.

After his wife had left him, the Chief Inspector strolled into the bar. The front door was closed and the light was on. In one corner, four men were playing cards with a grubby pack. They thought deeply and played slowly, as though all the world depended on the next card. They had a glass apiece of red wine. Sombre, taciturn peasants who didn't look straight up when Littlejohn entered, but gave him side-long, furtive glances. He passed through the room and went into the open air, following the direction of the voices and noise of bowls until it took him round the far corner of the inn. There, he found about ten men playing on an irregular plot of undulating gravel which stood in front of an unoccupied old house. The bowling pitch might once have been the courtyard of the large dwelling. A dovecote, badly needing paint and rotted by the weather, rose at one corner. Inside it he could hear the birds moving. They might have been the remote offspring of those which had occupied this simple home when it was new and when the house to which it belonged was in its prime.

A bare electric bulb, now illuminated, stood at the top of another post, and by its light the men were busy playing. Littlejohn leaned against the lamp-post and watched them fling the small wooden jack and then hurl the heavy metal bowls after it. The skill lay in the throw of the ball, not, as at home, in the biased rolling of the wood. The best players were obviously expert in scattering their opponents' metals and leaving their own in good place after the slaughter.

Nobody spoke to Littlejohn until the dark-clad figure of the mayor suddenly bounded from a group of players.

"Ha, Mister Littlejohn! You are without your wife?"

"She's retired early. It's been a busy, tiring day. Don't forget, we were in London early this morning."

Nothing would do but that Littlejohn should join the bowlers. With a wave of the hand, Savini introduced him to a group of three men. He could not make out their features properly in the dim, diffused light. They merely acknowledged the introductions with grunts and made way for the newcomer with the tolerance accorded to a learner. As the game progressed, they grew more affable, for Littlejohn, who had graduated through schools of marbles, cricket, darts and billiards at one time or another of his life, had merely to acquire the skilled back-handed twist of the throw and he was playing as well as the rest. It was quite dark when they finished.

The mayor congratulated the Chief Inspector on his game.

"I don't often return to the inn. I have work to do. But to-night I'll go back and drink to our friendship and good fellowship."

The procession of bowlers wound its way back to the *Restaurant Pascal. A* few lights behind the windows of the cottages fronting the road, and stars overhead. The fountain splashed monotonously and, somewhere in the distance, a train whistled on the main line miles away. Littlejohn paused. There was a sound on the air like steady drumming. Silence, then another volley.

"There is a thunderstorm somewhere in the direction of Nice.... It has been sultry and cloudy that way all day."

The mayor explained and, taking his arm, led him indoors.

There were about a dozen men in the bar, lolling round the counter or sitting at the tables. They looked shy and uncertain as Littlejohn entered. Mostly peasant types, large and small, but all of them strong-looking and burned by the sun. The clock outside struck nine.

Littlejohn and Savini sat at a large table and, with a gesture, the mayor gathered together the rest of his bowling party. They sat down quietly and Marie Alivon brought red wine. The mayor introduced them all again. Marius Brunei, Augustin Mora, and Gaspard Léonidas.

Talk in the room began to flow as the wine went down. It was mainly a mixture of dialect and unintelligible French and Littlejohn was lost in it. His companions, however, once the ice was broken, spoke plainly the French of the south and the Chief Inspector could, by intelligent surmise, fill in the parts hard to follow.

Brunei, it appeared, farmed the fields behind the inn and lived in the house adjoining the back wall. A tall, thin, tough-looking man of middle age with a heavy moustache and shaggy brown hair. He had the broad cheekbones and tapering muzzle of a fox and the sly approach of the cunning. He had large, strong, ill-kept hands which he used with the eagerness of a miser when he was offered anything, and with the same slow diffidence when it came to taking out his own purse and counting out coins with a fond gesture of reluctance to part with them. He drank glass after glass of the wine paid for by Littlejohn and the mayor, and grew progressively more taciturn, helping himself now and then from the packet of cigarettes which Littlejohn had put on the table and, on one occasion, slipping one in his pocket.

The other two men were more sociable.

"I take it, sir, you've arranged to have your letters forwarded here. There's a post-office opposite in Madame Colomb's grocery shop. Just stamps and simple things, sir. The rest you'll get in Manosque or Mirabeau."

This was Léonidas, the postman, a very important man in St. Marcellin, to his own way of thinking. He wore his *képi* at the back of his head of rough black hair and missed nothing with his busy dark eyes, shaded by heavy bushes of eyebrows. To match the eyebrows, a large shaggy moustache covered his upper lip and, if he missed shaving again on the morrow, he'd be starting a beard. A thin, lined face, tanned hard by his outdoor job, and a long, scraggy neck emerging from behind his uniform collar, like that of a plucked fowl.

"I must say I can't imagine anybody staying long in a god-forsaken place like this. So I expect you'll pick up your mail at your next port of call, sir."

Littlejohn hoped to goodness no letters addressed to him would arrive there. Chief Detective Inspector.... The fat would be in the fire!

The mayor was explaining that Littlejohn was a writer and traveller.

"Hé ... A writer.... "

Léonidas dug his neighbour in the ribs.

"Augustin, here, is a writer, aren't you, Augustin? You should have read his report of the accident here in the early part of the year.... A masterpiece! You haven't heard of the accident, sir? Quite put St. Marcellin on the map for a week or two. An Englishman and his wife, killed in their car."

"Now, now, now.... The gentleman doesn't want to hear of misfortune during his stay with us."

Augustin Mora raised a fat hand for silence. He was the local gendarme, a very important man, too, in his own eyes. He and Léonidas vied with each other for public esteem and importance. Mora certainly had it in size. He was six feet tall and fat with it. His moustache was better tended than Léonidas's, too, and sprouted from his fat red face upwards in two points. He was the lowliest official connected with law and order and wore a humble uniform, like a porter on a station. A cap, a tunic without official ornaments, and a pair of old baggy trousers whose renewal was long overdue and eagerly awaited. He was mainly concerned with keeping down poachers, watching the forests for fires or loafers, generally seeing the villagers behaved themselves, and keeping any malefactors occupied or under restraint until his superiors from Manosque could get at them and take them away to town.

Monsieur Mora obviously was moved by this testimony from his rival about his literary skill, but he wanted urging to tell his tale. He wished that, in spite of his huge paw raised to restrain, someone would insist on an account of his handling of the Lovell affair.

"I'm most interested, sergeant."

Mora looked into Littlejohn's eyes to see if the promotion was ironical, but met a bland, interested look.

"I only did my duty. The road down the hill is bad in winter. Steep and snaky, if you understand what I mean. These two must have been coming down at a hell of a speed. They hit a tree. Eleven o'clock at night, it was. The car was smashed up and both their necks broken. Of course, I had to put all that down in my report."

He looked round at the circle of faces; Brunei asleep, Léonidas smiling ironically, the mayor nodding out of politeness because he wanted to impress Littlejohn, and Littlejohn himself wide-eyed and agog with interest. Mora gazed at his empty glass and licked his lips to indicate that his story was parching him. Littlejohn poured out some more wine.

"That was all, gentlemen. Of course, I had the administrative work to do. The examining magistrate came from Manosque and, with it being an important Englishman *and* well-known to Monsieur le Marquis, the Procureur from Digne even paid us a visit and complimented me on my work."

"Very good, sergeant.... The administrative part must have been heavy in such a case."

"It was. In case you want to put it down in one of your books, sir, let me say that I had to search for witnesses to the accident, of which there were none. I also had to make sure it *was* an accident, which it was. But you never know, do you, sir? Someone might have made it *look* like an accident, mightn't they? And since the Dominici business, we've got to be careful. We don't want the reputation of France and the French police to suffer because it ain't safe here for foreigners, now do we?"

"You must have done some hard investigating, sergeant."

"You bet I did, sir. I got Leclerc from the garage here to examine the car and see if it was in working order before the accident. Brakes and such, I mean. I was able to show Leclerc's certificate, which I took in writing, to the examining magistrate, and though they had an expert from Grenoble on the job, he didn't find anything different than Leclerc, who, though he only keeps a petrol station and does the odd motor jobs of St. Marcellin, knows a thing or two, because before he was a prisoner in Germany he was on aeroplanes in Paris."

The mayor yawned.

"Leclerc's usually here in the evenings, but the Marquis's car broke down to-day, and, as he can't afford another, Leclerc's got an all-night job."

The postman was looking bored, too. Anything which added a little glory to his official rival annoyed and made him jealous. He was sorry he'd started all this in an attempt to make fun of Mora. He'd thought the Englishman would have laughed at the adventures of a stupid country bobby. Instead, he was full of admiration. He decided to call a halt before Mora qualified to appear in the Englishman's next novel.

"Hé, Hénoch!" he called to a man just entering. "Come and join us."

Mora glared and then began to sulk at the interruption, which took the form of a little, thin man, who, in the half light of the doorway as he entered, looked to be in the last stages of consumption, but who, when he came in full view, was revealed powdered in flour down to his very boots. The mayor stirred himself and introduced him.

"Hénoch Rossi, our village baker."

Hénoch bowed, sat down, looked at the carafe of red wine which Littlejohn had just paid for, and received a glass of it.

"I'm as dry as a bone," he said, and downed it in one.

"Hénoch and his brother, Ernest, are our bakers. By the look of you, it's your turn on nights, isn't it?"

Hénoch nodded and drank another glass, as though the flour in his system needed thoroughly mixing.

"Yes, Monsieur le Maire, it is. ..."

The baker turned to Littlejohn. He had a lofty forehead and a bald head fringed with thin hair. His face was lined and he had shaggy eyebrows and a ragged, thin moustache stretching the whole length of his upper lip. His hair, on head, eyebrows, lashes, and lip was white with flour, for, in his haste to quench his thirst before he put in the oven the bread he would guard until to-morrow's breakfasts, he had not washed himself. In any event, his ablutions didn't seem to do much good. Whenever you met him, the lines of his face, hands, and at the back of his neck were etched in the white of his trade.

"I should explain, sir, that my brother and I take turns about. One week he works at the ovens through the night, whilst I make the dough and sell the bread by day. Then, next week, we change over. Nobody is inconvenienced. We are bachelors and it doesn't matter when we go to bed."

He smiled and looked eagerly at the last of the wine in the decanter.

"Dry work, baking bread."

Littlejohn filled up Hénoch's glass again. Back it went, as the baker's large Adam's apple rose and fell at his open throat, like a fisherman's float bobbing down and then up again as the fish gets away.

"As I entered, you were talking about the accident."

It was obvious that *The Accident* marked a red-letter day in St. Marcellin, just as, in other parts, men measure the days by their distance from the earthquake, the great wind, or some other natural phenomenon.

"Yes."

Littlejohn noticed the effect on the others at the table; the mayor didn't look bored any more, the village bobby sat up and began to take notice, and the postman, half-drunk, stretched out his long neck like a bird of prey or a snake about to strike.

"I know many things about that accident, monsieur. They say in the village you are a writer. You will be interested."

The mayor rose.

"You'll excuse me, Mister Littlejohn, but I still have work to do and it is ten o'clock. I must go. The rest will be going soon, too. They get up early on these fine summer days."

"Then you don't want to hear what I saw that night, sir? I was up baking, you see, and I heard the crash just outside the village. I ran out. Then, two minutes later, Augustin followed. He was just returning home and heard the noise, too. Mora said later he was the first there and there was nobody else. He forgot to say, I was the first there and there *was* somebody else, who ran away."

The baker shouted it, and then there was a hush in the room. All eyes turned on him, as he stood there, like someone who has been pulled from a sack of flour. He was quite drunk and had to hold on the table. The mayor rebuked him.

"You're drunk, Rossi. Get out. Your bread will be burned and we'll have none for breakfast."

"You never told me.... Why didn't you tell me?"

Mora, his official cap askew, was hurt. He'd been let down and kept in ignorance all this time.

"You never asked me, and you took all the credit for being there first upon yourself."

The mayor put on his hat and looked sadly at Littlejohn.

"I'm sorry about this, but Rossi's drunk. You gave him too much wine. He just can't take it, you see. We all know that."

Marie Alivon and her brother arrived to let them know it was time to pack up. They shook Marius Brunei, who'd been asleep all the while, and he awoke and without a word staggered to the door and into the night. The postman and the policeman between them took away the baker, who turned at the door and shouted back to Littlejohn.

"Thank you, sir, for the wine. I'm not drunk. If you call at the shop of myself and my brother, I'll tell you more about the accident. I was there first, wasn't I?... Well, wasn't I?"

They hustled him off into the street.

Littlejohn made his way upstairs. His wife was in bed and fast asleep, tired out after the day's heat and journey. He washed, and inspected the improvised bathroom. The bath was there, still full of tepid water.... He kissed his wife lightly on the cheek, undressed, and got in bed.

The night was warm now; not a breath of wind to disturb the calm and not a sound save the splash of the fountain and, as Littlejohn strained his ears, the song of a nightingale far away. He wondered whether or not to waken Letty to hear it.

Then the peace was broken and the song of the fountain and the nightbird disturbed.

A voice like a foghorn shouting in the middle of the village street.

"Help! Help! Quickly! Hénoch Rossi is dead!"

Chapter Four
The Diffident Priest

"Help! Help!..."

The second stentorian call found Littlejohn halfway down the stairs of the hotel. He wore simply his pyjamas and dressing-gown. It was warm enough.

The door was closed in front of the bead curtain, but unlocked. There were lights in the bar and the staircase and, as Littlejohn opened the door into the street, he found himself face to face with César Alivon. He had his pipe in his mouth and wore the same sombre, taciturn look. He might have been resolutely concerned with breaking-up a fight between two cats on the tiles, instead of attending at the death of the village baker. He was in his working clothes which, from all appearances, he had not yet removed before the alarm was given.

"You're going the wrong way."

Littlejohn said it more to make the man speak than anything else, for he was trying to pass without a word.

"I am getting something to help, monsieur."

Alivon went into the bar as though his purpose occupied all his thoughts.

Outside, in the road, no sign of movement. Lights were showing in the upper windows of the mayor's house, and down the road in the direction of Manosque, the whining of a drill sounded in a small illuminated shed, with the door open. Apparently Leclerc, working overtime in his garage, hadn't heard the cry for help. Beyond that and the lights in the hotel, the village was in complete darkness. Either the villagers were sound sleepers, or else the alarm in the night had made them thrust their heads under the clothes or refuse to be disturbed.

In the mountains to the south, the storms were still wandering. The steady drumming of the thunder and flashes of light like a gigantic firework display. The fountain splashed without cease and in the stables and byres the rattle of tether chains and the stamping and snorting of animals.

As Littlejohn's eyes grew used to the darkness, he made out a shadowy form crouched in the middle of the old street under the gable-end of the mayor's house. He hurried across. A flash-lamp shone in his face. By its diffused light he eventually made out the village priest, kneeling beside a form stretched on the gravel under a great plane tree.

"What is it?"

He could see little of the curé, except that he had removed his hat and was wringing his hands beside the limp mass. Judging from his shadow, a huge man. Littlejohn could hear his heavy breathing, like long drawn-out sobs, in the dark.

"I had to visit Madeleine Tatin.... She is near the end. Whenever I am out at night, I always call at the bakehouse. There is nobody else about and it is nice to hear a human voice."

The priest began it in a kind of dull chant, half weeping, half excusing himself, as though the disaster were his own fault. Littlejohn went on his knees beside the curé, took the torch, and shone it in the face of the still form. The lofty forehead and thin hair, and the flour covering it all. The nostrils were pinched and the lips unhealthily red.

"The door of the bakehouse is usually open on account of the heat and the fumes of the charcoal in the furnace for the ovens. The furnace is in a little shed at the back and the door leads into the bakery."

Littlejohn bent and listened at the lips of the half-closed mouth and then stripped open the baker's shirt and put his ear to the chest. The vicar was still droning.

"He must have gone in to attend to the furnace and someone had closed the door and fastened it outside. It is always full of fumes. I have warned him, but he said nothing could happen with the door always open. I carried him outside."

Littlejohn sat on his heels.

"Will you kindly keep quiet, Monsieur le Curé. I think he's not quite dead. Shine your light on him."

"*Deo gratias!*"

Littlejohn straightened and arranged the thin bag of bones and began artificial respiration and, as he did so, he became aware that César Alivon was standing by his side, saying nothing. Finally he found his tongue.

"He is not dead? Then give him a drink of this, quickly."

Alivon stooped with what looked like a bottle of brandy and Littlejohn, with a quick gesture, dashed it into the road, where it broke with a crash. The mayor arrived, fully dressed. He had been before, but his vanity would not allow him to appear in public without the dentures forgotten in his haste. So he had been back for them.

"Don't you know better than to give a suffocated man drinks?"

"I thought he'd had a heart attack."

The priest's voice came from the dark in reproach.

"I told you it was the fumes from the furnace, César ... You must have lost your head. After your first-aid training in the war, you ought to have known better."

"Do you two mind being quiet?"

Littlejohn bent to listen to the victim's chest again.

"Has anybody sent for the doctor?"

"He is with Madeleine Tatin."

"Get him! Anyone would think you wanted Rossi to die! You, Alivon, get the doctor right away."

Alivon left without a word at his usual countryman's pace, his footsteps ringing on the uneven stones of the squalid, dark alley.

"Run, damn you, run!!"

Littlejohn's blood was boiling. Dark fatalism seemed about. A man was at death's door. He might recover; he might not. It was in the hands of the gods. Even the mayor seemed helpless, breathing heavily, stepping now to this side, now to that, kneeling down, getting up again.

"How is he?"

Littlejohn pressed the thin bag of ribs rhythmically without response from the little baker. It looked to be all up with him. He paused.

"Where is everybody? Surely the noise the curé raised must have wakened more people?"

"Shall I get help?"

The mayor was relieved to find something to do. The curé was praying again.

"Requiem aeternam dona eis, Domine."

"He's not dead yet, Monsieur le Curé! Where is your presbytery?"

"Just across the way, under the trees there."

"Help me carry him. ... You, Monsieur le Maire, go and see if Leclerc is about. Does he do welding?"

"Yes, I think so."

The mayor was dancing with eagerness to help.

"See if he has an oxygen cylinder.... Go on. Go on."

It was like a nightmare. Nobody in a hurry, no help, the fountain splashing, the appalling illuminations of the distant storm lighting the sky like the crack of doom.

The curé picked up the baker in his arms like a child, without the least effort, and gently carried him across the road, along the garden path, and into the house beyond. Littlejohn followed and half-unconsciously noticed the sweet fragrance of the flowers in the beds as they stumbled along.

The priest switched on a light. An old woman in a nightgown and with hair plaited in two pigtails, appeared at the head of the stairs which rose from the hall.

"How is Madeleine Tatin, Monsieur le Curé?"

She halted and, with a little scream at the sight of the burden in her master's arms and Littlejohn on his heels, she vanished into one of the rooms.

Littlejohn became aware of a large, warm room with a polished oak floor, old furniture, a fire of logs in a large hearth, and an atmosphere of scrupulous cleanliness. On the wall as he entered, a wooden cross and a picture of the Holy Face. Under this veronica, a large oak couch. The curé gently laid the baker on it.

"Better have him on the floor, sir, and please open the door to give us plenty of air."

Littlejohn started the routine all over again, the bony frame of the thin man almost creaking under his efforts.

Footsteps along the path, and the mayor arrived with two other visitors. One was the postman.

"I found Léonidas at the garage helping Leclerc."

"Helping!"

The other man seemed to think that funny. Another tall, thin workman in a beret and overalls. He had the face of a comedian. Long features, sunken cheeks, prominent large teeth, and a wide mouth. The type Littlejohn had seen over and over again in French comedy films.

Leclerc and the postman were carrying a cylinder between them. They put it on the floor beside Littlejohn.

"What do we do now?"

There was a rubber tube dangling from the contraption.

"There's not much oxygen in it. I never use it much. I send most of my welding to Manosque."

"Put the tube in Rossi's mouth and turn on the valve. Gently, damn you!"

A doctor would have laughed, and Littlejohn himself felt singularly helpless and foolish, for he'd no idea of the real technique. He did his best to regulate the flow, removing the tube now and then and pressing the bony chest to circulate the air and the oxygen.

It went on for a quarter of an hour. The curé persisted in going on with his prayers for the dying. The rest stood like statues, breathing heavily. Littlejohn wished poor little Rossi would only start to breathe a tenth as hard. And then he did! The blue eyelids flickered, the baker uttered a gentle sob and gulped, clawed at the tube with feeble hands, and sighed again. Then he tried to turn over on his back. The blue, flour-ringed eyes were wide open in a puzzled, beseeching expression.

More footsteps, and Alivon entered with the doctor. The mayor sprang to life, ran to meet them, and almost embraced the doctor, a little old man with a small grey imperial, thickset, stooping, with dark pouched eyes.

"What is this?"

"This is Mr. Littlejohn, Dr. Mengali.... He has just saved the life of Hénoch."

The mayor began to stammer. He hadn't even asked how the accident had happened.

Littlejohn looked up.

"Good evening, doctor. He's breathing now. He's been gassed by charcoal fumes."

"Has anybody told his brother?"

Silence. They hadn't even thought of that!

"Go and get him, then.... You, postman.... Please get Ernest."

Léonidas ran out in his eagerness to help. Alivon stood like a statue, waiting for the next move.

"Shall we put him in my bed, doctor?"

"Yes, Monsieur Chambeyron."

The curé picked up the baker like a child again, and with gentle arms bore him aloft, the blue eyes still puzzled, and now resigned. The doctor followed, with Leclerc dancing attendance, and left Littlejohn with the mayor and César Alivon.

"If you hadn't been there, Mr. Littlejohn... our poor Hénoch would have died."

The mayor looked ready to embrace the Chief Inspector, who avoided his manœuvres and sat down in the large wooden chair in front of the fire. He felt that if he hadn't been there, poor Hénoch wouldn't have been molested at all! His arrival, he was sure, had started a whole train of events, of which this midnight catastrophe was the first.

Leclerc came jumping downstairs two at a time.

"Hot-water bottles! Hot-water bottles!"

He ran through the room and into what appeared to be the kitchen, and they could hear him rattling and fumbling about as though he worked there every day. He chattered to himself as he worked.

"I'll wait for the curé, if you like, Monsieur le Maire."

Savini's eyes flashed.

"There will be an enquiry. I shall investigate this to the bottom. I demand an explanation and I will have it, if I have to turn the village upside down."

He flung his arms all over the shop.

Alivon stood looking into the fire, puffing his pipe.

"We can do nothing until to-morrow, though."

To tell the truth, Savini didn't know where to start or what to do. The chance Littlejohn had given him of a dignified retreat was just what he wanted.

"I'll leave you, then, Mister Littlejohn. I shall not sleep. I shall sit up in my study and think this out."

He backed to the door and Alivon followed.

"Till morning, then, Mister Littlejohn.... Good night."

Alivon even found his tongue.

"I will tell your wife, monsieur.... You will soon be back?"

"When I've seen the baker settled."

Leclerc ran from the kitchen with two stone hot-water bottles in his arms. "Hot-water bottles," he said, and vanished upstairs again.

Littlejohn was left alone by the dying fire. In the corner, a large old clock ticked softly and then struck one. The cracked bell of the church answered it. He looked round the room as he lit the half-empty pipe he found in the pocket of his dressing-gown. Old, highly-polished furniture, whitewashed walls, age-blackened beams in the ceiling, an atmosphere of spaciousness and peace. A silver crucifix on the sideboard.

Another visitor. Hurrying feet along the footpath and a replica of the man in bed upstairs thrust in his head.

Obviously Ernest Rossi. He resembled his brother in every way, except that, whereas Hénoch had a fringe of grey hair, Ernest was totally bald, and, before retiring to his own bed, he must have washed himself thoroughly, for he had none of the floury, etiolated look of Hénoch.

"My brother!"

That was all he could say in his emotion. Being rudely awakened with bad news had almost paralysed him. The postman, following hard on Ernest's heels, took him by the elbows and piloted him upstairs. Littlejohn could hear the stumbling footsteps on the floor above and then the doctor must have asserted himself, for Léonidas and Leclerc next made a noisy descent and appeared in the room below. They looked put out.

"The doctor says we've to clear off.... He was rude about it. After all I've done getting the oxygen and the hot-water bottles, too."

They hung about a bit to show a little resistance to the rude dismissal.

"I'd better be off, then. I've a job to do for Monsieur le Marquis. I don't look like finishing before dawn."

They went into the night and left Littlejohn alone again. Then the priest appeared after a slow, heavy descent of the stairs. Littlejohn had more time to look at him now. A tall, ponderous man getting on for sixty, with a large square face, ruddy complexion and thin black hair receding from a broad, low forehead. The great nose, the wide, fleshy mouth, the big hands and feet were not of the ascetic, but a man of peasant stock, probably doing in St. Marcellin the work for which he was best cut out. His eyes were brown and troubled, with swollen lids and bile-shot whites. He sat in the chair opposite Littlejohn and brushed the dust from his soutane.

"A poor beginning to your holiday, monsieur. And yet, it was God's mercy you came. Otherwise, poor Hénoch Rossi would have died."

His delivery was monotonous and wheezy, as though he suffered from asthma. And yet, he could shout to some tune, as Littlejohn well knew from earlier events.

"You don't mind my pipe, Monsieur l'Abbé?"

"Not at all. On the contrary...."

He rose and took a bottle from the heavy cupboard behind him, and two glasses, which he filled with dark wine.

"This is a cordial which Lydie, my housekeeper, makes. You must excuse her non-appearance. She is now with the sick man. She is shy with strangers. Your good health, monsieur."

"And yours, Monsieur le Curé."

The wine caught Littlejohn's throat and made him cough, and then diffused with a pleasant feeling of exhilaration.

The priest put down his glass and twisted his large hands. A troubled man, for some reason, and wondering what his guest was thinking of the night's events.

"Why didn't half the village come running to answer your call for help, Monsieur l'Abbé? You shouted loud enough."

Again the worried expression, the half-suspicious side-long look from the brown eyes.

"I didn't expect them to. You see, our people here are a bit noisy and boisterous when they get drunk. It is nothing strange to hear loud cries in the night from some enthusiastic reveller. One merely turns over and goes to sleep again."

"And the baker's accident? Did you get the impression that someone had deliberately closed and fastened the door of the little furnace room purposely to suffocate Monsieur Rossi?"

The priest remained perfectly still and tense, looking, this time, in the fire, on which he had thrown another couple of logs.

"I spoke hastily... on the spur of the moment. When I entered, the bakehouse was empty. I thought Hénoch was putting more fuel on the fire, so I went to find him. The door was closed and... well, it is a primitive kind of fastening. Just a leather thong, held by one nail and passed over another to keep the door to. It must have slipped over the nail as Hénoch went in."

"Yet, knowing the fumes were dangerous, wouldn't Monsieur Rossi have left the door open?"

The priest threw back his head and gave Littlejohn a pleading glance.

"You need not worry, monsieur. Don't let it spoil your holiday. The mayor will look into it all with our good Mora to-morrow and there will be an explanation. Hénoch is safe now, thank God, so you need not worry."

He paused and searched Littlejohn's face to see if the excuse was accepted and if he was content not to pursue matters further.

"I've no doubt, sir, they'll find a satisfactory solution to the problem. One must admit that the baker had drunk a little too much wine on an empty stomach."

A great sigh of relief from the priest.

"Another glass of Lydie's wine, monsieur?"

"Thank you.... Before he left us at the café, Rossi was telling me about the accident here earlier in the year. One of my fellow countrymen and his wife were killed?"

"Yes; it was a sad affair."

The brown, protruding eyes again beseeched him not to go on.

"A motor accident, Rossi told me. They hit a tree. Or so it was said..."

The curé jumped in his chair.

"It is not suggested otherwise? Surely...? There was a full enquiry. They even brought men from Digne to assist. Men from the office of the Prefect himself."

"So I believe. Yet, just before he left to meet what might have been his death, Rossi had promised to see me again and tell me of what he called strange happenings. Do you know what he meant, Monsieur l'Abbé?"

The curé was flushed and breathing heavily again. His hand trembled as he put down his glass. He gave Littlejohn a suspicious, curious look and leaned forward to emphasize what he was going to say.

"It is diabolical the way people make a crime out of the simplest misfortune. In this isolated place they have little to do but watch one another, pretend they learn secrets... evil secrets about each other; profess, in their vanity, to know of dark things which don't exist, and are merely the creation of their own sinful imaginings. They have a lust for power and... and..."

He paused as the doctor entered the room.

"He will be all right now. I have given him a pill and he should sleep. We must leave him where he is till to-morrow and then we'll see. Can you manage, Monsieur le Curé?"

"Yes, Hilaire. I can sleep on the couch for the rest of the night. Is Ernest there?"

"He will leave when his brother falls asleep. Nothing more we can do till to-morrow and I have a lot of work to do then. Good night, Monsieur l'Abbé; good night, sir."

The house fell silent again. Littlejohn could hear the night bird singing in the distance. The storms seemed to have subsided and the splash of the fountain was louder than ever. The priest was on his feet, anxiously waiting for Littlejohn to go.

"You are staying here long, Monsieur Littlejohn?"

"A day or two, that's all. My wife has some sketches she wants to make.... You have been here long, Monsieur le Curé?"

"Twenty-five years."

He said it with a sad sigh, a kind of flat boredom of a man played out, one who had given all he could and was yet asked for more.

"A long time."

"Yes. I shall probably end my days here now."

"You have always ministered in these parts?"

"I was in Paris once. I didn't like it much and they didn't like me. I am a countryman, you see. My father was born in St. Marcellin, although he was living in Lurs when I was born. He died thinking I would one day be a bishop. 'Even if it is only a little bishopric, like Riez,' he would say. But here I am.... My father was a bailiff on the estate of the Marquis de St. Marcellin for many years and, in the end, the Marquis used his influence to get me moved here.... But I am boring you, monsieur."

"Not at all. I am keeping you from your sleep. Good night, Monsieur le Curé."

"Good night, and call to see me again. I don't get very much company or news from outside. I have grown like my flock, a peasant again."

Outside, the stars were shining and the village was in darkness, except for the glow diffused from the open door of Leclerc's garage, where the whine of a drill was going, and the solitary light of the Littlejohns' bedroom at the *Hôtel Pascal.* He crossed the road, and found they had left the door of the inn open for him and a lamp on over the stairs.

Littlejohn turned and gave a last look at the dark road, with the darker forms of the trees and the fountain shadowed against the back-cloth of night. Beyond the village, in the direction of the mountains, there was a light in the sky which moved as he looked at it. The headlamps of a car travelling in the direction of St. Marcellin. The Chief Inspector waited to see who was abroad in those desolate parts at that hour. The glow in the sky drew nearer, turned, and entered the village. Littlejohn found the switch, extinguished the stair-light behind him, and waited.

A small car shot in sight, slowed down, turned, and entered the open doorway of the garage of the mayor's house. Then M. Savini emerged, closed the garage door, locked it, and quietly entered his home.

The church bell ringing the Angelus and tolling for service merely caused Littlejohn to turn in bed and sleep again. It was the arrival of Marie Alivon which got him up. She had come to say the bath was ready. The Englishman who had initiated this pleasant ceremony and even dragged the bath from distant parts had evidently well-trained the people at the hotel, for they seemed to regard the whole affair as a slight eccentricity to be tolerated with pleasure and cheerful service. The bath itself was of the old-fashioned variety, made of enamelled tin, and filled from many large jugs. Littlejohn was obliged to bathe himself by instalments, for it was impossible to sit properly in it, and his contortions were in the nature of early-morning Swedish drill. He was ready for the breakfast of fresh bread, honey tasting of thyme, and coffee, which Marie Alivon served for them on the balcony.

"There's bread after all, then, Madame Alivon?"

She raised her hands and uttered a strange cry at the thought of last night's events.

"And when it was all ended, Monsieur Ernest had to start all over again and bake the bread, because the loaves poor Monsieur Hénoch was making were all burned to a cinder."

As they ate, they looked down the village street, where women were already abroad shopping at the store opposite or gossiping. A woman passed pushing her bundles of linen on a wheelbarrow. Léonidas, his box strapped across his chest, was delivering mail and news about Hénoch at the same time. He had a purposeful, busy expression on his face, the look of one who had a duty to do and first-hand reports of the accident to scatter far and wide.

The morning mists had lifted and the sun was already scorching everything under a dry, metallic sky. A horse passed, pulling a cartload of manure, which left a strong smell of ammonia in its wake.

Suddenly the door of the presbytery opposite opened and the mayor and Mora, the gendarme, emerged, talking volubly, gesticulating, making hurried tracks to the *mairie*. On their way they crossed the path of the postman, who paused to ask the latest news. The mayor raised his hands to the sky, as though accusing it of treachery, and shouted in a tone which travelled to where the Littlejohns were eating their bread and honey.

"Hénoch has disappeared! He left his sick-bed in the night, and he has vanished!"

Chapter Five
The Village Gossip

If Littlejohn had got up when the early Angelus sounded and taken a stroll in the village as the thin crowd of old women were coming from the first Mass, he would have found himself rather popular, for it had got around that in the small hours he had restored the village baker to life.

Now, however, at nine o'clock, things were different again. News of Hénoch Rossi's disappearance had travelled fast and the villagers were wondering if the strange Englishman was mixed up in that, as well. When he crossed the road to the church, the women washing clothes at the fountain and those standing gossiping in small knots at cottage doors, gave him sidelong glances and followed his progress out of the corners of their eyes.

It had been too late when he returned to tell his wife all the events and all his thoughts about the adventures in the dead of last night. So, over breakfast, he had given Letty a full account. He had certainly collected a fine gallery of characters, if nothing else.

César Alivon, for example, the very man under whose roof they were living, and who, as likely as not, judging from the tell-tale fumes of his pipe, was listening behind doors to their conversation whenever he could. He had entered the hotel as Littlejohn left it, just after the priest had sounded the alarm on finding the baker unconscious. Had he been abroad before the alarm? If not, he'd covered the ground to the scene of the accident and back in record time. He'd also, in spite of his first-aid training, tried to give the unconscious man a drink of brandy which might have choked him, and he had been corrected by the curé when he said he didn't know the nature of the accident. Then, he'd been in no hurry to get the doctor and Littlejohn had boiled over and told him to get a move on. César Alivon was in the employ of the Marquis de St. Marcellin...

The curé himself, Monsieur Chambeyron, was a bit of a mystery, too. He owed his job to the patronage of the people at the château, and showed signs of distress at the suggestion that the death of Lovell and his wife had been anything but an accident. A bitter, disappointed man, beholden to the Marquis, he was obviously anxious not to offend his master; otherwise, he might be thrown into the world outside again and end his days in some hole-and-corner parish far away from his native heath.

And what had the mayor been doing abroad in his car in the direction of the château in the small hours after the events of the previous night? Had he been giving a full report to his "boss", and had the disappearance of Hénoch Rossi followed it?

"The trouble is," complained the Chief Inspector, "I daren't make the least show of being curious about it all. It's supposed to have nothing whatever to do with me. I'm a casual visitor here and, if I ask questions, I shall probably be told to mind my own business. On the other hand, I'm sure our arrival precipitated poor Rossi's trouble. Whether it was just that he talked too much to the world in general after taking too much wine, or that he talked too much to *me,* I can't think. In the latter event, someone suspects already what I'm here for."

He tried to look casual as he crossed to the church. He smoked his pipe and enjoyed the fine morning. The storms in the mountains the night before seemed to have cleared the air. Everything stood out distinctly; the plane trees on the roadside, the cypress in the churchyard, even the pebbles in the road. A hot breeze moved the leaves of the trees gently, and brought the scents of lavender and thyme from the upland fields. Littlejohn paused and looked at the village and its situation, which seemed quite different from his first impressions of yesterday afternoon.

St. Marcellin was dominated on one side by crags and a kind of rocky plateau. On the other, the ground slowly rose from the village to a chain of gently undulating modest hills, with pastures and rows of vines and olive trees. Beyond, the rising ground grew wilder, covered with juniper, myrtle, thyme and lavender, and then, in the background, the rocky bastion of the alps of High Provence. It was as if St. Marcellin had grown up in a little fertile valley in the wilderness and the sullen, passionate peasantry were incessantly engaged in a battle with nature to hold their own; and that over their habitation hung an atmosphere of impending misfortune.

A group of hens, pecking in the road, scattered with noisy cries as Littlejohn approached them, and a gander, leading four geese under the trees, hissed at him and then went for him with open beak. He beat a retreat and entered the church.

After the bright sunlight outside, it was like entering a tunnel and Littlejohn paused on the inside of the door to recover his sight. Indifferent stained-glass took away the necessary light and the dirty condition of the windows did the rest. The place smelled of candle-grease and incense and the light came mainly from an odd taper or two burning before images and near the high altar. A dim sanctuary-lamp flickered in a side chapel, the only one in the place, and, unlike the rest of the church, was furnished with new rush-seated chairs and a prie-dieu, instead of batteries of hard, cheap benches. Presumably the chapel of the people from the château.

The sacristan shuffled about the building, preparing the altar for High Mass, collecting dead candle-ends and putting them in a canvas bag, dusting the two shabby confessional-boxes with a feather duster. He took no heed of Littlejohn, who was just going to ask him if the curé was about, when the Abbé Chambeyron himself emerged from the sacristy. He had his vestments over his arm. When the priest saw the Chief Inspector he looked ready to turn about and run for it. Then, he slowly walked to meet him.

"Good morning, Monsieur Littlejohn."

"Good morning, father. How is the patient?"

Littlejohn knew it already, but wanted the priest's tale without having to ask for it.

"You must excuse me if I leave you hastily, monsieur. I have to take the Viaticum to Madeleine Tatin."

Madeleine Tatin again! The poor woman seemed to be the excuse for anybody in St. Marcellin who wished to run away. Like the traditional dog men went to see about, at home in England!

"I am waiting for the choir-boy. They are always late."

It was difficult to assess the curé's expression, for his face was illuminated by the reds, yellows, greens and purples of a window showing Abraham about to sacrifice Isaac, but his whole attitude was one of nervous tension.

"…Meanwhile, I take it Monsieur Rossi is getting along well?"

"I don't know.…He left my house in the dead of night and nobody knows where he has gone."

"Indeed! Not even his brother, who was watching by his bed?"

The priest fidgeted with the vestments over his arm.

"I had fallen asleep in the armchair, just after you left me. I was very tired and I didn't wake until two hours later. I hastened upstairs to see how Hénoch was getting along. I found both brothers gone."

"Hénoch is not at home, then?"

"No. His brother says he left him sleeping and went back to attend to the batch of baking for the morning. He is as puzzled as we are.…I can't think.…"

"Do they live over their shop?"

"No. Once they did, but they made a little money and took a small house at the end of the village. It was healthier, they said, and I've no doubt they were right."

"It was a good thing you were abroad last night, Monsieur l'Abbé.…It saved Rossi's life. I must have been the first to hear your shouts for help and get to the spot."

"That is right, Monsieur Littlejohn. I shall never cease from thanking the good God for your timely arrival."

"Alivon wasn't there before me, then?"

"Alivon?"

The curé paused, but he had said enough.

The door opened and a small boy put in his head, greatly to Monsieur Chambeyron's relief. A young imp, with a peasant's face and a tuft of hair on top of his head, which wouldn't lie down in spite of the fat with which he'd liberally anointed it. He slid past Littlejohn and the priest, entered the sacristy, and then emerged transformed and looking like a little angel, clad in a surplice too large for him and carrying a small handbell.

"Excuse me, monsieur."

The Abbé Chambeyron hastily put on his vestments, took up his breviary, and, preceded by the acolyte ringing the bell, went solemnly on his way to comfort the dying.

Outside, the village was almost deserted. Another cart of manure with huge wheels grinding the road and the whiff of rotten straw and ammonia.... A man on an old bicycle.... The tumbledown bus to Manosque ready to leave in half an hour and already half full of peasants afraid it might start without them. Mrs. Littlejohn waving to him from the window of the bar at the *Restaurant Pascal,* where she was writing letters. Eiderdowns and pillows hanging over the balconies of the bedrooms. The sound of Marie Alivon washing glasses and moving bottles. Four men sitting outside at the tables, drinking together. They looked sheepishly at Littlejohn and saluted him respectfully. In the bowling-alley, a small group of players hurling the steel balls about the beaten earth....

Mrs. Littlejohn had asked her husband to get some stamps, and he turned in the small, dark grocer's shop next door to the mayor's house.

Another tunnel, with shadowy forms converging round the counter. The chatter of voices ceased when Littlejohn entered. There was a heavy mixed smell of coffee and spices, half-rancid fat, sour cheese, and garlic on the air. A sanded stone floor, and shelves, counter, doors and cupboards of dirty yellow wood, stained and time-worn. The light came from two windows at the front, filled higgledy-piggledy with anything from shoe-laces and string to soiled dummy packets of chocolate and jars of pickled olives. The dark figures in the gloom of the shop hastily did their business and trotted out, leaving Littlejohn and the woman behind the counter alone. Thérèse Colomb, according to the name above the door.

Littlejohn ordered his stamps and was served from a grubby portfolio which the woman took from under the counter. Then, he asked for cigarettes.

"I do not sell them."

The answer came with venom, as though this were a standard grievance. By the light from the window, Littlejohn could see the dark malevolent eyes of the slatternly, middle-aged woman flash with temper. She was more mercurial and eloquent than the other women Littlejohn had encountered in St. Marcellin. Tall and thin, she must have been good-looking in her youth and perhaps until the perpetual gloom of the shop had withered her in body and spirit.

"I do not sell them.... You are the Englishman staying with his wife at the *Pascal,* hein? You will get them there. It is easy to get a licence to sell tobacco when one has Monsieur le Marquis in one's pocket, like Marie Alivon has."

"They wouldn't give you a licence, then?"

"Tobacco licences are not easy to come by unless one has friends. I am a foreigner. I have only been here for ten years and that is almost to be a stranger. I came from Sospel. My first husband and I were happy there.... A happy place, monsieur. Then I married Colomb and he persuaded me I needed a shop in his native village. And here we are. You will have seen him. He is sacristan at the church. Twenty years older than me and a miser into the bargain. Every night he counts the money and almost takes stock to be sure I haven't cheated him."

The door opened, a woman appeared, and then withdrew when she saw Littlejohn.

"They are a secret lot here. That woman, the wife of the village policeman, is afraid you will find out how much she spends, so she withdraws until you have left. She is a secret eater of chocolate, which she buys from the housekeeping money her husband gives her. And then she takes cheap rancid ham and stale cheese and tells her husband it's my fault. He ought to beat her."

"A pity about the tobacco, though."

"A pity, did you say, monsieur? It's a scandal. I can see you are a just man. You will agree that it isn't right for the snobs at the château to dish out all the privileges. This isn't the Middle Ages, although you'd think so to live here. The Marquis has everybody under his thumb. He owns some of the farms and those he's sold have farmers who were so scared of the people at the hall in the past, that even now, when they're their own masters, they knock at the knees if Monsieur le Marquis says 'booh'. He bullies the priest, and the mayor licks his boots because the Marquis could get him sacked if he wanted. I tell you, if the folks at the château get their knife in you, you might as well pack up and go."

Thérèse Colomb had found a stranger to whom she could open her heart, and Littlejohn's apparent sympathy and understanding had got her in full spate. She leaned her elbows on the counter and began again.

"I daren't talk this way to everybody. You aren't like the rest, I can see. They'd run right off to the bailiff's office and tell him what I said, just to curry favour.... Then, I'd be out. As it is, they just say I'm a bit queer. I don't mind what they say so long as they leave me alone. I only hope one of my sisters-in-law will die soon and then I can go and live with one of my brothers in Sospel. I'll leave Colomb to count his money alone then."

"The Marquis is a friend of the Alivons?"

"Well ... César works on the estate and ... "

She lowered her voice and thrust her face further across the counter.

" ... You've seen that Blanche, who works in Manosque and gets herself up like a cheap little tart? I can see you have, monsieur, and I'm sure you're disgusted. She is Marie Alivon's daughter, you think? That's what *she* calls her. ... Ask any of the villagers and they'll say the same. They all hang together. But I know different. My lady Blanche is really Marie Alivon's niece. Her mother died years ago ... of shame. Went off her head and drowned herself in the lake at the château. An old woman I once did a good turn for, told me. The father was said to be one of the fine gentry at the château and, if it wasn't the Marquis, it was one of his philandering friends. Céleste Alivon, that was Blanche's mother, was a maid up at the house."

"A sad affair."

"Sad! It was shameful, and César Alivon hasn't been the same man since. If he'd any guts, he'd have taken a shotgun to whoever did it. But, oh no. ... Nobody must question the doings of Monsieur the Marquis."

"A funny thing about the baker. ... Did you hear about his accident last night?"

"Accident? Accident, did you say, monsieur? Some of my customers earlier this morning said Hénoch had been drunk last night and talking too much about another *accident*. ... Two people killed on the hill outside the village in February this year. Hit a tree in their car. More friends of Monsieur le Marquis. So the enquiry was hastily done, the doctor, old Mengali, to whom I wouldn't trust a sick cat, certified death due and proper, and the magistrate from Manosque found it accidental. Just as quick as that, sir."

She hit the counter with the flat of her hand.

"All so that the Marquis, whose friends they were, shouldn't have any trouble. And those two poor things lying in the church dead in the prime of life. An Englishman, like you, sir, and his pretty French wife...."

Her voice dropped to a whisper again.

"A pretty girl, whom the Englishman stole from the brother of the Marquis years ago. I was told, in confidence, the brother, who was then Marquis himself, killed himself for love of her when he lost her."

"So, you don't think the affair in February was an accident?"

"I could tell you things, monsieur."

She bent closer and then recoiled. Shuffling footsteps from behind the shop, and the man Littlejohn had seen pottering about in the gloom of the church earlier that morning, entered. A little dried-up chap, with sharp button eyes and a bald head, partly protected from the elements by a black skull-cap. He didn't even look at Littlejohn but, with grubby mean hands, emptied the till, separated the notes from the coin, and started to count the money on the counter. His lips moved as the notes' slid through his clawing fingers. "Ten, twenty, thirty, forty... Four thousand...."

Littlejohn bade the woman good day and left the shop.

The doctor's car was standing in front of the mayor's house. It was a tumbledown, out-dated model, almost like a hearse. Dr. Mengali was just closing the door of the *mairie.*

"Good morning, doctor.... How is the patient?"

"Madeleine Tatin, you mean?"

Again!

"... She's taken a turn for the better. We'll soon have her up and about."

In the distance, the priest and the choir-boy were returning with less ceremony than they went. The choir-boy was carrying his surplice over his arm and holding the clapper of the little bell to keep it quiet. He said something to the priest, who took both bell and surplice from him, boxed his ears, and sent him off in the direction of the school.

"I meant the baker, doctor."

Mengali waved his arms about.

"A perfect farce, Monsieur Littlejohn! The man recovered and then he must have gone off his head. He got up and ran away. Always a bit unstable...."

"Where did he go?"

"Don't ask me. They have relatives all over the place. Some in Marseilles, some in Paris, some in Grenoble. He might be anywhere. And after the time that was wasted last night.... It makes my blood boil to think I dragged him out of the very jaws of death... yes, death itself... and then he does this."

No mention of Littlejohn's efforts!

The doctor chattered on, his beard wagging like that of an old goat, flecks of indignant foam in the corners of his mouth. Littlejohn wondered when and where he'd graduated and whether he was really any good. A typical Balzacian country doctor.

"Hénoch was telling me last night you attended to a countryman of mine and his wife, killed here earlier this year."

"They were dead when I arrived. Killed driving their car against a tree on the hill there. The road is bad and they must have been travelling at high speed."

"Hénoch suggested it might not have been an accident."

The goat beard seemed to rise almost horizontally on the little man's chin. Give him a cheroot and he'd have looked like Captain Kettle himself, in a bad mood, too!

"Who told him that? He knew nothing about it. He was always a bit mad. I tell you, it was an accident. What else could it be?"

The doctor's watery, washed-out eyes searched Littlejohn's face, and the Chief Inspector got the impression that he was afraid, too. He shrugged his shoulders in true French fashion.

"I was only telling you what Hénoch said in his cups, doctor. It's no business of mine. The case was closed ... "

"Closed, yes, and *found to be an accident."*

The little doctor shouted it aloud in his emphasis.

"I mustn't keep you, doctor. You're a very busy man, I know. A lot of official work, I guess."

The doctor was mollified and smiled. He took out a battered packet of cigarettes, gave Littlejohn one, took one himself, and lit them both. His fingers were yellow with smoking and there was a nicotine stain in the middle of his beard.

"Very busy, my friend. I have the schools to see to, local sanitation, as well as being official medical man to the power station at Brômes-St. Eusèbe, just over the hill there.... And, of course, I'm physician to Monsieur le Marquis and all the estate hands."

Another of them! Probably he owed all his official jobs to the patronage of the big house. It paid to keep his mouth shut!

"I'll let you get on, then, sir.... Good day."

"Good day... or rather *au revoir*, monsieur. I may see you at the *Pascal* this evening. I hear you are quite a man at bowls."

He entered the car, eventually got it going after a struggle, shunted it back into the road, and went off in the direction of Manosque.

There was only one other call and Littlejohn would have to be careful there, too.

The bakery door was open and heavy metallic noises were emerging. Ernest Rossi was cleaning out the ovens. He raised a strained, flour-covered face to see who was causing the shadow in the doorway.

"Good morning."

"Good morning, monsieur."

Ernest looked nervous, too. He took off the steel-rimmed spectacles he was wearing and began to polish them on his apron, breathing on them and examining them carefully to avoid meeting the Chief Inspector's eyes.

"How is your brother after last night's misfortune, Monsieur Rossi?"

"He is better."

"Still at the parsonage?"

A pause. Rossi busied himself scraping the shelf he was holding.

"No. He improved and was able to get up. He thought it better to take a little rest, so has gone to visit some relatives."

"He was in a hurry, wasn't he? A bit dangerous?"

"No, I don't think so. It will do him good."

"I'm glad he is better."

"So am I, sir."

And that was all. Littlejohn wondered if poor Hénoch had bolted to safety, or been rushed out of the village to keep him quiet.

There was nothing more could safely be said, so the Chief Inspector bade the baker good morning.

"This will make you busy, I fear, Monsieur Rossi."

"My nephew is coming to-day. I have sent for him to Gap, where he is an apprentice baker."

Out in the street, the bus for Manosque was throbbing heavily, ready for off. At the grocery shop something was happening, too. Loud shouts and screams, and Monsieur and Madame Colomb appeared. He was carrying a cheap fibre suitcase and pushing his wife along with his free hand. She was putting on her hat and trying to slip her arms through a costume coat at the same time.

"Get along, woman, the bus is going."

"I'm not ready.... I haven't packed my things.... If you send me off now, you old miser, I'll not come back. I'll stay in Sospel where I'm wanted, and you and all your money and your precious Marquis won't get me back to this hell-on-earth again. Take your hands off me."

Higher up the street people were holding back the bus. The Colombs had halted in the road to have it out. Arms flying, shouts splitting the air. People came to their doors to listen, never moving a muscle, quite unamused, taking it all in.

"You talk too much.... I'm sick of the sound of your voice. It never stops.... "

"I've no money. I can't go without money, you old skinflint."

Colomb took out a black calico bag from his pocket and began to count out notes and coins.

"This isn't enough. It won't pay my fare to Manosque.... Here, give it to me."

She snatched the purse and tried to put it in her imitation crocodile-skin handbag. The driver and conductor of the bus got out, with cigarettes in the corners of their mouths, and came to help the pair settle their differences.

"She can go to-morrow. There's always the next bus."

"She's going with *you*. I'm sick of her tongue. I want a rest. It's driving me mad."

She wouldn't give up the calico bag and clung to her own handbag, defying the sacristan and calling him all the names under the sun. Then she spotted Littlejohn.

"Monsieur... monsieur... I call on you to bear witness I wasn't gossiping or telling lies to you.... Was I... ? Now, was I? Do you hear? He's sending me home to my brother."

Before Littlejohn could gather himself together, the bus crew had hustled Thérèse Colomb on the vehicle and her husband, who tried to board it with her to rescue his money, was thrust off. The conductor rang the bell and they left him, waving his fists and shouting oaths quite out of keeping with his sacred duties.

Littlejohn couldn't help laughing when he got indoors, although it was really no laughing matter. Another important witness had been sent off into exile for talking too much.

Things had warmed up with a vengeance!

Chapter Six
The Lawyer who was Disbarred

Mrs. Littlejohn finished her letters and looked through the window. Her husband was still deep in the gloom of the grocer's shop opposite. It was time to make some show of following her purpose of sketching the village, so she went upstairs, found a pad and pencil, took a shooting-stick, put on a wide-brimmed native straw hat she'd bought in Marseilles, and went in search of copy.

The by-road which passed the side of the inn wound upwards into the hills. On either side were scattered clumps of cottages with dilapidated tile roofs, faded pink-washed walls, and crazy shutters. Some were empty and from those apparently occupied there came no sounds of life. Now and then a farm with a fetid smell of manure and straw. Here, more than elsewhere, was the evidence that St. Marcellin was dying on its feet.

The farm which backed on the hotel was better kept, with a clean yard, a threshing floor, and a small garden full of vivid sunflowers and with a knotted old vine climbing over the lintel. A shrill quavering voice arguing with a deep gruff one, and then silence, as though the contestants had paused to watch the passer-by.

The view from the adjoining field, through which a small footpath snaked its way, covered the old houses leaning on one another for support, a copse of dwarf oaks, and a background of rising hills. Mrs. Littlejohn found a place there and, sitting on her shooting-stick, began to draw.

She was so engrossed in what she was doing that she did not notice a new arrival for some time and then, raising her head, found a little slender woman, dressed in black and wearing a black straw sailor-hat on the top of her head, entering the field. Before her ran a little fat dog, a dachshund, whose busy legs were hardly visible and which looked like a large brown sausage sliding across the grass. Hardly had the little dog started to enjoy himself, than two mongrel wolfhounds, sheep dogs from the farm, tore into the field and made for the intruder. The dachshund slithered hither and thither, yapping with fear, seeking a way back to the old woman who, hampered by her long skirts and old bones, was frantically trying to reach it before the curs which were relentlessly rounding it up.

Mrs. Littlejohn entered the ring of dogs, seized the small one, and lifted it in her arms. At the same time she raised the pointed end of her stick in a forlorn effort to keep the snarling hounds at bay. The dachshund kicked and snapped and its claws tore a sharp gash in Mrs. Littlejohn's arm.

The farmer himself, an elderly man, loose-limbed and with a leathery face and the moustaches and the appearance of a tumbledown Viking, appeared on the scene, kicked his dogs away, muttering something in dialect, and then made himself scarce without another word.

The old lady arrived and took the little dog, her bright black eyes flashing first at Mrs. Littlejohn with gratitude and friendship, then at the receding back of the farmer with venom.

"A thousand thanks, madame.... He loosed his dogs deliberately. He doesn't like my bringing Mirabelle through his fields.... I shall tell Mora, the policeman, about him, but it won't do much good.... Your arm is bleeding, madame."

"Just a scratch."

"You must come to my house and I will clean it. I hope it isn't a bite. They are dangerous, especially from great hounds like those."

"It's just a scratch from Mirabelle's claws."

"All the more reason why..."

Mrs. Littlejohn was just going to brush matters aside and say she would go back to the inn and clean up; and then she remembered how few friends she and the Chief Inspector had made to help them.

It ended by her following the old lady, who introduced herself as Mademoiselle Malicorne, to her home.

The house was on the main street, the last of any size before the country opened out in the direction of the mountains. A stone building entered by a flight of stone steps with rusty iron railings on each side. The shutters to all the windows of three floors were closed.

Mademoiselle Malicorne opened the heavy front door and they found themselves in a dark hall, from which a staircase wound up in the gloom. The place was flagged and cool, with straw mats here and there, and smelled of old leather and floor polish.

The dog ran ahead and disappeared in the back regions, and somewhere a canary started to chirp.

"Who is it?"

A loud, domineering voice shouted from a room at the back just as Mrs. Littlejohn and her new friend entered. A highly-polished room, with a lot of heavy furniture, hanging cupboards, bookcases full of calf-bound volumes, two easy chairs in front of a stove. It was bright and sunlit from a large French window at one end. Beyond that, a walled garden, neglected and deserted, with a statue of a nymph with one hand and her nose knocked off, rising from the middle of a bed of overgrown and untended geraniums.

A fat, comfortable man with a swelling paunch was sitting in one of the chairs. Even if he had had a good head of hair, his forehead would have seemed abnormally high and large. As it was, he was bald and the height of his brow made him almost a freak. A smooth face, firm chin and straight nose. Dark eyes, like his sister's, shone through gold-framed spectacles.

"My brother, Maître Malicorne, late of the Bar at Grenoble.... He retired some years ago."

She did not say he had been disbarred for unprofessional conduct!

Monsieur Malicorne rose to be introduced and proved to be small into the bargain. He was dressed in black with spotless white linen as though ready just to put on his gown and go into court.

"The Brunels' dogs almost killed our poor little Mirabelle again."

At the sound of his feminine name, the little sausage appeared and howled as if to confirm the statement, although the noise was meant to imply that his food dish was empty.

"...And Mrs. Littlejohn saved his life by beating off the curs with her own hands.... I must attend to your injury, madame."

Mademoiselle Malicorne scuttered away for water and plaster. Her brother, however, was not listening. He flung his fists in the air and waved his arms.

"Scoundrels! Scum! Peasants! Hooligans! I will clear up my affairs and we will go down to the coast to live. I won't stay a day longer."

He said it every day, but his money was running low and he was dependent on the house his parents had left to his sister and the dowry she'd never needed.

Then the excitement subsided and he apologized.

"You must not take it amiss, madame. It is not your affair, but we are grateful for what you have done. Should the occasion arise, we will not be tardy in proving our gratitude. How long are you staying here?"

He looked at her anxiously, as though she might be about to ask him to fulfil his promise.

"A day or two. We are exploring the countryside and I am doing some sketches."

"You are an artist? In my youth I was thought to be good.... Those are my work...."

He indicated two heavily-framed water colours. Mrs. Littlejohn had seen better in children's exhibitions at home but did not say so. They looked to be bad copies of picture post-cards of the Riviera.

Mademoiselle Malicorne was back, quickly cleaned the scratch, on which the blood had dried, and stuck a piece of black sticking-plaster over it.

"You ought to have that seen to," said the ex-lawyer. "Those Brunei lurchers are sure to have rabies."

Mrs. Littlejohn tried to explain that it was a mere scratch from Mirabelle, but the little fat man was not listening. His arms were in the air again.

"But not by that incompetent noodle, Mengali. A quack, madame, a quack, if ever there was one. He ought to have been struck from the register long ago."

He mowed the air in a striking-off gesture, forgetting his own taste of the same medicine.

"You are English, madame. Are you aware that earlier this year that quack Mengali certified two of your countrymen… or rather a man and his wife… as having died from a motor accident when he hadn't even performed a post-mortem?"

There was a small tarnished mirror over the fireplace and Mrs. Littlejohn saw through it Mademoiselle Malicorne placing her finger on her lips and trying to warn her brother to guard his tongue. But the Maître wasn't having any. He was on his favourite hobby-horse.

"An incredible ignoramus, he couldn't perform an autopsy if he were told to do it. I doubt if he even has any surgical instruments. Cupping and bleeding, yes, but they are no qualifications for police evidence."

"English people, Maître Malicorne? Who were they?"

"Married people, touring, I presume. Lavalle or something, the name was…."

And, as he thrust his face in her own to pronounce the name, Mrs. Littlejohn received a blast of brandy and she realized the lawyer was half drunk. By the side of the stove stood a large coffee jug, a cup, and a bottle from which the drink had apparently been copiously laced.

"It was all a mystery."

He sat down, after drawing up a large carved chair for his guest and, obviously showing-off now that he had an audience, spoke in a heavy whisper.

"I could tell you things…."

His sister was in great distress, shaking her head, putting her finger to her lips, trying to interrupt his flow by irrelevant remarks. He completely ignored her.

"Why, madame, was the car said, at the enquiry, to be travelling *from* the Manosque direction, when all the time I saw it going *to* Manosque? I was standing at the door in the darkness whilst our little Mirabelle paid his final call before bed. It was between ten and eleven o'clock and the car came through the village first, struck a tree where the road begins to mount steeply to the forest, and then darkness again. At the enquiry, it seems they found that the car was *entering* the village from Manosque."

"And you did not give evidence as a witness to the contrary, Maître Malicorne?"

The little lawyer had been holding forth in his best court style and had screwed a thin monocle in his eye as though this mannerism were one of the tactics of his professional days. He paused when he heard Mrs. Littlejohn's voice. He wore a startled expression, as though someone had dared to halt his peroration in a court of law.

"I beg your pardon, madame."

"You weren't called as a witness?"

"Certainly not. I had no wish to be mixed up in the affair. I quarrelled with the parties to the enquiry some years ago. The magistrate from Manosque, the Procureur from Digne.... It would have been awkward to meet them, to say the least of it."

"And where could the car have been coming from at that hour, if it hadn't travelled from the main road from Manosque?"

The lawyer sketched in the air with his little podgy hand.

"Maybe from Nice or Riez, or even the château. Though why the château, I can't think. At that hour they would surely have stayed the night."

A buxom girl, with red cheeks, strongly-built and with bare arms, entered and served coffee. The canary chirped, the dog whined for attention, the sun shone in the room, and they made small talk. Then Mrs. Littlejohn left them.

"You will call again and bring your husband next time."

The house lapsed into its silence, with buzzing flies and the smells of lunch in preparation, garlic, stew and hot olive oil. Outside, the priest was passing with a party of small boys he was preparing for their first communion, and another little group of girls in the charge of a sister made up the rear.

Littlejohn was waiting for Letty at the inn.

"There's a nice roast duck for lunch," Marie Alivon told them. "It will be ready in half an hour."

They strolled along the road in the direction of Manosque and the spot where the death of Lovell and his wife had occurred. Mrs. Littlejohn told the Chief Inspector all she'd learned from the Malicornes.

"It's obvious the Maître has a grudge against authority. He took no steps to correct the official impression about where the car came from. And he hates the doctor, who's probably the only other professional man in the village, and hence a kind of rival."

Littlejohn lit his pipe and smoked in silence for a time.

"We'd better go down to the coast to-morrow. Christopher Lovell's father-in-law lives at Cap Ferrat, not far from Nice, and he may be able to throw a little light on matters. I must also call and say 'How-do' to Dorange, at Nice. He's probably been advised that I'm here and will perhaps have guessed what I'm after. The two people who could have helped me, Madame Colomb and Rossi, the baker, have vanished, and from what your new friend says, there was something funny about the enquiry. It will be safer to have the police at Nice in the background."

They had reached Leclerc's garage. The owner, dressed in dirty overalls, was repairing a tumbledown car, and when

Littlejohn appeared in the doorway, he drew himself from under the chassis and bared his long teeth in his comedian's grin.

"Good morning, Leclerc."

"Good day, monsieur."

"We're going for a trip to the coast to-morrow and I'd like you to overhaul the car, grease and oil it, and rub it down."

"With pleasure, sir. Bring it in any time, or shall I collect it?"

He wiped his greasy hands, stuck a cigarette in the corner of his mouth, and emerged for a talk in the open air.

"No news of Hénoch Rossi, Leclerc?"

The garage owner squinted in the sun.

"No, sir."

"A funny thing, the way he vanished without anybody hearing him. Did he own a car?"

"They have an old van."

"You were working, according to what you told me last night, long after you left us?"

"Yes."

"Did any vehicle pass your place after you returned?"

Leclerc flicked away the ash from his cigarette and gave Littlejohn an inquisitive look.

"No vehicle passed. ... No vehicle."

"A mystery. ..."

"Yes, sir. A mystery. Hénoch will turn up. He was always a queer, timid man and yet, get a drink in him and he was as brave as a lion and as talkative as a monkey. Well, sir, I must be getting on."

"We're just going to see the spot where the English people were killed early this year. Where is it exactly?"

For a moment they stared one another in the face, as though each were trying to read the other's thoughts.

Leclerc only read mild interest in the eyes of the Chief Inspector; his own were full of cunning and suspicion now. Leclerc wiped his hands again on his oily rag and pointed his long arm in the direction of the road, just where the hill rose steeply into the forest of firs.

"At the steep part, just where the road turns the corner. A very dangerous place, sir, especially when there's ice on it, as there was when the accident happened. You'll see the very spot where a tree has been dug up. The car hit the tree and it had to be cut down. They dug up the roots and will perhaps plant another in the autumn. There's nothing to see.... Not a thing...."

"Did you examine the car after the smash?"

"Yes. It was a complete wreck."

He kicked an empty sardine tin which was lying beside the door, twisted out of shape by forcible opening with a spanner. It had held Leclerc's lunch, which he'd already eaten.

"A wreck as much as this tin here."

He kicked it again into the road and a thin cat emerged from a side lane and started to lick the oil from the metal.

"Did you make a report on it?"

"Yes. Nothing to report, though. It was too smashed up even to examine the brakes."

The Littlejohns made their way to the spot described by Leclerc, who watched them listlessly for a minute or two, threw his cigarette in the roadway, and then vanished indoors.

There was, as the garage man had said, nothing to see. The road was a secondary one, with a loose surface, and turned sharply just where the disturbed soil showed the tree had been removed. There was good room for two cars to pass. Thence the road went into the thickness of the Forest of Cadarache on its way to Mirabeau and Manosque. From the spot where presumably the car had hit the displaced fir, the ground fell away and the slope of trees presumably ended far below at village level.

Littlejohn entered the forest just near the spot where the accident had occurred. Half a dozen paces and he was lost from the road. The trees had closed round him and he stood in the half-light on a carpet of dead leaves, cones, and pale slippery grass.

If, as Maître Malicorne had said, the car had been travelling *from* the village, instead of *to* it, it was incredible that it should have hit a tree hard enough to convert the vehicle into a mass of tangled wreckage, smash down the tree, and break the necks of the occupants. As soon as the skid occurred, the driver, unless a complete idiot, would take his foot from the accelerator; then the gradient would immediately act as a brake.... Coming downhill would be quite different, with the engine and the steep slope acting together.

On the road, a few yards away, he thought he heard voices, and quickly made his way back to where he had left his wife.

A large, old-fashioned open sports car had drawn up opposite where he had entered the wood, and the occupant was talking to Mrs. Littlejohn.

"Ah.... Is this your husband, madame?"

The man in the car spoke good English. He turned to Littlejohn, leaned out of the car, and pointed to the spot where the Chief Inspector had been exploring.

"You are right, sir. That is exactly where the accident happened."

From what Littlejohn could see of the newcomer, he was muscular and well-built with a trace of flabbiness setting in in his big frame. A bit soft... that was it. A good head of jet-black hair, a long, thin, intelligent face and dark, gay, mocking eyes with lines of early middle-age appearing round them. The hands resting on the wheel of the car were large and well cared-for, with a big signet ring on the left little finger.

"I took the liberty of stopping, because I had heard some English people were staying at the Alivons' place. I guessed you were curious to find the spot where your fellow-countryman and his wife..."

The mocking eyes sparkled as though there were something very humorous in the situation.

"By the way, allow me to introduce myself to you. I have already met your wife, sir."

Letty's eyes were almost as mocking as those of the newcomer.

"I am the Marquis de St. Marcellin—Arnaud de St. Marcellin, to be precise. And you, sir, are Monsieur Littlejohn, on a sightseeing tour. Well, you won't find much to see here different from a hundred other decaying villages in these parts. A peasant population... apparently surly, but actually shy with strangers, especially from foreign parts. And by foreign, I mean anywhere a few leagues away."

"It's a pleasure to meet you, Monsieur le Marquis. We've already heard a lot about you in the village."

"Nothing but good, I trust. I gather that you and your wife have already earned an excellent reputation. The natives are... How do the Scots put it...? Rather *dour*... yes, dour is the word. But they have already taken to you. You are quite an expert at bowls, they tell me, and that last night you rescued our village baker from a nasty end. As for your good wife, there was, this morning, an incident about a little dog.... You see, news travels fast here."

The mocking eyes looked straight into those of Littlejohn. The Marquis knew all the questions and all the answers. He never stopped talking.

"I am just leaving for a short time. A matter of some land to be settled at Brômes-St. Eusèbe, where they are building an electrical barrage and want to buy part of my estate. I shall be away for a few days. The shooting is too good to miss whilst I am there. But I'll be back about... let me see... Thursday. You will still be here?"

"Very likely. We are enjoying the place and the rest is doing us both good."

"Very well. The curé usually comes to dinner on Saturday."

Come with him to the château, both of you. You'll be most welcome. Although past its prime and in a state of some decay, it is still one of the sights of the neighbourhood, where sights are few. I think I can promise you an interesting time."

"Thank you, sir. That's a date, then."

"Yes. A date."

The Marquis pressed the starter and the large car began to throb. He extended his hand to Mrs. Littlejohn, took her own, and kissed it gallantly.

"*Au 'voir,* madame. Charmed to meet you."

He let in the clutch and the car began to move slowly. The Marquis leaned over and shook Littlejohn's hand. He was chuckling.

"Till Saturday, then. Charmed to meet you, too, Chief Inspector Littlejohn. You must tell me all about Scotland Yard next time we meet."

Chapter Seven

At *La Folie*

The astonishing day ended in a quiet evening, and the routine of the night before began and finished as though nothing out of the ordinary had happened. First an excellent meal in the gathering dusk to the accompaniment of the cracked bell of the church over the way. Olives, tomatoes, foie gras and crawfish for an hors d'œuvre, then *poularde demideuil* of boiled chicken and truffles, followed by cherries and cheese. The whole washed down with a Châteauneuf du Pape from the vineyard of a cousin of the Alivons. They had also put candied fruits from Apt, nearby, on the table in honour of Mrs. Littlejohn.

The church bell ceased and a melancholy silence fell on the village. Alivon had taken the bath upstairs, wearing it on his head like a monstrous oversized helmet, and smoking his pipe placidly beneath it. Water had been put to boil in the kitchen. The bar was deserted, for the men had adjourned for the nightly game of bowls and the mayor had invited Littlejohn to join them again. In the sad dusk, someone was playing a guitar.

As Littlejohn made his way to the bowling pitch, he saw lights burning dimly in the church and a small band of dark figures entering, like ghosts, for a saint's-day service.

The bar was full and there was a regular fug of tobacco smoke when they returned from their game. Men of all shapes and sizes. Some powerful, full-blooded and large-boned; others wiry and shapeless, the oldest of them knotted like old roots and with joints swollen like drumsticks. Most of them complaining of drought, rising costs, falls in the market prices of lavender oil, eggs, olives, livestock. Drinking was slow and steady, and mostly of cheap wine. Those who ordered coffee laced it with brandy. The scraping of chairs, the click of the bead curtains, greetings and leave-takings were going on all the time.

For some reason, perhaps for rescuing Hénoch Rossi, or even because earlier in the day someone had seen Littlejohn shaking hands with the Marquis de St. Marcellin and passed the news round, the Chief Inspector was treated with great civility, and even respect. The villagers took care to greet him with a nervous nod or an awkward salute when they entered, and to wish him good night before the bead curtain cut them off and they vanished unsteadily in the dark. The mayor and the doctor were sitting with Littlejohn. Monsieur Savini wore, as usual, his smart business suit and shiny patent-leather shoes and the doctor, who seemed to have been enjoying a country ramble or an afternoon's sport, had on a shooting-suit a size too small for him, and gum-boots.

But nobody mentioned Hénoch Rossi or his mishap and disappearance, which, in a village which lived on gossip and the remoteness of which from the busy world made even small things loom large, was very strange. And then, after a spell of steady drinking, Mora, the gendarme, rose from a nearby table, walked unsteadily to Littlejohn, placed a large forefinger on the lapel of the Chief Inspector's jacket and addressed him respectfully.

"I know, sir, that famous people often like to travel unknown on account of being troubled and worried by the curious, but I would just like to say... and I assure you, monsieur, I shall be silent on the matter afterwards... I would like to say that this village, and particularly myself as guardian of law and order here, feel highly honoured by the presence among us of a famous *Commissaire* from *le Scotland Yard.*"

Mora paused and looked round. Those near enough to hear had ceased their noise and were listening; those on the periphery were still shouting their bids at cards or conversing loudly. Mora cleared his throat and looked as if he suddenly realized that he'd been indiscreet and let the cat out of the bag.

The mayor and the doctor exchanged glances and then the mayor silenced the policeman with a savage look.

"You fool! Wasn't it agreed that the Inspector should be left in peace to enjoy the rest of his stay with us. He had obvious reasons for wanting to remain incognito. He is here for a rest... you blundering fool, Mora."

Littlejohn lit his pipe calmly. Now that the news was out, it might be easier.

Mora was still standing almost at attention, taking the mayor's abuse like a naughty schoolboy under the eyes of all present.

"Sit down, sergeant.... Have a drink with us. And thank you for the speech of welcome.... Come on, man, here's some wine."

The policeman pulled himself together, smiled, heaved a sigh of relief and drank his wine in one. Everybody relaxed, and talk and card-calls started again.

"How did you find out about me?"

Mora looked at the mayor, who said nothing. Instead, Savini poured himself a glass of wine, mopped his sweating forehead, and drank deeply.

"It was Monsieur le Marquis, sir. The mayor usually reports all unusual events in the village to him and when your name was mentioned in connection with Hénoch's little accident, the Marquis at once rang up Manosque, who had never heard of you, and then Marseilles, who had. They said you were a famous detective from *le Scotland Yard....*"

Another pause.

"We didn't want to disturb you, Mister Littlejohn—or should I say Chief Inspector? You must have had good reasons for not disclosing."

The mayor had chipped-in and looked uneasy about it.

"Are you here about the Englishman and his wife who... who met with an accident?"

"I am taking a rest from official duties, Monsieur le Maire. Even a policeman needs a holiday, now and then. To-morrow we're making a trip to Nice for a day or two. We have friends there. But we like your village and we will probably call again on the way back home."

"So you are not on a case, Chief Inspector?"

"No."

The mayor drank up and looked anxious to be getting along. It was becoming obvious that, on his own or someone else's behalf, he was out to find the real reason for Littlejohn's presence in St. Marcellin.

Littlejohn took the opportunity to call it a day.

"I must retire, too. We leave early."

Half those present had been listening again, and now everyone gathered round him to advise him on the best way to take from St. Marcellin to the coast. It was obvious that many of them had never been near the sea and gave advice from hearsay. Some even suggested a wide detour to Digne and then down the main road. They were still squabbling about routes when the Chief Inspector said good night.

The Littlejohns left at seven the following morning before the sun got too high, and half the village saw them off. They took the by-roads south through magnificent country with rich orchards on the low ground and wild undergrowth on the heights, and then through many towns of old Provence, with vast wildernesses between them. They lunched at Draguinan, struck south again to St. Raphael, and followed the coast all the way to Cap Ferrat. It was too late for Littlejohn to call on Monsieur de Barge, so they found a hotel for the night at St. Jean-Cap-Ferrat.

Next morning they had no difficulty in finding the de Barge villa. The manager of the hotel grew lyrical about it. *La Folie.* Near the end of the Cap, with the sea on three sides and its own private swimming-pool into the bargain. An earthly paradise! A garden famous on the Coast. Money no object. The manager added that the de Barges were smart, calm-loving people. He had evidently obtained these credentials from the English guide-book, which described the whole of the clientele of those parts in similar terms.

La Folie turned out to be a large, tastefully-built villa of whitewashed concrete, with a background of pine trees and a full view out to the lighthouse and the open sea. Large expensive wrought-iron gates shut it off from the rest of the world, but the shouts of people enjoying themselves somewhere in the extensive grounds showed it was not deserted. Littlejohn handed in his official card at the lodge and, after a pause—presumably whilst the porter communicated by telephone with the villa—the gates were opened and the Littlejohns drove along a drive of sharp white pebbles to the house, and parked the modest, hired railway *Simca* cheek-by-jowl with a flock of racing, luxury and extravagant cars which would have graced any motor-show. The gardens on the way and surrounding *La Folie* were a blaze of exquisite colour. Not a plant out of place, not a flower out of taste, not a solitary weed to be seen, sweeping green lawns between the beds, and batteries of water-jets whizzing round to keep it all cool and blooming.

Below the house, the land sloped away to a private beach where, in a large swimming-pool surrounded by tables shaded by coloured parasols, about a dozen young people were sporting around in bathing dress, plunging in and out of the water, and chasing one another up and down the sand and across the edge of the pool. A busy mass of *élan vital* making the most of the sun and the exquisite surroundings.

A manservant in a striped waistcoat immediately took the Littlejohns in tow and preceded them indoors. A large, cool white marble hall, a fine marble staircase, a balcony of the same stone with bedrooms leading from it. On the ground floor, the open door of a huge sun-lounge with wide windows, every one with a different view of the coast and the sea. The servant led them to another closed room, knocked, and showed them in. Here the shutters were drawn, but the half-light revealed a tall, fat man, sitting at a desk in what must have been his study. He waved the servant away before the poor fellow could open his mouth and say his piece. Monsieur de Barge seemed made that way. Impatient, highly-strung, querulous....

The room was of medium size and cosy. A large, unstained, modern mahogany desk with chairs to match, upholstered in yellow leather. Walls on three sides covered half-way in books, some of them used, others bought en masse for furnishing purposes. Above the shelves, three large pictures of the Matisse school. Pottery all over the shop. A perfect museum of Provençal ceramics.... On the desk facing de Barge, three photographs of the same girl as a small child, in her First Communion gown, and as a beautiful young woman. There were no papers before de Barge and he might easily have been taking a rest from the busy whirl of energy going on among his guests. A massive, dark, bald man of sixty or thereabouts, wearing an expensively-tailored yachting suit. His shoes and shirt and tie were probably the most exclusive anybody could buy. And, in spite of it all, he looked provincial and middle-class. He was holding Littlejohn's card and taking a drink from a long glass in which ice was clinking. He seemed surprised to see Mrs. Littlejohn, as though, somehow, he expected famous detectives to be celibate, like priests. All the same, he brightened up at the sight of her. He rose, revealed himself to be even taller and fatter, and shook hands firmly with them both.

"I'm so glad to see you. I'm not satisfied with the way the local police handled the affair. Now perhaps we'll get somewhere."

He spoke in good English. It was obvious the death of his daughter was still heavily on his mind and he thought about it before the courtesies due to his guests.

"You'll stay here, of course."

"No, sir. We're making St. Marcellin our headquarters."

De Barge nodded. He had a heavy, square jaw and good living had made the flesh of his cheeks loose. A large Roman nose, a broad, low forehead, and bright little eyes with heavy upper lids and baggy dark skin under them.

"Have a drink."

It was obvious that Monsieur de Barge took too much of it!

As though the banker had summoned the genie of the lamp, the manservant in his striped vest appeared wheeling a trolley of bottles, glasses, ice, shining tools and receptacles, like a surgeon's equipment. He did not speak, but raised his sad eyes, like those of a spaniel, and gently passed his white hand over the mass of bottles and paraphernalia to indicate that it was all theirs if they wished.

"Two long Italians with some ice and perrier, please."

The manservant looked pained and surprised at the simplicity of the order and, like a conjuror mixing ingredients from which he will eventually produce flags of all nations and a pair of doves, he made the drinks and gently handed them over.

"I'll have one, too."

The flunkey looked sadder than ever and gave his master a look which beseeched him not to insult his powers of concocting subtle mixtures.

"And then you can go."

The man bowed his head and handed over the third glass.

"Will your wife want to be in at this?"

Monsieur de Barge was asking out of courtesy, but his deep, melancholy voice made it sound as though some male secret, unfit for her to hear, was about to be divulged.

Before either could answer, he had pressed a key on the house telephone before him.

"Is your mistress at the pool?" he asked in French.

"Yes, sir."

"Get her."

"Yes, sir."

"And be quick about it."

He must have paid his servants well!

"Please be seated. You'll find the easy chairs the best. Cigarette?"

He handed round a silver box and took one himself, lighting all three from a gold lighter which he produced from his pocket. The cigarettes bore a crown with *de Barge* over it.

"You are staying long in France?"

"Not long, sir. Just until I can see through the affair of last February."

"You also suspect that it was not an accident?"

"There are one or two peculiar features about it."

"Such as?"

"I was watched from the first minute we entered St. Marcellin and the behaviour of the whole village has been, to say the least of it, odd. The place is feudal and everyone seems to obey the Marquis implicitly. They've evidently had orders to tell me nothing."

De Barge flicked the ash of his cigarette on the carpet.

"I could have told you that from the start. I have had my own private investigators on the case and they drew a complete blank. I suppose you are here on behalf of the brother of Christopher?"

"Yes. He didn't advise you of my coming?"

"Not exactly. He said he would do what he could from his end."

"You are not satisfied about the affair?"

"No. Although all the official work of the enquiry seemed honest and efficient enough."

"Why weren't you satisfied, then?"

De Barge put down his glass and settled in his armchair with a sigh.

"For the same reason that you must be dissatisfied. It was stretching coincidence too far for them to be killed on the very doorstep of the family whose ruin they seem to have brought about."

"Ruin?"

Another large car drew up at the house and a young man and a girl got out dressed for bathing, and made straight for the pool at the bottom of the garden. Littlejohn, his skin pleasantly damp from the heat of the room, felt envious, and could have done very well with a swim himself.

"Yes, ruin. When Elise broke her engagement with Bernard and decided to marry Christopher Lovell, Bernard met with a so-called shooting accident and his younger brother, Arnaud, succeeded to the title and estates. Arnaud, by his extravagance and drunkenness, has in a few years dissipated the already declining family fortune."

"You mention a *so-called* accident."

"In my view, it was suicide. In the first place, Bernard loved my daughter to distraction. In the second, I know he hoped, with Elise's considerable dowry, to make good some of the losses and dilapidations in the estate. I do confess that I never favoured her marrying an impoverished aristocrat from the start, but Bernard seemed to sweep her off her feet. And then I found she didn't love him when Chris turned up."

"You were glad she preferred Lovell?"

De Barge grimaced slightly as though some memory or other hurt him.

"Yes.... Lovell was a nice fellow. But we'd always hoped she might marry her cousin Charles, with whom she'd been brought up from childhood. There was a kind of unspoken understanding and it would have pleased our family. We are a large family from Lyons. I admit I've done well for myself. I began as a clerk in a merchant bank and rose to own it. Elise would have been very rich one day."

The old provincial idea of keeping the money in the family!

"Wasn't the cause of Bernard's death definitely established?"

"In a way. There were witnesses. Four of them; all soldiers."

"Who were they?"

"Lovell, himself; the present Marquis, Arnaud; a colonel named Latour, who died just after the war; and a sergeant, I think, who was acting as loader for Bernard."

"Where *is* this sergeant?"

"He left the army after the war and is now caretaker of a villa near Antibes. His name is Albert Lapointe. My son-in-law visited him once or twice at Antibes.... A villa called *Montjouvain....*"

"And they all appeared as witnesses at the inquest?"

"Yes. And on their testimony it was declared to be an accident. There was a proper inquest, of course, and medical evidence."

"By Dr. Mengali?"

De Barge looked up hastily with just a touch of malice in his glance. He resented Littlejohn's knowing so much!

"How do you know Mengali?"

"He is official surgeon in St. Marcellin and I met him there."

"I think the whole affair was dealt with like that of Elise and Chris. Things were hushed up on the feudal authority of the Marquis."

"But that is fantastic!"

"Why? The only witnesses were friends of the Marquis. Even the enquiry was conducted by a judge politically beholden to the family. I have had both affairs investigated to that extent."

"All the same, you aren't suggesting corruption?"

"No. But you don't know those parts. It is a land apart. Influence can be so powerful as to make people *believe* strange things."

There was a timid knock on the door and a woman of about sixty entered the study. Thin and dejected looking, she seemed quite out of place in the luxurious surrounding of *La Folie* and its fashionable company. De Barge introduced her as his wife. His huge bulk completely dwarfed her and she looked years older than her husband.

Madame de Barge shook hands awkwardly. She was grey-haired and obviously still grief-stricken from the loss of their only child. Dressed in expensive clothes, which on her figure looked ready-made. Fundamentally a peasant type, the kind who might do her own shopping in the local markets and haggle about prices, and insist on doing her own housework in spite of a score of servants. De Barge had married her when he was a bank clerk and she had failed to rise with him and his increasing fortunes. She had been a draper's daughter in Lyons and had brought with her the comfortable dowry her husband had used to make his millions. And yet, De Barge had remained scrupulously faithful to her, and consulted her and relied on her shrewdness in all the business he did.

Madame de Barge found relief in Mrs. Littlejohn.

"Would you like to see round the house whilst the men continue their talk?"

Littlejohn wondered why the couple persisted in keeping up such an establishment and a crowd of frivolous hangers-on of half their own age. The answer arrived as the women left the room.

A young man, probably in his late thirties, dressed in a bath-robe over his bathing costume and with espadrilles on his feet.

"My nephew, Charles."

"I didn't know you were ... "

"Chief Inspector Littlejohn, of the London police."

The young man began to look awkward, as though he ought to explain his sudden intrusion.

"I just wanted to say that the hot-water system has given up the ghost again."

Littlejohn studied the face of the newcomer. Not so stupid and lackadaisical as he tried to appear. Dark; high, narrow forehead; small set-back ears; and a resemblance to his uncle in features. Crisp black hair with a curly lock hanging over one eye and which he kept thrusting back with a hasty habitual gesture. Large brown eyes and a long straight nose, with close-set narrow nostrils, a thin mouth, and a sensual nether lip. He was six feet tall and slim, and he looked fighting fit.

De Barge was gesticulating excitedly.

"Well? Why bother me? Tell Eustace ... I'm engaged. ... I'm busy ... "

Charles merely smiled, lowered his head, and remained perfectly calm.

"I only came to say that I told you so, uncle. You insisted on letting Larsen do the plumbing and I said how it would end. However, I'll speak to Eustace. Excuse me, Mr. Littlejohn. Glad to meet you. I expect you're another on the case of Elise and Chris. I hope you succeed, but I don't think you will. I keep telling uncle, *there is no case.* It was an obvious accident. Perhaps I'll have the pleasure of seeing you later."

He shrugged, turned his back, and left them.

"My nephew, and the only relative ... close relative, I mean, since we lost Elise. He has been in sole charge of my bank, de Barge & Co., of Lyons, since I retired. He is likely to inherit all this."

With a sigh almost of despair, he passed his hand with a sweeping gesture round the house, the estate, the beach, the swimming-pool, the lawns, the flower-beds.…

"All this… for what it is worth. We established ourselves here because Elise loved it and liked to entertain friends here. One day we hoped she would marry and bring a family to make it all young and happy again, as it was when she was with us. There was a child on the way when she died.… Now…"

He shrugged his shoulders wearily and fixed his sad, bloodshot eyes on the picture of his daughter dressed like a little bride for her First Communion.

"My wife and I would be better in a little cottage. But Charles likes it and, after all, he has tried to make up as best as he can for our loss. We are, as yet, too stupefied to know what to do. Sometimes, Littlejohn, I find myself waiting for Elise to come through that door again, fresh from the sea, and shake her wet hair over my desk to tease me, as was her habit.… And then I remember.…"

He began to sob—hard, dry, gulping noises, without tears, like the cries of an injured animal, and he reached for his empty glass, filled it with whisky, and poured it down his throat in a single draught.

"I'm sorry. If I only knew how she died and why."

De Barge rose to his feet now, his face livid with fury, a quick reaction to his grief. He seized Littlejohn by the coat and shook him.

"She was murdered. I know it. I know it. Don't ask me why. But I know. Find who did it and let me kill him with my own hands."

He stretched out his large podgy fingers and moved them convulsively. The women returned just in time to prevent a scene.

"You'll stay to lunch? We can have it quietly on our own. The rest will be picnicking on the beach."

Madame de Barge had been weeping, too. She had taken to Mrs. Littlejohn, a woman nearer her own age and sympathetic enough to open her heart to.

"Don't go so soon. I want to tell you about Elise. Such a sweet child and a bit delicate.... All her photographs are in the album and her room is just as it was when she was here with us."

So it was decided that they should stay and that, afterwards, the Chief Inspector would leave Mrs. Littlejohn with Madame de Barge and go himself to talk with Albert at *Montjouvain* in Antibes.

Outside, there was a scene of great animation as a servant arrived at the swimming pool with hampers of food and bottles of wine. Little tables were assembled and striped parasols erected over them. There was a rush for the food, the men taking advantage to cuddle the girls and chase them about. One of them poured a glass of champagne over the red bathing cap of his partner.

De Barge was out of patience.

"Never mind that, Littlejohn! I want to say this. Do the job properly, this time. Get to the bottom of it and I'll pay you well. We've had a lot of police around here already, asking questions about Elise and Chris. Cocky, bossy little local chaps, who smoked and kept their hats on till I asked them who they damn-well thought they were.... And there was an examining magistrate from Digne who wore kid gloves.... And after all was said and done, they found it was a pure accident. Well, I don't believe it."

Littlejohn looked him in the eyes.

"Do you really want me to find the truth, Monsieur de Barge?"

The banker looked ready to blow up.

"What the hell do you mean? Of course, I do. That's what I'm asking you to do, and I'll pay you more for it than you earn in five years at your job. Why do you ask a damn silly question like that?"

It was Littlejohn's turn to shrug his shoulders. He was watching Charles de Barge through the window. The man whom the family hoped would marry Elise, whose first lover had, according to the reckoning of her father, shot himself, and whose second lover, her husband, had been killed along with her in a motor accident. Young Charles showed none of the grief of the old couple whose large fortune he would eventually inherit. He was now passionately kissing the girl in the red cap over whose head he had poured a glass of wine, and the rest of the party were cheering and waving their glasses and foie gras sandwiches.

De Barge didn't seem to see it. He was sitting slumped at his desk, his eyes on the photograph of his daughter at the time of her marriage. "To Daddy, with all my love, Elise. ..."

Chapter Eight
Surprises at *Montjouvain*

Littlejohn tried to drive slowly over the short distance between Cap Ferrat and Nice. He wanted to enjoy the scenery, but the rest of the traffic wouldn't let him. The coast road was humming with heat and cars, and vehicles of every kind whizzed past him, hooting, in both directions. Now and then, a passing motorist waved his fist at the Chief Inspector for going too slowly. Here and there, where nonchalant workmen had dug a hole in the road, he found himself engaged in a crazy battle for existence and grew hot and angry in the fierce competition. He ended by driving hell-for-leather like the rest and blowing his horn with displeasure.

There was a shimmering mist over the calm Mediterranean. Expensive yachts and motor launches moved past at various speeds, displaying themselves along the stretch of nautical fashion-parade between Cannes and Monte Carlo. The glare of the sun gave everything the appearance of shadows, passing boats, cars, and pedestrians scantily clad and dodging in and out of the traffic.... Slow and incongruous among the hurly-burly and trembling heat, a cab-horse was gravely pulling an open landau containing three fat men in panama hats. As Littlejohn slowed down to let it pass, the horse, its sad eyes hidden under a fringe of little tassels to keep off the flies, gave up the ghost, halted, and neighed loudly.

He was soon in the outskirts of Nice. Villas hidden among flowers and trees on the slopes down to the sea; green, pink and orange-coloured awnings, or else closed shutters at every house; neat little squares with gardens and fountains in the middle. And then the busy dock area with heavy traffic coming in all directions. An American destroyer was tied-up at one of the quays and white-clad sailors were landing from a motor-boat for an afternoon out.

Littlejohn felt it would be a shabby trick not to call on his friend, Inspector Dorange, of the Nice Sûreté, so he turned off the promenade, parked his car among a mass of vehicles ranging from extreme poverty to the height of luxury, made for headquarters, and asked for his colleague at the enquiry desk. A sleepy policeman with a cigarette dangling from the corner of his mouth took his card, eyed it, sprang to attention, and vanished like a shot. He was soon back, all smiles.

Dorange hadn't changed a bit. He was small, slim, dapper, and smiling, in spite of the heat, and was sitting at a shabby desk in a shabby chair, with a solitary shabby file before him. He was in his shirt and trousers with a pair of snakeskin shoes on his feet and a snakeskin belt. He slipped on his jacket of light pearl-grey material, like nylon, and patted the red carnation in the lapel affectionately. Then, he embraced Littlejohn.

They didn't stay indoors, of course, but Dorange nimbly led the way through the flower market, halting at a stall to pick another carnation which he threaded through Littlejohn's buttonhole. Then they reached the sea-front at the Quai des Etats Unis and sat under the striped awning of a café terrace. On the left, a large florist's shop made the air heavy with the sweet smell of roses and the heady scents of exotic blooms. Expensive cars parked along the kerb....

"*Deux Pernods....*"

Littlejohn might never have been away. The pair of them were smoking cigars, watching passers-by, glad of each other's company. The holiday feeling soaked right into Littlejohn's bones. A head in a turban passed in a gold-plated Rolls-Royce with ivory fittings.

"That's the Maharajah of Jikinir."

And so it went on. St. Marcellin might have been at the other end of the earth, instead of just a stone's throw away over the hills behind.

Dorange let the sun and the sea and the *anis* do their work on his friend; then he gently raised the subject they both had in mind.

"How are things going at St. Marcellin, old chap?"

The whole affair had now taken on a new perspective. Littlejohn explained everything in fluent French. It didn't seem as difficult with Dorange there to help.

The open carriage with the horse and the men in panamas appeared again. The horse was, by this time, gone at the knees from its exertions, and halted in front of Littlejohn. It seemed to have taken a fancy to him! It gave him a sly look from between its tassels as the fat men dismounted, and neighed again as they began to argue with the cabby about the fare.

"There are a lot of queer things about the case, Jérôme."

The two Inspectors had long been on Christian-name terms.

"In the first place, although I tried to arrive incognito, the Marquis was quick to find out who I was."

Then followed Littlejohn's list of suspicious circumstances.

The man smoking a pipe behind doors and spying on them.

The talkative baker and the postmistress, the former of whom had seen strange goings-on as he baked his loaves on the night Chris and Elise Lovell died, and the latter who chattered too much about the influence and business of the château.... Hénoch Rossi had almost been murdered and then had completely vanished. Thérèse Colomb had been sent home to her brother at Sospel out of the way.

The queer behaviour of the parish priest, and of the doctor who had examined the bodies. The peculiar story of the Malicornes, who had seen the fatal car travelling in the opposite direction from that given at the enquiry.

The mysterious death of Bernard de Saint Marcellin; shooting accident or suicide.

In fact, the reserve, almost the antipathy, shown to Littlejohn by everyone in the village from the mayor downwards....

And finally, remote from the scene of the crime, living a life of wealth and ease, Charles de Barge, cousin of Elise, and, now that she was out of the way, heir of the wealthy banker. The man all his relatives had hoped would one day marry Elise and keep the money in the family. If Charles had hoped so, too, and happened to love his cousin, as well, he had been richly revenged in the death of the two men who had loved her, and the family fortune would be thrown in for overweight by fate when Monsieur de Barge died.

Dorange listened carefully, puffing his cigar, drinking his *Pernod,* watching the holidaymakers passing on the promenade. Beautiful young girls, elegant and sporting young men, middle-class trippers with young families hard to control, and elderly spruce old flâneurs with that touch of sadness which comes with the realization that one is too old for anyone to give a second look. An Arab in a red fez carrying an armful of carpets and leather cushion-covers, approached Littlejohn with a hopeful look in his eyes, and then spotted Dorange and fled like mad.

"And now, Tom, you are going where?"

"A villa called *Montjouvain* at Cap D Antibes. One of the witnesses to Bernard's death is caretaker there. An ex-army sergeant. He may be able to throw some light on the first death at any rate. As I said, de Barge is sure it was suicide."

"He, too, may prove difficult. If the present Marquis has made a point of silencing all the talkative ones, who knows what might have happened to the ex-sergeant? I'll come with you."

"Splendid!"

Littlejohn didn't say it with much enthusiasm, however. It wasn't that he didn't need the help of Dorange badly; it was the holiday feeling. It was the blaze of sunshine, the pleasant lethargy of sitting in the shade and watching the white sails moving across the calm sea ahead, and the whole of the coast from Cap Ferrat to the Estoril stretched out before them in a thin mist of heat.

"What is the man's name?"

"Albert Lapointe."

"I wonder if we've anything on the files about him. We'll call at the office and see on the way to the car. Shall we go, then?"

A 'plane drew in and landed at Var airport beyond the Promenade des Anglais, the Maharajah passed again in his luxury car, four film stars on location arrived followed by a crowd of admiring autograph-hunters. One of them stared hard at Littlejohn and gave him a queer look. The Chief Inspector had once hauled him in in London on a drug charge.

Littlejohn got to his feet. It couldn't go on like this! It was like a poster in a travel agent's shop. The blue sea, white sails, dim mountains behind, a few palm trees, and everybody dressed in white holiday clothes like the chorus in a musical comedy. He felt so stupefied by the sun and the scene that the passers-by began to assume the appearance of a lot of dummies showing off a range of holiday wear.

"We'll get the car, then."

Littlejohn climbed in the hired Simca and waited for Dorange to look up Albert's record in the files of the Sûreté or the city police. It was like sitting in an oven and he could hardly bear to touch the upholstery.

"Yes, I thought so. Nothing serious. A little matter of smuggling currency on the Mentone frontier. Everybody does it at one time or another, but this gives us details of Lapointe which might be useful."

Dorange had returned, carrying a grubby file, which he spread out on his knee after getting in the car.

Lapointe, Albert.... Born Dijon, 1902.
Regular Army, 1918–1940.
Served Algeria, Tunisia, Home Garrison Tarascon.
Resistance 1940–1945. Honourable discharge. 1926, Married Margaret Paty.
Oct. 4th, 1948, Smuggling currency and goods, Mentone.

"A pettifogging offence.... His war record saved him and he was fined and the goods and currency confiscated. Algeria, Tunis, Tarascon. That means he was in the Spahis. Tarascon isn't far from St. Marcellin and perhaps Bernard took Lapointe home with him now and then."

They left Nice along the Promenade des Anglais and reached Antibes in less than half an hour. The policeman on point duty recognized Dorange and held up all the traffic whilst he told him where to find *Montjouvain.* It was a villa on the Cap D'Antibes, a very nice one too, owned by an Englishman who spent three months there in the summer and the rest of the year in Manchester. The foolish fellow! Yes; Albert Lapointe and his wife looked after the place. A decent couple, enjoying a "cushy" job, which the policeman said he could very well do with himself in his spare time.

Littlejohn turned the car in the direction of Cap D'Antibes and saw the gendarme still holding up the long rows of traffic whilst he furiously ticked-off the leading vehicle for daring to blow a horn at him whilst he was in conference with his colleagues.

Montjouvain was an older type of villa standing back in neat grounds just off the Esplanade and facing a magnificent view of Nice and the snow-capped Alpes Maritimes behind. A compact little château, with a pepperpot tower rising from each of four corners. A terrace overlooking the sea. Gardens neatly laid out in beds of red and pink geraniums, mimosas, eucalyptus and palm trees, with orange and lemon groves on the slopes facing south. Littlejohn drove up the short approach to the house.

In the basement kitchen there were sounds of work going on, and at the noise of the car pulling up a pleasant, dark-skinned, buxom woman appeared at the door and approached. An Alsatian dog followed at her heels, lazily sniffed at the car, anointed one of the tyres and, apparently satisfied, sat down on the grass and fell asleep. Out of sight, someone was watering the beds with a hosepipe, for they could hear the swish of water.

Dorange left it all to Littlejohn and sat slumped down comfortably in the car smoking a cheroot.

"Madame Lapointe?"

"Yes."

The woman looked them up and down anxiously. Visitors of their type were rare and, with the native intuition of her class, she scented official status.

"Is Albert here?"

She paused again and eyed Dorange, who casually cocked one eye in the direction of the swishing water.

"Alberrrrrt... Alberrrrrt...."

She made no more ado but threw back her head and shrieked for her man as though someone were trying to murder her. The dog merely growled in his sleep.

Almost at once a man appeared running down the slope. He was bare-headed and wore navy blue dungarees. Medium-built, slim, agile, he soon covered the distance and reached the car.

"Messieurs?"

A handsome face, sunburned, clean cut, and with a high, bald forehead and blue eyes set deeply under heavy lids. A Roman nose and a firm chin. A man used to discipline and who knew his place, and with a cunning worldly look of wide experience.

"We are from the police."

Lapointe smiled pleasantly; he didn't seem disturbed by the news, although his wife did and hastily retreated to the house.

"From the English police, sir?"

Dorange replied.

"The English police and the Sûreté at Nice."

Lapointe gave a slight, almost imperceptible bow and another smile. He carried a short hoe in his hand, as though his wife's cries had alarmed him into finding a weapon of sorts. He quickly flung the hoe on a flower-bed with a gesture which struck Littlejohn by its grace. In fact, Lapointe's every movement was graceful, the way he ran, the way he stood, his slim, well-kept body and its movements. Like a ballet dancer ... or ... Littlejohn nodded to himself. ...

"At your service, gentlemen."

They climbed out of the car and casually strolled to the terrace, led by Lapointe. There, on a stone seat, the two detectives made themselves comfortable. Lapointe almost stood at attention in a manner reminiscent of his days as a Spahi.

The view from the terrace was magnificent. The full sweep of the Baie des Anges as far as Cap Ferrat, with Cagnes and Nice in the foreground and the mountains behind, rising to peaks capped with snow. The hillsides terraced in lush vegetation, with neat villas dotted over them. The sea calm and blue. White sails and motor-boats passing to and fro and the luxury yacht of an oil king gliding to Monte Carlo. The heat of the sun was smothering, and Littlejohn was glad to shift his position and sit in the shade of an old well-head—a lovely wrought-iron winch standing *on* a stone plinth with a vine twining itself around it. Impossible to think of work in such surroundings with the dazzling light making his cigar-smoke transparent, and a red carnation in his buttonhole.

"We are here for some information, Albert, and hope you will be able to help."

"At your service, sir."

"You knew Bernard, Marquis de St. Marcellin, well before his death?"

On guard! Something in the pale blue eyes indicated caution. Something almost like a deepening of their colour, as though the lids had closed slightly to protect them.

"Yes, sir. He was my superior officer in the army."

"Whilst you were stationed at Tarascon?"

"Whilst I was at Tarascon, as you say, sir."

"You were present when he died?"

"I had that unhappy experience."

"A shooting accident."

"Yes, sir."

Lapointe was now standing completely relaxed. Littlejohn knew instinctively that this was a deliberate technique, practised by an adept who knew that the surest way of lowering his guard and becoming vulnerable was to grow tense and excited.

"Tell me how it happened, Albert."

Lapointe shrugged his shoulders.

"In just the way that I and my companions testified at the enquiry. We were going to shoot duck in the marshes a little way from the château and, as we passed through a thicket, Monsieur Bernard's gun must have become entangled in the briars. We were separated. We heard a shot and went back. He was dead with a wound in the head."

"And you all testified as to how the affair happened?"

"Yes, sir."

"And that was all?"

Another shrug.

"What else could there be, sir?"

Littlejohn paused and looked Lapointe in the face.

"It has been suggested that the Marquis committed suicide."

Dead silence, broken only by the persistent swish of the hosepipes on the flower-beds and the distant rumble of traffic on the road.

"But that is ridiculous, sir. Why should Monsieur le Marquis wish to kill himself? He was a happy man with all his life before him."

"Are you sure? Hadn't the lady he was betrothed to just broken their engagement?"

"That had nothing to do with me. It was not my affair. I was there because Monsieur le Marquis knew I liked duck shooting, and after we parted at Tarascon and he went home, he used to invite me to the château from time to time when the birds were plentiful."

"I see. You know the present Marquis?"

"Yes, sir. I knew him as an officer of our regiment. When Monsieur Bernard was alive we sometimes met at the château."

"He was one of your shooting party when Monsieur Bernard met his death?"

"That is so."

"Have you seen Monsieur Arnaud lately?"

"Only once since the Occupation ended. He was passing and called."

"The other member of your party was Mr. Christopher Lovell?"

"Yes. A very nice gentleman indeed, sir."

"He sometimes called to see you?"

"Once or twice after his marriage when he and his wife were staying at Cap Ferrat."

The answers came calmly and quietly and Lapointe stood patiently, smiling slightly and inoffensively, apparently happy to reply when he could.

Littlejohn paused and flung away the stub of his cheroot. Dorange sat in the sun, his head bare, staring across the blue water, apparently not very interested in what was going on. From time to time, he turned and looked appreciatively at the villa as though approving fully of it and envying the man who owned it.

"You were a fencing instructor in the army, Albert?"

Another broad smile, but no surprise at Littlejohn's perspicacity.

"Monsieur is very observant."

"You betray it in almost every movement."

"Yes. I was an army instructor at Tarascon. For a number of years I was champion there."

"And Monsieur Bernard.... Was he also an expert at *l'escrime?*"

"He was a very good swordsman."

"A duellist?"

Again the light blue eyes darkened.

"Monsieur means a competitor in the championships?"

"I mean what I say. Did he ever fight any duels?"

"There were quarrels from time to time among the young officers. Nobody was hurt very much. It was forbidden, and as a rule..."

"When such duels were fought and any injuries sustained, was it understood, as a matter of honour, that the seconds and those present passed them off as accidents?"

"I don't understand what you mean, sir."

Dorange rose to his feet and casually strolled towards the house. He seemed to have decided to leave it all to Littlejohn and to pass the time exploring the grounds. He vanished round the corner of one of the pepperpot towers in the direction of the main door.

"Perhaps you don't understand, Albert, but I'm making a suggestion that Bernard de St. Marcellin met his death in a duel fought in the grounds of the château with Mr. Christopher Lovell."

Lapointe seemed to be striving to relax even more, like an expert fencer who, finding that pressure is causing him to lose ground and grow confused, eases off to take a fuller measure of his adversary.

"But that is not true, sir."

"It seems strange to me that all of you were soldiers."

"That was natural, monsieur. Monsieur Bernard's friends were all soldiers. Most of his guests at the château were soldiers, too."

"You and Monsieur Bernard were swordsmen; I don't know about the rest. Was Mr. Lovell an expert fencer, too?"

"Not as good as Monsieur le Marquis."

"That might explain, then, why Monsieur Bernard died from a shot wound. Presumably he was the challenger and Mr. Lovell chose the weapons. What kind of a wound did Monsieur Bernard receive?"

"It was said, at the enquiry, that a single bullet of duck-shot penetrated his brain, sir."

"That sounds strange. Duck-shot is large, I know, and there are less shots than usual in a cartridge. But *one* only.... That puzzles me, Albert."

And then Lapointe licked his dry lips. Littlejohn sighed with relief. He had struck a vulnerable spot with a purely random aim. It was Albert's fencing and a few signs of his uneasiness which had started the whole fantastic theory.

"So you weren't acting as second to one of the parties, Albert."

"I don't understand, sir. There was no duel. As I have said, it was a duck-shooting party."

Before Littlejohn could press the matter further, a diversion occurred.

Noises round the corner near the front door. Dorange's voice, sounding very cheerful, another stuttering in protest, and a wild look from Lapointe, like that of a trapped animal which doesn't know where to run for refuge.

And then Dorange appeared gently leading an indignant man by the arm. It was Hénoch Rossi, the little baker of St. Marcellin!

Chapter Nine
The Affair at St. Marcellin

For a brief instant all movement died away from the scene. They all stood transfixed like figures in the *Sleeping Beauty*. Littlejohn in the process of filling his pipe, and Albert, wide-eyed now and uncertain what to do next, like a thief caught in the act. Dorange perplexed and wondering humorously who the man might be he'd just caught behaving suspiciously. Rossi like a rabbit in a trap, waiting for the blow or twist of the neck which would put paid to him. And Margaret, her arms full of dirty linen, peeping round the corner expecting trouble. The whole set against the background of the pretty little villa like a scene in grand opera.

Dorange was the first to speak. He seemed amused.

"I had just gone in the house to put through a call to Digne for some information and, as I was telephoning, I saw this little chap eyeing me through a crack in the door of the first floor. So I brought him along to see if you know him, Littlejohn."

Hénoch Rossi's distress was painful to behold. He had obviously been caught on the hop and without time to make up a tale of excuse. He recognized Littlejohn at once and would have fled had he dared. Instead, he cast upon Albert a regretful look which was returned by a scorching glare.

Rossi looked different, too. Divorced from his bakery, he had been able to clean himself up and get out the flour usually embedded in his pores. He wore a cheap navy blue suit, too, and a cream, soiled open-necked shirt which made him look like an excursionist.

"Well, well.... It's my friend the baker."

Littlejohn could have laughed outright, partly from relief at the solution of a knotty problem of the case, and partly because little Hénoch, as an excuse slowly grew in his mind, was trying to look indignant.

"This is an outrage!" he said at length. "I am here on holiday and I find I'm followed and disturbed. It's not fair."

"It's a good thing I followed you the other night, Monsieur Rossi. Otherwise you wouldn't be here to tell the tale."

"I admit I'm grateful, Monsieur Littlejohn, but you will admit it isn't the right thing to do to keep following me about when I'm taking a rest for my health. It's disturbing to be involved with the police, in any case."

"So you know I'm of the police?"

"The mayor told me."

"Your mayor seems to do a lot of talking."

"Besides, I know Monsieur Dorange. His photo is often in the local newspapers. Everyone knows him."

"Let's all sit down."

Dorange was always out to make himself comfortable and drew up a wrought-iron armchair, sat in it, placed his feet on a little iron table, and admired his snakeskin shoes.

"And can't your wife find us all something to drink, Lapointe? We may as well make ourselves cosy whilst we have a little chat."

There was something ominous in the way the French inspector said it. Albert evidently thought so, too. He had lost a bit of his aplomb and reverted to subordinate rank as he hurried to seek his wife and tell her to get some wine.

"And you, Rossi.... Who are you and how do you come to be here?"

"I am a baker in St. Marcellin, Monsieur Dorange, as this gentleman will tell you, and I am on holiday with my friends, the Lapointes."

"What are you so scared about, then?"

"I'm not scared, sir."

"Don't contradict. Now, my friend, Inspector Littlejohn, has some questions to ask you, and see that you answer truthfully. Otherwise, you can answer me at Nice."

"I'm sure I only wish to tell the truth."

"Well, get on with it, then."

Lapointe and his wife arrived almost at the double with glasses and two open bottles of wine. It was obvious that Albert didn't want to miss a word of what was going to be wrung from his baker friend.

Margaret filled up the glasses.

"Good health!"

Dorange took a sip.

"Mon Dieu!"

It was the cheap raw wine used by the Lapointes with every meal.

"Can't you do better than this?"

"I regret, sir, the cellars are locked and Mister Taylor, who owns the villa, has the key in England."

They were all sitting now; Albert and Rossi on the edges of their chairs.

Littlejohn lit his pipe to take away the fire of the wine.

"How did you get here, Hénoch?"

The baker hesitated, caught Dorange's eye, and seemed eager to reply after that.

"The mayor brought me. He said I ought to have a holiday by the sea after my accident."

"So he got you up in the small hours, soon after you'd almost died, and rushed you over the mountains to hide. Is that it?"

"He said he was busy next day and wouldn't have time if we didn't come to Antibes right away."

"Suppose you tell me exactly what happened.... Or else, let *me* tell *you*, and correct me if I'm wrong. You promised me earlier in the evening, before you were gassed, that you would say more about events on the night of Mr. Lovell's death. After that, someone tried to kill you by locking you in your fire-hole among the charcoal fumes."

"Nobody locked me in! It was an accident."

"The priest found you in the place with the door closed and fastened."

"It was an accident!"

"Let me go on.... You were restored to consciousness and put to bed in the presbytery. By morning you had disappeared. Why?"

"As I said before, the mayor came and suggested ... "

Dorange was out of patience. He took a drink of wine, spat it out, and turned angrily on the baker.

"For the last time, both you and Lapointe will speak the truth and nothing else. Otherwise, we go to Nice to investigate a charge of kidnapping."

"Kidnapping?"

"Kidnapping. It will take several days and we shall accommodate the pair of you in the cells instead of the luxury of *Montjouvain.* Proceed."

He put his feet on the table again, lit a cheroot, pulled his panama over his eyes, and seemed to fall asleep. Then, in the villa, the telephone bell rang and he had to jump up and hurry in to take the call.

"Now, Hénoch, let me get on with my tale. Whilst you were in the curé's bed recovering, the mayor motored over to the château to report to the Marquis. Monsieur de St. Marcellin didn't wish you to talk to me, so arranged for you to be kidnapped ... or else scared you into coming to Antibes of your own free will. The mayor drove you here through the night. Meanwhile, the Marquis had fixed up with his former sergeant, Albert, to hide you for a time. In other words, you had to be stopped from telling me your story."

Albert thought it wise to join in.

"Monsieur le Marquis telephoned to ask me to find accommodation for one of his friends who had been ill. That was all. I swear it."

"Very well. ... But what have *you* to say, Hénoch? Having failed to kill you to keep you quiet, the Marquis succeeds in kidnapping you—with your consent, if you like to put it that way—to prevent your seeing me again?"

"Monsieur le Marquis wouldn't think of killing me. I tell you the affair in the furnace room was an accident."

"Why then was he in such a hurry to rush you away in such a serious condition?"

"I ... I ... "

"He wanted to prevent your talking to me. Now, tell me the story of events on the night Mr. Lovell and his wife died."

"I had drunk too much. ... There was no story."

"Yes, there was. Instead of entering the village from Manosque, the car which was smashed up, ran through the village from the direction of the château. At the enquiry, the reverse was said in testimony. Why?"

"I don't know anything about it."

"You were baking at the time, went to the door when you heard the car, and saw it pass. You also heard the smash, didn't you?"

"I can't tell you anything."

"If you don't tell me now, the French police are waiting to hear your true story at Nice, and there you'll stay until you tell it."

Rossi turned the colour of putty, and Albert shuffled on his chair.

"I admit I did see it, as you say, Monsieur Littlejohn. That was all I had to tell you. The mayor said you were a busybody with no authority to ask questions, and that if I remained in St. Marcellin you would worry the life out of me, in spite of my not being well."

"Did he also say that whoever had tried to kill you once, would try again? So you'd better go into hiding?"

"You have been talking with Monsieur Savini and he has told you? It is not fair to try to trip me up after he has told you everything."

"He hasn't, but I'm glad you've had the good sense to come out with a proper tale. What else did you see that night?"

"When?"

"The night of Lovell's death."

"Nothing else, I swear."

"Don't perjure yourself, Hénoch. Who was first on the scene of the accident?"

"I don't know.... That's the truth."

"But you saw someone there?"

"Of course. You could hear the impact with the tree all over the village."

"Did you run to see what had happened?"

"No, sir. All the loaves were in the ovens and at a critical stage. I couldn't leave them and go all that way. I'm not a rich man."

"Please don't be so evasive. Who *did* go?"

"L'Abbé Chambeyron.... There was a light in his house and he was the first to appear. I told him what I had seen and heard.... The car and the crash.... He ran.... Then Leclerc and others...."

"The priest wasn't the first person you saw, though. There was someone else.... Was he going the other way, *towards* the château instead of towards the car?"

"I thought I did see someone and hear footsteps, but it was dark. It was my imagination. We were all upset."

"And you gave no testimony at the enquiry?"

"No, sir. What could I say? They would have thought me mad. The car was in a position which pointed obviously to the fact that it was travelling down the hill from Manosque to St. Marcellin. It might have been another car. After all, the one travelling from the château might have had nothing to do with the accident, and gone on to Manosque."

"Who told you to keep your mouth shut about what you saw?"

"Nobody, sir.... I swear."

"Now, now. No perjury.... Remember what Inspector Dorange said."

"I casually mentioned it to the mayor, who confirmed that I'd imagined it and said I must not mention it, or people would think I'd lost my wits."

"Very well. And then..."

Dorange was on his way back, smiling and rolling his new cheroot between his strong white teeth.

"That was Digne. They had looked in the records concerning the death of the Marquis... Monsieur Bernard... By the way, has Rossi told the truth?"

Rossi could not wait to reassure Dorange.

"Yes, Monsieur le Commissaire.... Oh, yes. I told M. Littlejohn all I know."

"Good! Two army surgeons certified the death of Bernard de St. Marcellin. Toselli, of Digne, and Mengali, of St. Marcellin. Permission was then given for burial, which took place in the vault of the chapel at the château. I put it to you, Lapointe, that a duel was fought between Mr. Lovell and Bernard de St. Marcellin. As is customary in such cases where the parties and seconds are army officers, there is a binding oath before the duel that, in the event of death, the rest will testify that it was a shooting accident. Toselli and Mengali were formerly stationed at Tarascon with the Spahis, so that was easy, too."

Dorange seemed to grow a couple of inches in height as he faced Albert.

"THE TRUTH! It was a duel, and the Marquis fell."

Lapointe hung his head, but was still silent.

"Never mind the oath. That is over and done with and, in any case, was immoral. Tell me here and now, or else come with me to Nice and we will re-open the whole affair."

"I shall go to gaol in any case."

"Nothing of the kind. The duel is a thing of the past. We are now concerned with a recent disaster which may have been an act of revenge arising from the duel. Now speak, or I will arrest you."

"Very well, sir. It was a duel. We swore, as you just said. The Marquis challenged Monsieur Lovell on account of the way he had stolen the affection of Mademoiselle Elise. I acted as second for Monsieur Lovell; Monsieur Arnaud was second for the Marquis. The late Colonel Latour was the *arbitre,* the one in charge of the arrangements."

Littlejohn could imagine it all. The early morning and the group of officers in the misty park of the château. The referee laying down the conditions, the stern ring of men, the two separating themselves from the rest, pacing and turning ... the shots. ... All so out of keeping with the present surroundings. The distant hills with the still, blue sea between, and the spread sails of little boats. Families in bathing dress sporting on the beaches, little pedal-craft skimming across the water. ... And in the garden round them pigeons strutting about and, almost at Littlejohn's feet, a pair of blackbirds listening on the grass, like black-coated doctors auscultating a patient, and then plunging their beaks in the turf and dragging out worms.

"There was a surgeon present?"

"Dr. Mengali. ... He was of the regiment, you see. It was all kept private. He was accompanied by Monsieur Charles de Barge, who also had been in the regiment. ... "

"And then?"

"I could not understand why the duel was fought. Monsieur Bernard was a kindly, philosophic man; the kind who would have resigned himself to his ill-luck and wished his friend and Mademoiselle Elise well. It seemed to me that some of his friends had fomented the quarrel. Monsieur Bernard being the challenger, Monsieur Lovell had the choice of weapons. They were both swordsmen and we were surprised when Monsieur Lovell chose pistols. It was certainly to his advantage, for Monsieur Bernard was the better of the two with the duelling sword and ... I am sure, sir, had it been with swords, it would not have ended in death. The Marquis would never have killed his friend."

Albert was in distress. Dorange poured him out a glass of the red wine and he drank it in two gulps without the least trouble.

"Proceed."

"Colonel Latour gave the instructions.... Twelve paces each."

"The weapons?"

"Duelling pistols, which belonged to the Marquis."

"Not revolvers then, with one chamber loaded?"

"Oh, no, sir. The pistols were a beautiful set owned by the grandfather of the Marquis and with which it was said, he, too, had once killed an adversary.... They were loaded through the muzzle, and with a single ball.... Lovely weapons, they were, well-kept, precise."

"The two men took twelve paces and ...?"

"They were both good shots, sir. I think the Englishman was, this time, the better of the two. The Marquis fired a fraction before Monsieur Lovell. He missed. I'm sure he never tried to injure his friend. He must have hoped they would be reconciled afterwards. Monsieur Lovell fired immediately after; so soon after, that the two reports sounded like a single prolonged one. Monsieur Lovell shot the Marquis right between the eyes. He fell dead without a word or a sound. It was frightful."

"Listen carefully, Albert.... Did Mr. Lovell seem to take deliberate aim, and did he seem surprised when the Marquis fell?"

"As for aim, how can I tell? One has to be behind the pistol. But Monsieur Lovell seemed surprised and dismayed at the result. He kept trying to assure us that he didn't intend to kill the Marquis. But we all shrugged our shoulders.... It could hardly have been an accident, a misfire.... Monsieur Lovell left almost at once and we never saw him again.

Colonel Latour dismissed me, too. They wished to be alone with the dead. That is all."

"Where was Monsieur Arnaud de St. Marcellin when the fatal shot was fired?"

"With me, of course, and the doctor, and Monsieur Charles. We stood in a group."

"You're quite sure?"

"Quite sure. Where else could he be, sir?"

"Who else was staying at the château when this occurred?"

"Quite a number of people. It was a house-party, sir. It is so long ago, I can't remember all of them."

"Mademoiselle de Barge was there?"

"Yes. And her parents. It was very awkward, sir. I believe the party was to celebrate the betrothal of the Marquis to Mademoiselle Elise. On the day before the announcement and the signing of the contracts, Mademoiselle Elise and Monsieur Lovell had told the Marquis they were in love and she did not wish to go on with the arrangements."

"And the Marquis challenged his friend at once?"

"Later that evening and they fought at dawn next day. It was horrible. The servants told me the news was broken to Mademoiselle Elise when she went down to breakfast and by that time Monsieur Lovell had left for Paris. She joined him there later and they were married."

"And that was the last you saw of either of them?"

"Until after their marriage. Monsieur Lovell called here from time to time to see me when visiting his wife's parents at Cap Ferrat."

Dorange looked enquiringly at Littlejohn in case he had further questions.

"He was here just before his death in February?"

"Yes, Monsieur Littlejohn. They had only arrived from England the day before. He had motored over to see me. We had met again during the war. He knew these parts so well that when the English and Americans invaded again, he was posted with the troops and actually landed at Antibes. He was here for some time on staff work and we met. The past was all forgotten, and he used to like to call and see Margaret and me when he was in the neighbourhood.

Margaret was maid to Madame de Barge for a time during the war when I was away."

"And did Lovell seem in any way upset when he last saw you?"

"No, sir. Nor did he say anything about returning to St. Marcellin. The place was never mentioned between us. After leaving us, he must, for some reason, have decided to motor there with his wife. He may have received some message."

"He would, I take it, go over the mountains?"

"Not direct from Nice in the winter. The roads are passable, but difficult. Probably through Cannes and Grasse."

"And that is all you have to tell me?"

"Yes, sir. I hope you will keep it confidential. I did promise on my honour as a soldier.... You understand? You have made it very awkward for me."

Dorange intervened.

"And on your honour again, you will say nothing to anybody. You hear. Not a word of our visit here, or what you have told us. Rossi will remain here, too, and he will say nothing either. It is understood?"

Hénoch eagerly agreed and swore another oath.

"An oath is not necessary. If either of you—or Madame Lapointe—says a word to anyone, *anyone*, of this, it will be the worse for all of you."

Littlejohn lit his pipe again and they made for the car.

"Thank you all for what you have told me, and thank you, Madame Lapointe, for the wine... *Au revoir.*"

Littlejohn and Dorange parted in Nice.

"We'll meet again soon, I hope, Jérôme.... We must spend a day or two together when this is all over."

"Certainly. Meanwhile, carry on with the case and let me know if you need any help whatever. I've arranged for the files to be available for you at Digne, if you need them. And I shall keep an eye on you from a distance, you know. *Au revoir,* Tom."

All the way back to Cap Ferrat Littlejohn kept his eye on the road. He didn't see the sea or the panorama of hills with their spread of flowers and fine villas. His mind was on Christopher Lovell, the English officer, who had killed his disarmed friend stone-dead with a shot between the eyes.

Chapter Ten

The Melancholy Factotum

Back at *La Folie,* Littlejohn went through the ceremony at the lodge gate and was taken in custody by the manservant in the striped waistcoat, whose name was Edouard. A melancholy general factotum was Edouard, who undertook every duty from mixing an unusual cocktail to taking the dog for a walk, and he sighed gently from time to time, as though attention to the follies of the rich had filled him with resignation and despair.

Everything about the villa was quiet and the bathing pool was deserted. The absence of the cars around the door indicated that Charles de Barge had taken his friends on some excursion or other. A gardener was lighting a charcoal fire at a large open-air fireplace where Charles was going to hold a barbecue dinner when he returned with his followers.

De Barge was in his study, and the sad manservant took Littlejohn there. The master of the house was reading financial papers, following the ups and downs of investments which no longer interested him. He did it mechanically and out of boredom, for he had enough cash for all his needs and the rest would, on the death of himself and his wife, go to an heir whom he was growing to dislike more and more as time passed.

"Did you find anything out?"

He didn't even greet Littlejohn, but, as was his custom, spoke first of what was on his mind.

"I found Lapointe very interesting. He agrees with you that the death of Bernard wasn't accidental. It occurred in a duel with Christopher Lovell."

De Barge jumped in his seat and then smote the table with the flat of his hand. The glass from which he had been drinking toppled over and the other odds and ends and photographs vibrated. He started to mop up the whisky which trickled slowly over the red leather top. He was perspiring greasily and his eyes stood out.

"That explains everything! The sudden disappearance of Chris, the strange behaviour of those with whom Bernard was supposed to have been shooting, the conferences behind closed doors."

"Conferences.... What about and by whom, sir?"

"As far as I remember, Arnaud, my nephew Charles, a Colonel Latour, who happened to be among the guests, the doctor, and Lapointe did a lot of talking locked in the study, and then the examining magistrate arrived and a doctor from Digne. No wonder we never knew the truth! It was all hushed up because of the military... because it was an army affair of honour."

"That's quite likely."

"Chris had left for Paris in haste the morning Bernard died. Elise followed almost at once. There was a lot of talk about her strange behaviour. After all, it didn't seem right, with Bernard dead in the house, for her to rush off in such a hurry, but there was no holding her. The party was supposed to be for the betrothal of Elise and Bernard. Arnaud told me later that they had broken it off the night before Bernard died, and that Chris and Elise were in love. I never thought the two men would fight over it. Bernard wasn't that kind, or didn't strike me that way."

De Barge cast a bewildered look round the room as though he couldn't recognize the familiar surroundings. His eyes fell on the photograph of his daughter again and filled with tears.

"What a mess."

He sat down heavily and looked at Littlejohn as though all the strength had gone from him.

"Had the death of my girl anything to do with the death of Bernard? I can't see how it could have resulted from it, but I can't think properly. The whole thing beats me."

Edouard entered with his cocktail apparatus again, looked at the damp marks of whisky on the desk and the wads of wet blotting paper lying about, sighed, and cleaned it up with a duster which he drew from his pocket like a magician. He mixed fresh drinks and left, trundling his wagon before him. De Barge didn't seem to notice him, and took and swallowed his drink automatically.

"I'd like you to try and cast your mind back to the betrothal gathering at St. Marcellin, in 1939, was it?"

"Yes. In the spring before the war. What do you want to know?"

"Who was there in addition to the names I already know, sir?"

De Barge took up a pencil and doodled on his writing-pad as though it helped him to think.

"By the way, Littlejohn, our wives are having tea in the summer-house in the garden. I promised to take you there when you got back. What did you ask me?"

"Those who were at St. Marcellin?"

"Ah, yes. My wife and myself. Some relatives on both sides. Uncle Ambrose, Uncle Jules, Aunt Adèle, Aunt

Mélanie.... All dead, so they won't interest you. Some aunts and uncles of Bernard... All dead, too. The war killed off a lot of the old ones.... One or two official friends of the St. Marcellin family.... A Deputy who was shot for collaborating with Laval.... A sub-Prefect who... What good is all this going to do? It was a duel, wasn't it? And they all thought it was an accident. Every blasted one of them thought it was an accident.... I can't remember it and if I do, it can't be any use."

"Was Monsieur Charles there?"

"Yes. And his father, who killed himself after the Occupation. His brother Antoine, too, who was killed at Lake Chad in the war. It hurts me to remember them all. The war swept them all away like dead leaves and there's nobody left of either of our families.... Ours or the St. Marcellins, except Charles, my uncle Sylvestre, who's in a Catholic home for the aged, and my aunt Eulalie, who's in an asylum. Come to think of it... I wonder if Uncle Sylvestre knew anything about the duel. It was all very mysterious."

He paused, looking into space before him.

"What was, sir?"

"About Uncle Sylvestre.... He was a retired captain in the army.... He's eighty now and, right to the time he went into retreat, he was a perfect martinet. He used to get up at five in the morning, take a bath, and go out for a route march, as he called it. It usually consisted of walking five miles from home at Le Bô, where he lived in retirement, and back before breakfast. When we were young men, we stopped going to visit him because he insisted on our going marching with him."

De Barge was rambling in the past.

"Was he a guest at the betrothal party, sir?"

"Yes. I was coming to that. On the morning of Bernard's death, he'd apparently gone out for his usual route march and when he returned, he sought out Colonel Latour and was closeted with him for a long time. I remember it well, because we could hear my uncle shouting loudly behind closed doors and we thought it highly improper in view of the death in the house. Colonel Latour called in Monsieur Arnaud and the doctor, and whatever happened in private affected Uncle Sylvestre for the rest of his life. I begin to see it all now. Being an old army man, the rest of them must have made him join in the oath of silence. He must have seen the duel on his way out for his walk and when they reported it as a shooting accident, he must have objected until they called on him to obey the army convention. He's a very religious man and it would go hard with him to join in so obvious a lie, especially when a man had died. He didn't even stay for the funeral and, shortly after, entered a retreat and grew more religious than ever."

"Do you ever visit him, sir?"

"No. He's a bit queer and doesn't welcome visits from his relatives."

"Where is he to be found?"

"You're surely not thinking of disturbing him?"

"I may.... Subject, of course, to the consent of whoever is in charge at the home."

"It won't do much good, I'm sure. But if you insist, he's at a monastery just outside Aix-en-Provence. He's not a monk, of course; just a sort of paying guest, and has been, since 1939. They didn't disturb them during the war, seeing it was turned into a military hospital, as well, at the time. L'Hôpital du Bon Samaritain, it's called. Ask for the Father Superintendent.... Although what good it will do, I can't think. It's up to you, but I wouldn't mention the family, if I were you. He seems to have taken a dislike to his relatives and when my Aunt Clotilde asked for him just before she died, he got quite nasty and said he didn't want to be disturbed."

Outside, the young people had returned in their cars and gathered in a party, laughing and shouting, and made their way to the little châlet near the swimming pool to change again into bathing attire. Charles de Barge was among them and Littlejohn saw Edouard hurry towards him, speak to him, and point to the house. Charles followed him indoors.

"What happened to you all during the war, sir?"

"We were separated from Elise, who was in England whilst her husband was in the army. We lived here, in the lodge. The villa was occupied by the German staff. They were very proper and very officious, but didn't trouble us much."

"And when the war ended, Elise and Chris came back to see you? Did you or they ever go back to St. Marcellin?"

"Not until the time they met their death."

"Did you know they were going then?"

"No. On the day after they arrived here, they received a telephone call. It was about three in the afternoon and they said they had a visit to make and must go right away. They were very secretive about it, and simply said it was an urgent message from a friend and they would be back next morning. They left almost at once and we never saw them alive again."

"You had no idea where the call was from, then?"

"No. Now it seems very likely it was from Arnaud, at St. Marcellin, although when I asked him during the enquiry about their deaths, he denied it. It seems to me that their deaths were an act of revenge for the killing of Bernard in the duel.... "

De Barge rose with a flushed face again, otherwise he showed no excitement.

"If that is so, I, in turn, will avenge *them.* I shall re-open the whole case in the light of what you have told me, and I'll see it doesn't close again until..."

The voice was icy and the protruding eyes alive with hatred. Littlejohn put a restraining hand on de Barge's shoulder.

"Better leave it all to me, now. If it gets beyond my powers, I can refer it to a friend of mine at the Nice Sûreté. You can depend on us not to let the matter drop until we have a satisfactory explanation of the whole business."

"Very well. But if I think there is any more lagging or trying to hush up matters, I shall act. I have influence in Paris. I shall know what to do.... And now, if there is nothing more, shall we join the ladies? They'll wonder what in the world is happening."

Madame de Barge and Mrs. Littlejohn were taking tea in a small stone summer-house overlooking the Baie des Anges. Madame de Barge had obviously been weeping and raised her tired eyes to her husband and then to Littlejohn as they entered.

"You have been a long time."

De Barge patted her hand gently.

"The Inspector has been giving me an account of his excursion to Antibes. He has discovered that Bernard was killed by Chris in a duel."

He turned to Littlejohn, half excusing himself.

"I tell everything to my wife, as I said before. The blows of fate have been more than one soul can bear. We have to comfort one another."

Madame de Barge had covered her face with her hands.

"Horrible! How horrible!"

"It was not the fault of Chris, my dear. From what the Inspector has told me, it looks as if both of them were the victims of some evil influence which forced them into a situation neither of them wanted. Don't weep. Nothing we can do will alter things. The Inspector has promised he will get a true account of everything. We must trust him."

Madame de Barge's eyes were still wide with horror.

"So... So, the spot marked by the memorial is not where Bernard accidentally shot himself, but where Chris killed him.... Horrible."

De Barge shrugged his shoulders helplessly. Then he turned to Littlejohn.

"The memorial my wife mentions marks the spot where Bernard fell. It is in the grounds of the château, a small column which his family built, with his name and the date of his death.... It is near a little shooting-lodge in a quiet clearing in the woods."

Mrs. Littlejohn did her best to comfort her stricken companion. Grief seemed to have brought back the two de Barges from their wealthy, frivolous world to the simple homely companionship they knew when they set up house together in a small villa when they were young.

Madame de Barge dried her eyes and sniffed.

"I'm sorry.... Forgive me. I had forgotten the courtesy due to guests. You'll have some tea, Mr. Littlejohn? This is cold. We'll get some more. Ring for Edouard, please, Sylvestre."

De Barge tugged at a rope hanging by the wall, and a bell in a little turret on the roof of the summer-house clanged. Edouard soon appeared walking across the lawns with a dignified melancholy tread. Without a word, he understood the situation, picked up the silver tray with its contents, and with a sigh made the journey back to the servants' basement.

Littlejohn and de Barge sat on rustic chairs made comfortable by rubber cushions.

"The Inspector has been asking me about those present at the house party at the time Bernard died. I tried to remember as many as I could.... Our family, the Marcellins, those army fellows.... He was interested in Uncle Sylvestre."

Madame de Barge smiled for the first time.

"Why Uncle Sylvestre...? He has been out of this world since war broke out. After Bernard's death, he turned strangely religious and went to live in a retreat with some monks."

"The Inspector is talking of paying him a visit."

"Whatever for? You'll be lucky, Mr. Littlejohn, if he sees you. He has refused to allow any of his family to visit him since he entered the hospice."

Littlejohn asked permission to smoke his pipe and filled and lit it as he talked.

"From what your husband tells me, his uncle behaved strangely at the time Bernard de St. Marcellin was killed. It appears he left the château hastily before the funeral, after a somewhat stormy interview with some of the army officers present."

"That was true. But surely uncle had nothing to do with the death of Bernard...."

"He might have seen it occur. It's worth asking him, even if he knows nothing particular about it."

In the distance, Edouard was carrying the tea, balancing the tray and crossing the sloping terraces like a ballet dancer.

"Your manservant is a melancholy fellow...."

Littlejohn made the remark more for something to say than anything else.

"He has never got over the death of Elise. You see, he has been with us for almost thirty years without interruption, except during the war. When Elise was little, they were great friends. He used to take her every day for a ride on her pony and after she grew up, they remained on very good terms. She treated him like an uncle."

"Who received the telephone call on the afternoon she and her husband died?"

"Probably Edouard."

"May I ask him?"

"Of course."

The butler's steps crunched on the gravel and he appeared in the doorway, sad and silent, laid down the tray, and raised his eyebrows to ask if he must pour out the tea.

"Thank you, Edouard. I'll see to it."

De Barge intervened.

"Edouard, this is Inspector Littlejohn, from England. He is looking into the matter of Elise's death again. Have you anything to say to him?"

The man looked faintly surprised at being addressed at all, but continued to hide his feelings behind his melancholy poker-face. He bowed slightly.

"Monsieur. May I say I hope you are successful?"

"Thanks, Edouard. I want to ask you something. You remember the afternoon Mr. Chris and his wife left here ... the day they met their death?"

"Yes, sir. There was a telephone call and they went almost at once."

"Who was the call from?"

"I cannot say, sir, who spoke to them, but I answered it and it came from the château at St. Marcellin."

"How did you know that?"

"When I picked up the instrument, Claudius, the butler at the château, was speaking. We know each other. I have been there with madame and monsieur. We exchanged compliments and then Claudius asked to speak to Monsieur Christopher. I went for him ... and that was all."

"You don't know for whom Claudius was putting through the call? He didn't say?"

"No, sir."

"Who else but his master, Monsieur Arnaud, might he have been speaking for?"

"I do not know, sir."

"Monsieur Arnaud has denied he spoke to Mr. Lovell that afternoon. So, you see, it's rather important I should know."

De Barge was growing impatient again.

"Are you holding something back, Edouard? Because, if you are ..."

The manservant did not turn a hair.

"I assure you I am not, sir. All I know is, Claudius asked for Monsieur Lovell."

De Barge was on his feet, gesticulating angrily.

"You don't mean to tell me, knowing Claudius as you do, you didn't ask him who wanted Monsieur Chris! You're lying, and if you don't speak, I'll damned well find out myself. I'll ring up Claudius. Stay here till I come back."

De Barge stormed out of the pavilion and hurried across to the house, with Edouard on his heels, now completely shaken, gesticulating, too, and running to keep up with his master. They halted, Edouard gently fawning, de Barge shouting and bullying. Then they turned back and rejoined the party in the summer-house. De Barge looked thoroughly put-out. He drank a cup of tea in a single gulp, made a grimace and mopped his face and neck with his handkerchief. Meanwhile, Edouard stood humbly by.

"Tell the Inspector what you've just told me, you rascal."

The butler gulped.

"I'm very sorry, sir, but you will understand I was asked to say nothing about the call. Nobody asked me until you mentioned it. I have my duty and loyalty... and my word of honour."

"Get on with it, you... you... you little ingrate. Tell him at once."

"Claudius asked for Monsieur Lovell. I have strict instructions, sir, strict instructions from Monsieur de Barge, not to keep him or any of the family waiting on the telephone. If they are asked for by a third party, I must insist on whoever wishes to speak being brought to the instrument, so that Monsieur or Madame hasn't to hold on."

"Get on with it, you ruffian.... Hurry."

"I insisted that Claudius put through whoever wished to speak.... It was Monsieur Charles."

"But what was Charles doing at the château?"

Edouard shrugged his shoulders, and cast a beseeching look at his master.

"We never know where he is from hour to hour, Littlejohn. He goes out without saying anything. He may be away a week, and then we'll get a card from Antibes or Cannes. He's been staying with friends and suddenly remembered that we didn't know. His aunt and I don't count for much."

"Don't say that, dear."

"I repeat, we don't count for much.... But go on, Edouard. You've wasted enough time already."

"That is all, sir. It was Monsieur Charles. He asked me not to mention that he was at St. Marcellin. He had forgotten to tell Monsieur de Barge where he was and would not like him to learn from a servant. I forgot all about it afterwards. I gave my word not to speak and I have kept it. I trust I have done nothing wrong, sir."

"No, Edouard. Did you know what Monsieur Charles was doing at the château?"

"I didn't even know he was there until he telephoned. I was very surprised, sir."

"You know the château well?"

"I have stayed there during visits of Monsieur and Madame de Barge."

"He's an excellent chauffeur, Littlejohn, and my wife is only happy when he's at the wheel on the dangerous roads in the mountains. Besides, it's useful to have him with us on holidays. Although he doesn't deserve the least tribute after what he's done, I've got to admit he's the best valet I've ever had."

The factotum-paragon bowed slightly and gave a wintry smile, knowing his place was still secure.

"You were at the château when Monsieur Bernard died?"

"Yes, sir."

"Was there any talk below stairs about him and the way he met his death?"

"We were all very distressed, sir. It was very sudden, sir."

"And that is all you have to say about it?"

Edouard, already in his master's bad books, was trying his best to be helpful now.

"The servants of the château were weeping, sir. It upset all of us. Some of the women were overwrought. The assistant cook, a big fat woman, I recollect, had hysterics right in the middle of serving lunch. It would have been funny in other times, sir. Alivon slapped her face, and she picked up and went on with the cooking."

"Alivon? Is that César who lives at the village inn?"

"Yes, sir. He was chauffeur to the Marquis at the time. During the war, when there was no petrol, César went to help on the estate, and then, afterwards, the Marquis couldn't afford a chauffeur. Times have changed, sir, and he drives himself."

"Did you know his sister, Céleste?"

Edouard gave Littlejohn a queer, sideways look as though wondering how much he knew.

"Yes, sir. She had been dead some months when Monsieur Bernard died."

"Well?"

Edouard looked at the ladies and then at the men, licked his lips and paused.

"Go on, you wretch! What are you waiting for now? We can't wait all day. Answer Mr. Littlejohn."

"She had died six months before. Very sad."

"Yes. She threw herself in the pond in the park, didn't she, Edouard? Did you know?"

"Yes, sir. Everyone knew her sad story, but we didn't expect she would go off her head through it. After all, if I may say so, the same thing happens every day. Such accidents and misfortunes are provided for. Very foolish to take her own life, sir. But very sad, all the same, for she was a nice young woman."

De Barge had given it up. His mouth fell open and he gazed at his servant in puzzled anger.

"What the hell are you talking about?"

"Sylvestre!"

"I'm sorry. But this fellow would make a saint swear. Now, Edouard, what is all this gibberish? Explain yourself."

Edouard cast his sad, resigned eyes on Littlejohn.

"He means Céleste had a baby. She wasn't married. She committed suicide after it was born and her brother and sister have since brought up the child, whose name is Blanche."

"That is so, sir."

"Do you know who was the father, Edouard?"

"I cannot say. The girl was the quiet, sombre kind. Very good-looking. Nobody knew who had betrayed her."

"Any of the servants?"

"I don't think so, sir. Claudius had a wife who was housekeeper in the château. She watched his every move. As for the rest... Céleste wouldn't have found any of them good enough. She was said to have ideas above her station... ideas above stairs, if I may say so, sir."

"Very well, Edouard. That's all, I think. I may want to talk with you again later, if Monsieur de Barge will permit."

"It will be a pleasure, sir."

De Barge took another swig of cold tea.

"Right, Edouard, you may go. We'll overlook your lapse of memory, but don't do it again."

"Thank you, sir."

"And you can go and tell Monsieur Charles I wish to see him. We've guests here and it's discourteous of him not to call and pay his respects. He's probably chasing some half-naked woman round the bathing-pool. ... Get him. ..."

Edouard's Adam's-apple rose from below his collar and then vanished again.

"Well?"

"Monsieur Charles is out, sir."

"Well, I'm damned! Where is he this time? And don't say you don't know, because ..."

"There was a telephone call an hour ago. He spoke to someone and then left in his car."

De Barge ground his teeth and then spoke through them.

"History repeating itself, eh? Only this time, even if you're sworn to secrecy, you're going to tell us at once, or else I'll personally wring your blasted skinny little neck. ..."

"Sylvestre!"

"Am I master in my own home, or am I not? Who was it this time?"

"It was Monsieur Arnaud de St. Marcellin, sir. Monsieur Charles left right away for the château."

Chapter Eleven
The Confidences of Uncle Sylvestre

The Littlejohns left Cap Ferrat after tea and drove fast along the Corniche D'Or from Cannes to Saint Raphael and thence inland to Aix-en-Provence. It was quite dark when they reached that delightful little university city, but lights blazed everywhere; among the great trees which march four abreast down the Cours Mirabeau, on the many splashing fountains, and from the cafés where a colourful crowd of students were vigorously enjoying their evening meals and drinks on the terraces.

They found a good hotel, a former aristocratic town house in the Cours Mirabeau, and, after they had dined and Littlejohn had made enquiries about the Hospital of the Good Samaritan, they turned-in, ready for an early start next day.

The following morning they were off before nine. The hospital was just outside the little village of St. Luc, twelve kilometres from Aix on the main road to Grenoble. They reached it in half an hour.

A dirty, shabby little village with a dilapidated church, a few tumbledown houses, and a couple of impoverished farms. There was an inn of sorts and, when he saw it, any hope of taking morning coffee there died out of Littlejohn's mind. The place was flyblown and ill-kept and, on a ramshackle terrace outside, a number of surly natives were drinking. The landlord, in shirt, trousers and rope-soled sandals, eyed the Chief Inspector suspiciously as he pulled up. He was obviously very unwelcome.

A very old priest, wearing a soutane splashed from neck to knees with food stains, with long, matted dirty-white hair and his ears stopped up with plugs of cotton wool, was among the company and he, at least, rose and said good-day.

He drooled as he spoke and bubbles of saliva formed at the corners of his mouth.

"Can you direct me to the Hospital of the Good Samaritan, father?"

The abbé uncorked one ear and turned to Littlejohn.

"Eh?"

Littlejohn repeated his question.

"Le Bon Samaritain, eh?"

It was obvious he knew the answer, but he paused, wondering whether or not to ask the Chief Inspector what he was wanting there. Finally, he gave the directions.

"Turn right through the village.... At the end of a blind alley... an *impasse....* "

The men listened but scowled and made no reply. The hospice wasn't there at all, but they didn't correct their priest, whose aged wits had long ago gone woolgathering. Eventually Littlejohn found it by turning *left* through St. Luc and following the sound of a cracked bell, which suddenly started to toll and whose melancholy note filled the valley.

The retreat was quite different from the village of St. Luc. A tall surrounding hedge of clipped cypress broken by wrought-iron gates under a stone arch, with gold lettering across it. *Hospice du Bon Samaritain.* Beyond, spacious grounds, mainly consisting of shrivelled lawns and thick coppices of myrtle and almond. There was a main single-storeyed white building, surrounded by innumerable small pavilions, probably built as annexes to the main block as time passed. Patients were wandering about the grounds, some being pushed by others in bath-chairs. A general atmosphere of quiet and contentment.

Littlejohn dragged at the chain which hung down at the side of a wicket gate. A bell on the inside of the stone gatepost clanged and a fat, black-bearded brother wobbled from the lodge, smiled broadly, summed up the Littlejohns and their car with shrewd blue eyes twinkling behind round gold-framed spectacles, folded his hands over his enormous paunch, and indicated that he was ready to hear what they had to say.

"Is Captain Sylvestre de Barge in, *mon frère*?"

The brother seemed to think that funny and gave a satisfied little chuckle.

"No, monsieur.... But Monsieur Sylvestre *Barge* is.... The old gentleman abominates the *particule,* the little *de.* He insists the family name is simply *Barge* and that his relatives have assumed the other out of pure snobbery. I warn you, if you see him, do not, on any account, address him as Monsieur *de* Barge. He will turn on his heel... and that will be that.... By the way, sir, I must remind you that this is not ladies' visiting-day and madame will regretfully have to stay outside."

He bowed to Mrs. Littlejohn and tried to indicate that it pained him very much, but regulations were regulations, and the reverend abbot was a terror for the conventions....

"Come inside, sir.... As for madame... she can be very well occupied in the lodge here. We have a little shop with souvenirs and bottles of wine we make ourselves.... "

The idea of a bit of business during Littlejohn's absence delighted the brother so much that he rubbed his hands and couldn't get Mrs. Littlejohn in the shop fast enough.

"Does the captain smoke?"

"Like a chimney, monsieur."

Littlejohn took a tin of English tobacco which he carried in the car, put it in his pocket, and joined his guide again. The monk handed over Mrs. Littlejohn to a junior colleague, who at once took her to a trestle table set out with a mass of pictures, medals, paper-weights bearing a picture of the monastery, rosaries, bottles of cordial....

"This way, monsieur."

They crossed the grounds where black-robed figures were engaged in gardening and other menial tasks. The fat monk who accompanied Littlejohn made one or two enquiries and then led on.

"He seems to be in his cell.... Follow me, monsieur."

They finally reached one of the small annexes near the main block. A single-storied concrete structure, built in the shape of a U, with a grass plot in the middle and about a dozen small doors giving on to it. Each door closed off a separate little lodging for a single inmate. The monk halted before the middle one and tapped. A low room, with a comfortable single bed, a table, a plain and an easy chair, a reading lamp, and a prie-dieu. The walls were plain whitewashed and there was nothing on them except a wrought iron crucifix facing the window. The latter was in the outer wall and gave a view of wide fields rising in the distance to the hills. Another little window by the door showed a view across the courtyard with its fountain playing, and then the gable end of the abbey building itself.

A tall man was writing at the table and he rose to greet them, an enquiring look in his eyes. A very well-preserved old man, who, in spite of his years, maintained a clear blue eye and stood upright like a ramrod. He was completely bald and clean-shaven and his eyebrows and eyelashes had fallen out, the latter making him blink from time to time as though somehow he grew dazzled. He was wearing gold-framed spectacles halfway down his nose and looked at Littlejohn over the top of them. Only the knotted, gnarled old man's hands gave his age away.

"You have a visitor, monsieur."

The monk placed Littlejohn's card close to his short-sighted eyes and read from it in a monotone.

"Chief Inspector T. Littlejohn, Criminal Investigation Department, New Scotland Yard, London."

Barge bowed a bit impatiently.

"What does he want with me? I have been out of the world too long to…"

"Please be patient, Monsieur Barge. The Inspector has come a long way and doubtless has good reasons. I will leave you together. You will not stay longer than midday, please, monsieur. You will hear the great bell."

"May I sit down, monsieur?"

The old man was standing facing him, formally dressed in black, with a spotless linen shirt and a tall collar held together by a thin black tie. The little button of the Legion of Honour sat on the lapel of his coat.

"Please forgive me. I get so few visitors. I never liked my family much. They are milksops and I don't wish to see them. So they never come. Please take that chair."

He indicated a plain walnut chair with a seat of delicate petit-point tapestry.

"You like the tapestry? I made it myself. It is one of my diversions… needlework.…"

"It is very beautiful, sir. You smoke, I understand. May I light my pipe?"

Littlejohn took out his quarter-pound tin of fresh English tobacco and slid it with a smile across the table.

"A souvenir of my visit, sir."

The old man looked surprised, touched the tin, took out his own pipe, and started to fill it from the pouch Littlejohn also offered.

"Thank you. That is the first gift anyone has brought me for at least fifteen years.... I venture to say, however, that is not the purpose of your visit, Inspector? What can I do for you?"

Littlejohn explained the reasons which found him in France. He made it as short as possible.

"You knew Christopher Lovell, sir?"

"I met him for the first time at St. Marcellin in 1939 on the occasion of the betrothal fiasco of my niece, Elise Barge. It is incorrect to call them *de* Barge, as you do, sir. They are not nobility, but plain middle-class. They assumed it falsely.... I did not know that Elise and her husband had died tragically... I never see the newspapers and the family never visit me. I have forbidden it. They don't write."

All the same, the old man seemed upset by the news. His blue eyes grew filmed, as though he'd suddenly forgotten where he was and who was there.

"And you are here because foul play is suspected?"

"I was asked to make sure that there was no foul play, but now I have grave doubts."

"In what way?"

The old man was shrewd and easy to talk to. None of the military snob about him. He had served his time in the commissariat and the finer points of top-rank etiquette had passed him by.

"I have been obstructed in my enquiries and the fresh details I have unearthed about the duel, for example, have come as a grave shock."

"The duel.... Ah, yes... the duel. That carries my mind back a long way, Inspector. I was under oath not to mention it, but as you seem to know about it, perhaps we can talk it over together. That would be an immense relief to me. How much do you know exactly?"

Littlejohn told him.

The old man rose, walked to the large window, and looked out at the hills, apparently making up his mind. Then he turned.

"As for the obstruction you mention. That is quite understandable. You see, in spite of his lost fortune, the Marquis is a very powerful figure in local life. You might think them petty, tinpot nobility, but the St. Marcellins are a very old family, and, in spite of the so-called modern democratic ways, of which I don't approve at all, although I am a republican, the old houses have great power. Even the communists will kowtow to them on occasion. It is inborn habit from generations and generations of custom.... As for the local power of the Marquis... You have noticed it among even the farmers who own their own farms and, therefore, seem quite independent of him?"

"Yes, I've noticed it, sir."

"In Provence, as in most of the rest of France, there is a feverish restlessness among the peasants and country-people for the land. They will sacrifice anything to acquire more and more of it. When the impoverished gentry sold it off from their estates, they were cunning enough to keep the whip hand by disposing of it piecemeal.... A block here, a block there, with a tiny field which the Count or Marquis retained as a threat in the very heart of the land he had sold. Such holdings prevent what we call "ploughing in the round". That is, they make the farmer have to *go round them,* lift his plough, so to speak. The farmers detest that. Such little fields which don't belong to them in the heart of their farms are like rodent ulcers which annoy them. They try to curry favour with the Marquis to get him to sell them. They dream of them by night or else lie awake plotting how to acquire them. Such little alien plots are the blackmail by which the aristocrats hold the landed proprietors in their power. St. Marcellin owns a lot of such nuisance plots around his village and the farmers will obey him to the letter in the hope that, by doing him a favour, he, in turn, will do them one and sell."

Littlejohn rubbed his chin, wondering where it was all getting to. The old man was obviously riding his favourite hobby-horse.

"I know the village very well. The mayor, a fellow called Savini, was born there and went away to make a fortune. Having done this, his heart's desire was to become mayor of his birthplace and he owes it to the St. Marcellins.... If they whistle, he comes running... otherwise... a new mayor...."

"You know the local doctor, sir, Mengali."

"Very well. He was surgeon to the regiment when I was stationed at Tarascon. There was a scandal. Mengali was almost ruined and, had his officers not hushed matters up, would have landed in gaol and disgrace. In the course of some banquet or other, a drunken fool fired off a pistol and shot a fellow officer through the calf. Mengali, in an intoxicated condition, tried to remove the bullet. His instruments were dirty. The man died."

"So, he, too, is beholden to the Marquis?"

"Arnaud de St. Marcellin was a fellow officer, if that is what you mean."

"Could you tell me about the duel, sir?"

Sylvestre Barge was excited about something. He remained silent for a minute and then went and looked out of the window again. Then they were interrupted.

A tap on the door, and a small man, almost the size of a child, appeared. Everything about him seemed frail and gentle. Small hands and feet, quiet movements, a thatch of silky white hair, delicate features. He looked very old and only his eyes seemed to retain any vigour. They were black, like little sparkling shoe buttons.

"You didn't come, Sylvestre.... I thought you were ill. Aren't we going to play our game of draughts this morning, Sylvestre?"

Barge turned sharply on him.

"Oh, do leave me alone, Swithin.... Here, a gentleman has arrived with a proposal which may mean a new life to me, and all you can talk about is draughts.... Please do go, Swithin, there's a good fellow."

"I only thought.... "

"If you'll only leave me alone now, Swithin, I'll play twenty, even a hundred games of draughts with you afterwards."

The tiny man put his head on one side.

"Will you really, Sylvestre? Then, I'll go, but I shall keep you to your promise."

He tiptoed out and silently closed the door and left them.

"Is this interview really so important to you, sir?"

"It is, Inspector. If it ends as I think it will, it will mean freedom for me.... The end of a long nightmare. What do you want to know?"

The old man sat down, sighed, and looked Littlejohn eagerly in the face.

"You have been under an oath of secrecy, Monsieur de ... Monsieur Barge?"

"Yes. An oath which has completely severed me from the world and my family. ... But you know all the facts and hence I shall break no oath if I tell you what you know, shall I?"

"No, sir."

"Very well. I was invited, along with others of my family, to the château at St. Marcellin in connection with the betrothal celebrations of my niece, Elise, with Bernard de St. Marcellin. I was to stay as a guest for four days. Quite apart from family affairs, I knew Bernard and Arnaud from the time when their regiment was stationed at Tarascon. I wasn't in it, but I was permanently at the barracks as an officer in the commissariat. They were trained at St. Cyr; I was a ranker. I also knew several other guests there from the army ... Mengali and Colonel Latour, as well as a fellow called Lapointe, who was a sergeant and a kind of hanger-on of the St. Marcellins. ... There was a hitch in the arrangements. It seems Elise had fallen in love with another military friend of Bernard's, an Englishman called Lovell, and broke off her engagement."

The old man shuffled across to a cupboard and returned with two small glasses and a bottle of green liquid labelled *Cordial du Bon Samaritain*. ... He poured out two helpings.

"Your good health, sir. ... I am in need of a little cordial."

It was sweet and very potent and Littlejohn felt the sticky fluid creep down his throat and make him slightly lightheaded.

"Good health, sir."

"It is my habit, from many years in the army, to take a long walk early every morning and then a cold bath before my coffee. I still do it, though our medical brother here has told me it can't go on at my age. However, I followed the custom on the morning after my arrival at the château at St. Marcellin. As I reached the boundary of the park, close to a little shooting-box, I saw that a duel was in progress. Arnaud, Bernard, my great-nephew Charles, Colonel Latour, Mengali, Albert Lapointe and the Englishman, Lovell, were there and Bernard and the Englishman were already standing at the ready to fight with duelling pistols. I remained stock-still and, before I could think what to do, they had begun to pace out their ground. Then they turned and fired simultaneously. Bernard fell, and from where I stood, I knew he was either badly hit or dead."

There was a pause as the old soldier gathered his thoughts and helped them both to another drink. Outside, a lawn-mower was droning and the 'plane to Nice passed overhead.

"...I did not reveal myself, standing as I was, beside a coppice of trees, and, almost before I had time to move deeper into the bushes to conceal myself from the party, two of them had brought a hurdle from the shooting-lodge, placed the body on it under a coat, and all had followed it away."

He removed his cold pipe and cleared his throat.

"Now, monsieur, please follow me closely. The place where I was hidden was midway between the duellists, and I had a full side view. I saw them both fire and *neither had taken aim at the other.* Their bullets must have gone over their heads. Yet, Bernard was dead. I must have stood for ten minutes, wondering, and then I finally reached the conclusion that, unless my eyes had failed me, or I was mad, someone outside the party, someone also with a weapon, had fired at and killed Bernard de St. Marcellin under cover of the double report of the duelling pistols."

He looked Littlejohn in the eyes and Littlejohn nodded.

"Making sure there was nobody about, I went and examined the spot. The positions of the combatants at the time of firing were: the Englishman had his back to the shooting-box and Bernard was ten yards in front of a large oak tree, facing Lovell. I found the spot in the wall of the lodge where Bernard's bullet, fired high, had broken into the mortar. The Englishman's must have missed the oak tree, for I could not find it. But I did discover the bullet which killed Bernard. It must have entered his skull, passed through, and buried itself in the trunk on a level a little below Bernard's head. It was embedded two inches in the wood. I removed it, and then kneaded clay, filled up the hole, and smoothed it with chippings of bark. From the position and angle of the hole, I judged the bullet, a rifle bullet, monsieur, had been fired from the shooting-box. If so, the assassin must be still in there and I must be in danger.... I need not have feared, however. In a frenzy of indignation and stupid courage, I rushed in the lodge intent on capturing the murderer, or dying. He had gone. There was a back door which led through the wall of the park to a track outside. This door was unlocked, and the bird had flown."

"But, surely, sir, those present at the duel must have known."

"They did not appear to at the time. They were in such a hurry to clear matters up, that they overlooked all else. You see, sir, it was obvious they never expected one to kill the other. It is rarely done. A challenge and a scratch or two.... Those are usually the tomfool conventions of a modern affair of honour."

"You told them?"

"When I got back to the château, I at once demanded an interview with Colonel Latour. The rest of the duelling party came, too, except Monsieur Lovell—who had at once left for England—and Charles, presumably because he was a relative of mine and they might have wished to avoid him any embarrassment. I told them what I had seen and I produced the bullet. I was at once instructed to keep my mouth shut; nay, ordered to do so as a subordinate under discipline from his Colonel. I quarrelled fiercely with them, but they were too many for me. They had agreed among themselves that the death should be sworn as from a shooting accident. If my own information came to light, the whole story would come out, and all those concerned would be disgraced, if not imprisoned. And that included myself, for they all vowed to implicate me if I divulged the truth. Finally, I was overcome and made to swear an oath on the Bible. I felt that, were I faced by poor Elise and her family, in the circumstances I could not keep my peace and abide by the vow. I therefore fled at once, avoiding my relatives ever after, and I ended in this place hiding from them, for, as you know, monsieur, nobody can compel an inmate to see visitors. Then came the war and the whole affair assumed different proportions. Death was everywhere. What did an odd life or two seem to matter? All the same, I had sworn the oath and did not intend to break it. Besides, as an old army man, I might easily have been victimized had I offended powerful, aristocratic officers like Latour and Arnaud de St. Marcellin. I might have lost my pension, or even worse, my life might have been forfeit.... I have heard of such things happening."

Old Barge shook his head sadly.

"They are all dead now who matter, and there's only my godson, Sylvestre, left. I wonder what he thinks of me and whether he's interested in seeing me again. All these years I've been afraid to face him because of what I did in connection with the man who was to be little Elise's husband. I've been a coward.... And yet, it is a fearful thing to die without one's family around one. I wake in the night sweating to think of it. I cry out.... "

"I wouldn't worry, sir. I saw Monsieur Sylvestre and his wife only yesterday, and they spoke very kindly of you. They would be delighted to see you again. They are very lonely since Elise died and are eating their hearts out in their villa at Cap Ferrat. They are bored and you, who have been a part of their lives in better days, will cheer them up."

"You think so?"

The old man blew his nose in a silk handkerchief and paused to gather himself together.

"I'll write to them.... Your visit has brought me new hope and new life, sir. Have I told you all you want?"

"More than enough."

"And the broken oath.... You don't hold me culpable?"

"No. As you say, they're all dead who matter.... And the rest.... Well, I knew, and the French police knew, without even a word from you. You have done your part."

Barge saw Littlejohn to the visitors' lodge and there left him, returning with a light step to write at once to his forsaken relatives.

Mrs. Littlejohn was sitting talking to the young Brother in the little shop. There was a large parcel on the counter and the Brother looked well satisfied.

"Have you three thousand francs, Tom?"

"Good heavens. Have you bought the whole monastery!"

The big fat monk and the little Brother-shopkeeper looked sad and anxious until they saw Littlejohn was shaking with laughter. The monks waved the Littlejohns goodbye as the great bell began to toll.

Chapter Twelve
The Chateau

They drove back to St. Marcellin over the now familiar dusty road. The air was so oppressive that they gasped for breath. The heat hung like a pall over everything. Littlejohn was glad to reach the uplands of the Durance again and thence they had intermittent shade and coolness for most of the remaining way.

It was about five o'clock when they arrived in St. Marcellin and history seemed to repeat itself. The deserted main road through the village, the shade of the plane trees, the curé asleep in his garden with a handkerchief over his face, the ceaseless splash of the fountain, and the final coolness of the *Restaurant Pascal,* where Marie Alivon received them with a show of placid pleasure.

"The room is ready and there will be a duck for dinner."

She did not ask them about the trip they had made. She seemed to take it for granted that they had enjoyed themselves and to have no curiosity about what they had done since last she saw them.

"There is a note from Monsieur le Marquis, sir. My brother brought it from the château last night."

Marie Alivon calmly handed him an envelope which she had been carrying in the pocket of her apron. A cheap envelope and, when Littlejohn tore it open and removed the letter, the notepaper was plain and cheap as well and covered in spidery handwriting done with a thin pen in violet ink. The sort of thing you write in a café with writing materials you've borrowed there.

It was dated Wednesday evening, and reminded Littlejohn of a barrack-room instruction.

ST. MARCELLIN.

I would like to see you urgently as soon as you return. I am expecting Madame and yourself to lunch on Saturday and this does not cancel the arrangement, to which I look forward with pleasure.

I shall be at home at any time on Thursday, when I presume you will be returning.

A. DE ST. MARCELLIN.

Littlejohn felt nettled. The note was too peremptory. Who did Monsieur le Marquis think he was? The Chief Inspector would much rather have taken a cold bath in the antique tub and washed away the heat and dust of the journey. He excused himself to his wife, who said she'd take a hot bath instead, and after dipping his handkerchief in the fountain and mopping his head and neck, he soaked his hands in the ice-cold water and the heat of the day dried them in the short space it took to reach the car, which stood under the cypress trees of the presbytery opposite.

This was Littlejohn's first trip to the big house and he already knew the direction in which it lay. He followed the road for half a mile on the route to Peyrolles, turned right, and then, in the distance, he made out the compact mass of trees which surrounded the park. The by-road along which he was now driving was monotonous and bordered for as far as he could see with straight parallel lines of poplars, and on either side, into the far distance, stretched vast tracts of poor land, apparently under cultivation until it reached heights on the foothills where nothing profitable would grow, and sheep were pastured. Here and there, where the soil improved for a space, were odd groves of oranges and lemons. Where it grew poorer, smooth silvery-leaved olives of the type which yielded small, hard, sun-resisting fruit, fought for sustenance. A farm or two with a poor homestead badly roofed in leaking, moss-covered tiles, which the farmers couldn't or wouldn't repair. There had been no small landed proprietors here until the Marquis had started selling-off portions of his one-time ten thousand acres, and now the small landowners were intent on accumulating more land before they tackled their tumbledown dwellings, which had once been small cottages.

The heat here was moist and droves of flies plastered the windscreen of the car and flew in through the open windows and tortured Littlejohn.

The château was enclosed by a spacious park of old trees and protected from sight by deep thickets of pine, fir and a spruce. Eventually the living wall of foliage broke and revealed large rusting wrought-iron gates, mounted on great stone columns which had once been topped by heraldic figures of one sort or another, but the features of which had now been totally weathered away.

There was a lodge behind the gates, but, as nobody appeared, the Chief Inspector had to let himself in. He passed into the park itself. The afternoon sun had lost its strength and failed to dazzle him or create any illusions, and there was no mist now to soften the outlines. Everything stood out stark and cruel. Neglected trees, dead trunks with bare, fantastic branches, thickets of untended bushes, sheep grazing on what had once been lawns, and at the end of the weedy, overgrown drive, the château itself, shabby, with most of the shutters drawn. The details of the great house grew plainer as the car advanced. Two corner pepperpot towers, a large frontage, a wide stone staircase leading to a heavy front door which badly needed paint. Below, the barred basement windows, behind one of which Littlejohn spied a fat woman plucking a duck.

The car pulled up at the foot of the steps and Littlejohn got out and mounted to the door. He tugged at the chain which hung at one side, and he had to repeat the performance before a man appeared, a butler of sorts, still shuffling his way into a shabby tail-coat which covered a black, sleeved waistcoat. This was presumably Claudius.

"Good afternoon, Claudius."

Littlejohn wanted to make sure.

"Good day, monsieur."

A tall, heavy man of sixty or more, grey-haired, and with a full, round face. Obviously a robust peasant type who'd been trained for the job from boyhood.

"Monsieur le Marquis is expecting me. Chief Inspector Littlejohn."

They passed through a small vestibule and then the interior opened out. A vast place, with a long corridor from which numerous rooms branched to left and right, and a huge marble staircase rising from an archway halfway along the passage.

Dust everywhere. Moth-eaten tapestries hung faded on the walls, ancestral pictures spoiled by the damp, faded patches here and there where good pieces of furniture had been moved for sale. Littlejohn had heard in the village that antique dealers were often around... and others less expert. "Monsieur le Marquis does quite a trade, I can tell you, buying old furniture and selling it at a profit as genuine stuff he's inherited."

They walked along the uneven parquet, dotted with holes where it had rotted and collapsed. A large window at the far end of the corridor gave on the back of the house and revealed it to be right in the middle of a park.... Forest all round it; beeches, oak, elm, hornbeam, box.... All struggling for life amid the shambles. And blowing down the draughty passages, the perpetual smells of rotten wood, decaying furniture and hangings, the scent of burning leaves.

Claudius left Littlejohn for a minute whilst he sought out his master, and returned to lead him into a small room midway down the hall. It was a library, and here the aroma changed to that of decaying calf. The damp had, in places, even spread a furry fungus over the leather binding of the hundreds of books on the shelves which surrounded the room. Some of the backs were hanging off the large volumes. A wood fire in the hearth. Arnaud de St. Marcellin was standing before it. To the left, another door stood open, disclosing what must have been the salon, a huge place where once the elegant aristocracy of the neighbourhood on occasions had danced and enjoyed themselves. A marble fireplace and a gilt-framed mirror were visible, and the floor, where the parquet had collapsed and left it shabby and forlorn. The ceiling, once beautifully ornamental, was smashed and torn where the lustre chandeliers had been removed for sale.

"Ha! My friend the police-officer.... Come in."

St. Marcellin shook hands languidly. He wore the same ironical smile as when they'd first met. Standing, instead of sitting in the car, he looked broader and more plump, and taller. A well set-up fellow, but a bit soft and flabby, as Littlejohn had thought on first encounter.

"Sorry, we can't receive you in better style. The place is mortgaged, you know, and our only visitors nowadays are mainly creditors and a few antique dealers from Grenoble and Lyons, sniffing round for bargains.... Last week, we sold the piano Chopin once played when he stayed here with George Sand...."

The Marquis seemed to enjoy mocking himself as well as others.

"You've met Charles, I believe... Monsieur Charles de Barge."

De Barge rose from a large, shabby chair and bowed without offering his hand.

"Yes.... I met him at his uncle's place at Cap Ferrat. I heard he'd come here to see you, sir, presumably to report on my enquiries on the coast...."

De Barge looked put-out.

"I... I..."

"Don't, my dear Charles, try to deny it. I sent for you because I knew the Inspector was down your way, presumably pursuing his most stubborn investigations.... Won't you sit down, Inspector, if you can find a chair that'll hold you...? Try this."

Another shabby chair which groaned as Littlejohn lowered himself in its damp grasp. De Barge sat down, too. He was obviously embarrassed and kept his eyes on the threadbare carpet, avoiding Littlejohn's glance.

There was whisky in a decanter and glasses on the table. St. Marcellin poured out three helpings.

"Your good health, Chief Inspector Littlejohn. Success to you."

"Good health, sir."

"Come, come, Charles. Drink! We *do* wish the Chief Inspector success, don't we? Why else have we brought him here to-day? We don't want him to make a fool of himself, do we?"

The Marquis drained his glass in one, put it down, and then turned to Littlejohn.

"I thought I'd better send for you and talk things over. It seems you insist in regarding the accident of February last as a murder and that you're determined to find out who killed Lovell and his wife.... I do advise you, Chief Inspector, not to persist. You are only likely to make a complete ass of yourself."

Littlejohn calmly filled his pipe and lit it.

"You seem to be very well-informed, Monsieur le Marquis. Everyone reports developments to you and everyone who knows anything whatever about the events of February last is either as tight as an oyster or else disappears."

The mocking eyes returned Littlejohn's steady look.

"I must defend myself, Inspector. If things go on like this, I am likely to be accused of a crime I didn't commit. I believe you have discovered that Lovell and his wife called here *before* they drove to their death and that they were leaving here and not driving in from Manosque when the accident happened. You see, Clara, the maid at the Malicornes, overheard the conversation between that dotty pair of gossips and your charming wife. She reported it at once to the servant of the mayor, who is her sister, and the news naturally found its way here. I'm like the father of the community. They tell me all their troubles and their little surprises. So, you see ... I know what you're thinking."

"You also have your reports from Cap Ferrat and Antibes, I have no doubt. The very presence of Monsieur de Barge here ..."

"Quite right.... You have been to see Albert Lapointe and found our little baker enjoying a holiday by the sea.... Lapointe is a good fellow who knows how to keep his counsel, but I'm afraid he was forced to tell you quite a lot to avoid a stay in the cells at Nice.... The duel.... You presumably know all about it?"

"Yes, sir. Not *all,* but quite a lot."

"And our friend Charles here found out from his friend the valet that something was said about Uncle Sylvestre.... I would make a guess that you visited the lunatic asylum at St. Luc on your way back to St. Marcellin."

"Right again, sir. But hardly a madhouse. Just a retreat for the aged."

"You're wrong there.... Excuse me, but I know the place better than you. It *is* a madhouse and any information you may have got from Sylvestre de Barge, I beg your pardon, *Barge,* must be discounted accordingly. Did he tell you that the duel was, in fact, a murder all the time? I see he did. We had great difficulty, at the time of poor Bernard's death, in persuading the republican captain or major, or whatever he was... that he was suffering from a grave delusion. Four of us, men of local repute, saw Lovell kill my brother.... You see where his strange ideas have led Captain Barge. Into a madhouse where he still persists in telling his crazy yarns. I observe you aren't convinced. Well, I hope to prove it to you later. Meanwhile, may I know why, when you arrived in St. Marcellin— presumably on a commission from Lovell's brother, the Minister of something or other in your government—may I know why you didn't come straight to me and place your cards on the table and ask for my help?"

"Because I had no authority to question anyone. My work was purely informal and, Monsieur le Marquis, if there were any suspects in case it did turn out to be murder, you were very near the top of the list, as the only remaining man in this place who knew the Lovells."

The mocking look had died out of St. Marcellin's eyes. Charles de Barge said nothing and his hands gripped the arms of his chair tightly.

"Look here, Littlejohn, I've told you the matter was officially declared to be an accident."

"Why, then, did you start at once to obstruct me at every turn? One would think you didn't want an impartial investigation, which, if what you say is true, would have put the mind of Lovell's brother at rest and closed the case for good."

St. Marcellin stood silent for a moment, gnawing the nail of his left index. The great ruin of a house seemed completely silent outside the door of the library, as though resigned to its fate at the hands of the mortgagees. A small clock on the mantelpiece, a ticking little fussy thing which looked as though someone had won it on a shooting-range at a fair, struck six. Outside, long sunset shadows were falling across the park and the sheep there stood stock still as though, like the house, expecting some awful judgment.

"Tell me what you know, Littlejohn," said St. Marcellin suddenly. "Or, rather, what you think you know."

Littlejohn made no bones about it. He didn't trust St. Marcellin, but if the Marquis could give a satisfactory answer to all the strange events of the past few days, light might be thrown on the case.

"You said when I arrived, sir, that you had to defend yourself. You seem to have done that very well by shutting up anyone with useful information. First of all, the innkeeper, Alivon, began to spy on me. He listened behind doors and, as he carried up the tin bath every evening, he doubtless took the chance to cast his eyes round our room for anything which might prove useful to you.... Yes; I'm sure Alivon wasn't merely eaten up with curiosity. He was spying for someone."

"He is in my employ, Chief Inspector. He works on the estate. He is naturally interested in all that goes on in the village and countryside. He likes telling me the news, and naturally goes to some trouble to find out what happens…"

"Very diplomatically put, sir. I don't quite see it that way."

"What do you mean?"

Littlejohn went on as though no question had been asked.

"…Then there's the mayor. He obviously owes his position to your favour. You are still a power in the land, sir, and your name is good for many things. Monsieur Savini also makes a point of being your watchdog.… One night when little Hénoch Rossi got drunk and talked too much, the mayor saw him hustled out and, later, Hénoch almost died from charcoal fumes in his bakery. I want to know who closed the door of the furnace-room. Can you tell me, Monsieur le Marquis?"

Again the ironical smile and the smug look which Littlejohn was growing to dislike heartily.

"No. Savini said it was an accident and the door had closed by mistake.… The wind probably."

"On a still, thundery night? No, sir. Until I get an answer to that question, I shall probably be staying here. That is unless you give orders for me to be thrown out of the hotel and forbid anyone else to take us in."

"Now, now, Inspector. I'm not so inhuman."

"Why, then, did you give orders for the baker to be moved or remove himself to Antibes to keep him out of my way? You can't deny it *was* on your orders. Savini came here hot-foot to report little Hénoch's malefaction and, before we knew where we were, the baker had vanished. *And* his brother, who probably knew where he'd gone, daren't say a word.… Were you prepared to chuck them out of their bakery, or forbid the villagers to buy bread from them, if they didn't do as they were told?"

"You're getting impertinent, Littlejohn. We have a way of dealing with impertinent officials."

"Not with me, sir. Kindly remember that."

The Marquis looked puzzled. He wondered now how far Littlejohn had the backing of the French police and how far the case had passed into their hands.

"Then there was the postmistress, Madame Colomb, whose husband also spied on her when she told me certain things and who at once sent her to her brother's in Sospel to keep her quiet. All these things add up, Monsieur le Marquis. And there's Leclerc, the garage man, who knows something, and remains mute when I ask him questions. And whether or not Father Chambeyron, your village priest, has heard things under the seal of the confessional, I don't know, but he almost grew hysterical when I asked him a few simple questions...."

The Marquis smiled again.

"You seem to have been received in our village with a woeful lack of hospitality, Littlejohn. But you do see, don't you, that the case was officially closed months ago, and our people don't like fuss and a lot of questions? They are a secret people and they resent attempts to wring information out of them. I ask you again, why you didn't come to me for anything you wanted to know? I would gladly have told you anything. I would even have put you in touch with the officials who conducted the case and you could have seen the dossiers. There's nothing to hide."

"Except, perhaps, that the car was travelling *to* not *from* Manosque. Suppose you tell me, now, exactly what happened on the night Lovell and his wife died. And suppose, also, you go back to the duel in which it is said Lovell killed your brother. And that you paint in all the background which will explain why Lovell came back to meet his death in a neighbourhood which, of all places on earth, must have been the most distasteful one to him."

The Marquis took out a battered packet of cigarettes.

"Cigarette? No? Smoke your pipe then. Cigarette, Charles?"

Charles took one and lit them both without a word.

"First of all, Littlejohn, Lovell killed my brother in a duel. He shot him dead, and of that there is no doubt. Later, I'll show you why. Lovell stole the affection of my brother's betrothed. They fought; my brother fell. The girl left and married Lovell. That was the end of the chapter, except for one thing. A half-mad and disgruntled ex-army captain, Barge, who turned out to be a great-uncle of Elise, my brother's betrothed, was for some reason invited here to the betrothal celebrations, and somehow blundered into the duel. My brother naturally challenged Lovell... Who would not have done? After the death of Bernard, Barge arrived and kicked up a fuss, said he'd seen the duel, and that a third party had shot my brother; that neither of the duellists had fired anywhere near his opponent. There were five witnesses; a doctor, the seconds, Charles here, and Colonel Latour who acted as umpire. We all swore that Bernard was killed by a bullet from Lovell's pistol. Barge persisted and even had the effrontery to produce a bullet which he said had killed Bernard and which he'd picked out of a tree after the event. It was fantastic, and we told him that unless he immediately withdrew his insinuations, we would see that he paid for his folly."

"In other words, he, too, might have met with an accident?"

"Please don't interrupt with impertinences.... He was living on his army pension.... Something was said about looking into it.... We have our ways with insubordination in the army."

"I'm sure you have."

"The result was, Barge left at once and, I hear from Charles, hasn't been seen since by the family. Now he's in an asylum. So far, so good.... The war intervened, we were all scattered, or involved in the Occupation, and nothing was heard of Lovell until, late one night, he arrived here with his wife and demanded to see me. I was naturally very cool with him, but found him persistent almost to dementia. He said that since we last met on the morning of the duel, he had been anxious to settle a matter.... He had left hastily and upset on the day of my brother's death, war had intervened, and he hadn't been able to seek me out. Then, he had been absent abroad. But all this time his mind had been obsessed by a single thought. He felt that the shot he fired had not killed my brother.... I knew then that somehow he had heard from Elise's great-uncle, the crazy Captain Barge, and that he, too, had become infected with the old man's mad idea. He went so far as to demand that my brother's body should be exhumed to find out whether or not the wound was from the ball of a duelling pistol, or a rifle. I refused absolutely. He grew almost violent, and his wife, who was there with him, also joined in the argument.... I ended by showing them the door. On his way out, Lovell said we hadn't heard the last of it and that if I wouldn't behave decently, he'd take official steps to get his question answered. He proposed to raise the matter with the Ministry in Paris.... He never did, for, driving dangerously, I presume under the influence of his rage with me, he smashed his car into a tree at a bad corner and killed himself and his wife.... And that is a true account of what happened, Littlejohn, and if you require it on oath, I am prepared to swear it before a proper notary."

"No need for that. I still can't understand why, if you were prepared to be so frank about it, you started a kind of shadow-boxing contest with me as soon as I arrived. I grant you, I might have approached you and asked you right away for an explanation or help. But I didn't. That was no excuse for issuing orders to all the village that nobody was to utter a word to me about the accident. It struck me as being very suspicious behaviour and I can't get it out of my mind."

St. Marcellin smiled good-humouredly.

"Well, I trust you're satisfied now, Chief Inspector. I've invited you here, which is apparently what you wanted, and I've told you the circumstances of the case quite candidly. I hope you are content and will make a real holiday of the remainder of your stay in St. Marcellin. It isn't much of a change performing your daily routine when you're supposed to be taking a rest.... Well?"

"I have met Sylvestre Barge, sir, and I still don't think he's mad. I find it very difficult to ... "

A look of intense hate lit up St. Marcellin's eyes. He was no longer the mocking, nonchalant spendthrift, but an arrogant aristocrat, a man of a world long past, whose word was being doubted.

"Very well, Littlejohn, you force me to measures which are extremely distasteful to me, and for which I shan't forgive you in a hurry. Wait."

He took from his pocket a bunch of keys and went to a cupboard in a corner near the fireplace. Thence he gently, almost with reverence, took out a large black box. He inserted another small key and opened the box. Then he brought it and laid it on the desk. It was a silk-lined, leather-covered casket, which at one time might have been used for holding a tiara or a coronet, and on the silk of the inside of the lid it bore the name of a jeweller in Rue de la Paix, Paris.

But the box didn't interest Littlejohn and de Barge, who had risen to inspect it. It was the contents which horrified them.

Reposing in the velvet interior was a human skull.

St. Marcellin was obviously deeply moved.

"After Lovell's visit and insinuations, I had to know the truth. I personally visited the family vault and examined my brother's remains. A bomb fell in the grounds near the mortuary chapel during the war and many of the tombs were damaged and cracked. Bernard's suffered such a fate, although I didn't know it until I opened the casket, which was split. Nothing but the skeleton remained. I inspected the wound, which, as you will see, is not from a rifle bullet at all. A rifle bullet would have passed in and out and left two fractures. This was made by a pistol-ball of soft lead, which, as you see, is lodged here in the cranium."

St. Marcellin, with an effort, was being objective, like a professor of anatomy, and pointed out his case with a trembling finger.

"I will now replace the skull, which I removed again only last night, in the hope that I could convince you that what Lovell and Barge said was a gross untruth."

He looked at Littlejohn, his face strained and his eyes blinking.

"I hope now, Chief Inspector, you are satisfied, and that the case will drop at once."

Littlejohn did not reply. He looked at St. Marcellin and then at the pathetic, grinning object in its velvet wrappings.

And this was the man who presumed to call poor old Sylvestre Barge a madman!

Chapter Thirteen
The old Woman of Digne

Littlejohn drove back to the village in the deepening dusk. The rows of poplars converted the road into a long, gloomy tunnel and he had to put on his headlamps to see where he was going. Frogs croaked in a raucous chorus and bats flitted about among the trees. The Chief Inspector had heard the ringing of the Angelus on the cracked church bell whilst he was in the château. Now, they were dismally tolling it again. This time for the dead. Madeleine Tatin had at last passed peacefully away. The doleful message rang through the village and far across the desolate countryside and everybody knew what it meant. In the far distance on the hillsides, Littlejohn could make out the fires of herdsmen and shepherds camping in the open.

Lights shone through the windows of the *Restaurant Pascal* and, in the alley behind, the men had started their evening game and the clash of steel on steel rang out as they threw their bowls. Before going to find his wife, Littlejohn parked the car in the wooden shed behind the inn which served as a garage, and then crossed the road and entered the dimly-lighted church. There had been a service of some kind and Colomb, the sacristan, was going round extinguishing the candles by pinching the wicks. The air was heavy with the smell of incense, candle grease and damp stone. The priest was in the sacristy taking off his vestments.

Littlejohn walked down the nave, turned past the dark confessionals, and made the abbé jump when he greeted him.

"Good evening, father."

"Good evening, Monsieur Littlejohn. You are back?"

The sacristan was shuffling about waiting to put out the last of the lights and lock up.

"All right, Colomb.... I'll lock up and take the keys."

"Good night, father."

"Good night, Colomb, and God bless you."

The sacristan, unaffected by the benediction, scowled at Littlejohn, turned his back, and shambled off.

"I heard the bell tolling, father. I hope ... "

The priest almost seemed to read Littlejohn's thoughts.

"No, my son; it is Madeleine Tatin who passed away to-night."

"I see. I have just got back from the château. The Marquis asked me to pay him an urgent visit. My wife and I are dining there with you on Saturday."

"Yes. I usually dine with Monsieur le Marquis every Saturday. It is a little joke of his to say that he feeds me up between the fasting of Friday and the work of Sunday."

The curé did not smile. He still wore the worried look which Littlejohn now knew so well.

"The château is a big place for so few servants to keep up.... "

"That is so. I remember days when I was young, when there were a score or more servants of one kind and another at the house. Now, there are four. All the same, much of it is closed, there are only a few rooms to keep tidy, and attendance on Monsieur le Marquis."

"I suppose the rest are dead or scattered."

"Yes. The two wars.... And nowadays, people don't like entering into service any more. There is more money to be earned in the towns. Strangely enough, speaking of Madeleine Tatin... she was once a lady's-maid at the château. She left when the mother of the Marquis died and there were no more ladies there to serve. The Marquis gave her a little house in the village. And that reminds me.... "

The priest shuffled his large forefinger among a mass of papers on the table of the sacristy, produced an envelope, licked the flap, and briskly sealed it.

"I must find a stamp in the presbytery and post this. It is to advise Madeleine's sister, Eulalie, of her death. Madeleine had no relatives living in St. Marcellin, and I promised her I would notify her family when she died. The funeral is next Tuesday and I have just been writing a note."

"I have a stamp here, father. Let me post the letter for you on my way across."

The temptation to save the price of a stamp was too great. The priest handed over the envelope, Littlejohn took a stamp from his note-case and stuck it on. They started to walk to the door.

"Yes.... Madeleine's sister is a great age, too. Eighty, if a day. She will follow soon, I expect. She also worked at the château as a maid in the old days. Her husband was head groom. When he died, ten years or more ago, Eulalie went to live in Digne with a married daughter."

Father Chambeyron turned in the porch, switched off the last of the lights, locked the door, and put the key in a pocket under his soutane.

"Why not come and dine with my wife and me at the hotel, Monsieur l'Abbé?"

"Please excuse me to-night.... Some other time. I shall be out to-morrow night and there's a lot to be done."

"Some other time, then, father."

"Yes, my son.... Good night, and God bless you."

It was like returning home. The priest seemed glad to see him and was using familiar speech, as though Littlejohn were a member of his own flock. It was the same at the inn. As he entered, Marie Alivon smiled and told him Madame had had her bath and was waiting for him to join her at dinner. The men in the bar, too, nodded or saluted him respectfully and one or two asked if he'd had a good trip. He suddenly remembered the letter, which he was carrying in his hand, excused himself for a minute, and turned to cross the road to post it at the box outside the village stores. Instinctively he looked at the envelope and, as he did so, an idea struck him.

He noted the address.

Madame Eulalie Bonjour,
122 bis, *Boulevard Gassendi,*
DIGNE.

Bonjour! That was a good one! A cheerful sounding name, if nothing else. He felt interested in Madame Bonjour.

As he went to their room to wash, the bath was being emptied. César Alivon, smoking his eternal pipe, and a lanky youth with a calf-lick of hair over one eye, were carrying the whole contraption, water and all, very gingerly down the stairs. They had removed a couple of bucketfuls and were now doing a grotesque balancing feat in bringing the rest below.

"Good evening, sir. Glad to see you back."

César, too! Even the laconic gamekeeper seemed in a good temper.

The evening passed as all the others had done. The well-cooked meal, the good wine, and afterwards, the return of the men from their games of bowls. The shouts of the card players and the steadily increasing voices of the drinkers as the wine went down. Savini, the mayor, was missing. Someone said he had gone to Manosque on business.

The Littlejohns retired early, and to the noises of croaking frogs and the splash of the fountain, both quickly fell asleep.

"To-morrow, I'd like to go to Digne, Letty. You've never been there. Not that it's much of a place.... A bit melancholy.... But there's an old lady there I'd like a word with."

They were up good and early next morning, a day promising to be like all the others, with a brief heat haze, and then the grilling sun until late afternoon. They told the Alivons they were off for a picnic, took lunch with them, and Marie Alivon had prepared it with her usual care. Fresh crisp rolls, butter, cheese, fruit, and a pot of genuine *foie gras* from Strasbourg. "My cousin lives in Strasbourg and sends us some now and then...." She seemed to have relatives in all the gastronomic centres!

They drove to the main road through Manosque again, and it took them two hours along the broad, weary valley of the Durance, and then along the fresher, lovelier course of the Bléone to Digne itself. This was familiar country to Littlejohn; he had visited it with Dorange when following the Dominici affair and pointed out to his wife the places where they had halted and where the tragedy had relentlessly unfolded. The depressing valley of the Asse with Brunet, Ganagobie, and Lurs, scene of the horror itself. And then Digne, a melancholy little city, capital of the Basse Alpes, crowded in by mountains, bulging away from the main road as if trying to hide itself from the busy stream of traffic flowing to and from the warm, joyful south.

"Don't be long."

Mrs. Littlejohn said it plaintively. Littlejohn had almost at once found the broad main thoroughfare, the Boulevard Gassendi, dusty and shaded by plane trees, and had parked the car in the Place de la Libération. The prominent and grim prison in the best position in the town, the secret-looking, silent natives who regarded them with suspicion, the heavy weight of the lowering peaks around, all gave them an unhappy, uneasy mood, which the shadows cast by the grim mountainsides across the streets did nothing to dispel.

122 *bis,* Boulevard Gassendi was a third-rate tenement over a seedy wine shop, and was entered by a narrow door which gave access to a shabby staircase leading to the flats. Sitting at this door on a hard wooden chair and making the most of the fresh air, was an old woman, with her worn hands lying placidly in her lap. She looked up at the Littlejohns and, for the first time since their arrival, they felt really cheerful.

"Does Madame Bonjour live here, madame?"

"That's me."

A little, smiling, dark-eyed woman with grey hair and shrivelled pink cheeks like ripe apples. She had a look of serenity difficult to describe, for it was obvious that, in spite of her age, she had a fund of vitality and humour rarely found in the aged of those parts.

"You have something to say to me?"

Littlejohn wondered just how to put it.

"Yes, madame. Last night I posted a letter to you from the Abbé Chambeyron, but, as we were visiting Digne, I thought I'd call and tell you beforehand. I'm sorry to say..."

"So Madeleine has died at last!"

No tears, just a sigh, a placid smile, and a nod of the head.

"It has taken a long time, monsieur. Five times she has been on the verge of death. Five times have I been ready to labour all the way to that wretched village to see her laid to rest. And five times she has risen from her bed again. She is in God's peace at last. I suppose they'll be asking me and Fonsine, my daughter, to the funeral.... Hé me; it'll be my turn next. I'm the last of us now. When is it to be? Luckily, I've got my mourning clothes ready."

"Tuesday, madame."

"It's a long way there and back in a day. All the same, I owe it to her."

A silence, as though Madame Bonjour were thinking about the past.

"We'd both have liked to be buried at home with our own people, but the good God has ways of his own."

"You aren't from these parts, then, madame?"

"Me? No; I'm glad to say. Madeleine and me are from Auch, in Gascony.... Now, that's the land, sir. Full of merry, cheerful people.... I remember the good times we had when we were girls. We both came in service at St. Marcellin. Madeleine never married, for some reason, although she was a lot prettier than me.... Nice arms and legs. I was a bit on the heavy side, but she... she was a beauty. She was too particular about the men. I married Bonjour and I never left these parts after, although Bonjour was a Gascon, too. I suppose they'll bury me here, now, among these mountains. It makes me shiver.... Still, it's nothing I can help. The good God has strange ways of making us settle down."

"You liked the château, madame?"

"The life was all right till they got short of money, But, if my husband hadn't got kicked by a stallion and died, we'd have had to move. They had to sell the horses and couldn't afford to pay us any more. ... As it was, Fonsine had married a policeman and he was posted to Digne. So, I came to live here with my kith and kin. It's a bit of a tight squeeze, too. They've four children and only three rooms."

The cheerful old woman prattled on, glad of someone to talk to.

"You're foreigners, aren't you, monsieur?"

"English."

"I like the English. My husband, God rest him, fought side-by-side with them in the first war. He liked them, too."

"We were at the château yesterday."

Madame Bonjour's eyes lighted up.

"A good place to live, once upon a time. Now. ... Is Monsieur Arnaud still there?"

"Yes. It's tumbling down now, though."

"I thought it would. They spent too fast. The St. Marcellins were always great spenders. That's all right if you have money to do it with, but ..."

"Claudius is still with them."

"He is, is he? The villain."

She cackled to herself and even looked a bit coy.

"The girls there always had to watch that Claudius. He had a wife with him who scarcely let him out of her sight, but he managed now and then to swing a loose leg. I suppose he's old and has lost his vitality now. I can't imagine Claudius without vitality, the wretch!"

"He's getting old and growing bald. ..."

The old woman chuckled again. The idea of the one-time philandering butler bald, aged, and living in isolation seemed to tickle her.

"At one time, any girl who valued her virtue did well to keep far enough from the château of St. Marcellin."

"We're staying with the Alivons at the *Hôtel Pascal* there.…"

"Ah, yes, the Alivons. Marie was always a nice girl. Her husband died in the war.… I'm surprised she didn't marry again. Many a man in those parts would be glad to have her. Money and good looks.… That's what the men are all after, isn't it, monsieur…?"

She gave Littlejohn a droll sidelong look and smiled knowingly at his wife.

"Marie's different from that brother César of hers. I always said he was a bit mad. And the affair of Céleste, his sister, made him worse. I don't suppose he's married, has he? He grew strange after Céleste made away with herself, although before the tragedy, César had an eye for a pretty woman. He's made a pass or two at me in his time. Seeing me sitting here with my old bones and eighty years, you wouldn't think I was good-looking once, would you, monsieur?"

The naughty old woman didn't wait for an answer, but prattled on.

"Is Céleste's baby still around St. Marcellin, sir?"

"Yes. She's called Blanche, is quite grown up now, and works in Manosque in an office. A good-looking girl."

"All the Alivons were good-looking. The girls never stopped chasing César and the men Céleste and Marie. Marie wasn't the flighty sort, but Céleste had her own ideas. She was one of the parlourmaids and had notions above her station. I think she thought one of the army officers who used to come would marry her. The stupid little chit. As if they ever did! They got what they wanted and then cleared off, married one of their own kind, and forgot those who were silly enough to get big ideas. I know…I've been through it all."

"I heard there was some scandal about Céleste. Marie, I believe, adopted Blanche as her own child after Céleste's death."

"Scandal, did you say, monsieur? Those things are not scandal in these parts. They are commonplace. Céleste was foolish enough to get herself a child out of wedlock. But that is no reason for killing oneself. It happens everywhere and if all the girls who suffer that way killed themselves, the churchyards here would be full. Of course, she would have had to leave the château, but there are plenty of positions elsewhere for pretty girls.…But Céleste was an Alivon, and they are a proud lot. Why, César even swore to kill whoever betrayed his sister. The foolish man. Time heals everything, but the Alivons couldn't wait. Like those who plant potatoes one day and dig them up the next to see if they are growing."

"Did César know the man responsible?"

"Of course he didn't. One or two of us made a good guess, but we kept quiet. We didn't want bother and bloodshed at the château, even if Céleste did drown herself in the lake in the park. No reason for causing another death, was there…? César thought it was one of the officers who'd taken advantage of his sister and he went about scowling and asking questions and finding no answers to them. If I'd dropped a hint about what I'd seen, there would have been a rumpus, I can tell you."

Two small girls arrived down the stairs of the tenement and clung to the skirts of the old woman, who started to straighten their frocks and smooth their hair.

"These are the youngest of my grandchildren. Twins, monsieur! As if we hadn't enough without Fonsine producing two at a time.…"

Littlejohn gave them some small change and they ran away without another word to spend it.

"I must be getting indoors. Fonsine is out shopping and if she finds me out here gossiping, the fat will be on the fire. ..."

Littlejohn felt he must act quickly or Madame Bonjour would be off before she'd told the critical part of her tale.

"You were telling us about Céleste, Madame Bonjour. Blanche isn't half an aristocrat, then?"

Madame Bonjour laughed until she coughed.

"How well you put it, monsieur! How well. ... Of course she isn't. I'm surprised you haven't guessed whose daughter she is. ..."

"Not Claudius!"

"Of course!"

The old woman rocked with laughter and even slapped Littlejohn on the thigh, as though the pair of them were enjoying a huge joke.

"You won't, I know, monsieur, tell anyone. ... I talk too fast when I get excited. It is our way in Gascony. ... But swear you won't say a word to anyone. If César got to know, there would be blood on the floor at the château, I can tell you."

"I promise to keep your secret, Madame Bonjour, but I'm surprised the Alivons never found out."

"Why? Céleste had obviously told nobody. The house had been full of visitors ... and some very persuasive young men in uniform among them, there were, too. It might have been anybody. But I'd seen Claudius after Céleste along the corridors of the house. He seemed crazy about her. I even caught him in her bedroom, the rascal. ... She wasn't there at the time, I must admit, but Claudius was, no doubt, spying out the land. I've never seen Blanche since she was a child in arms. She mustn't look like her father. Otherwise César would know. But I'm ready to wager, monsieur, that she looks *all*peasant. These children with even half a gentleman in them are different. ... You can tell, monsieur. Breed comes out, you see. They have an air. ... You have seen Blanche, you say. Is she part gentility, or all peasant? Tell me that."

"All peasant, I'd say. What we'd call a country girl at home."

"What did I tell you! Claudius was a farm labourer's son whom the father of the present Marquis took a fancy to, and trained as a house servant. And the Alivons were countrymen ... owned a little land. I'll bet Mademoiselle Blanche hasn't the hands and racehorse's ankles of the gentry. ... Now has she? And don't tell me you haven't noticed, monsieur."

Mrs. Littlejohn's turn to laugh at her husband's rising colour.

"Of course he's noticed. She's a very nice girl, but she has the strong features, heavy limbs, and the thick bone of country stock. Her taste in dress, too, wasn't inherited from the château."

"That's right. Madame is more observant than the men, as usual. A pretty face and a nice leg for them. ... Here comes Fonsine."

Another countrywoman, middle-aged, carrying a string bag full of vegetables with a long loaf of bread thrust among them and a bottle of wine under her arm. She paused and gave her mother a quick glare.

"Yes, I'm still here, Fonsine. I was just having a word with this lady and gentleman. They're English tourists. It's nice to have someone intelligent to speak to now and then. ... "

It went quite over Fonsine's head. She had a placid, heavy face and a mop of dark unruly hair. Perspiring and plump, she was obviously busy and bothered by her family duties and resented her mother wasting time.

"Bonjour, m'sieur, 'dame.... Glad to meet you, I'm sure...."

Her speech was very different from her mother's and difficult to follow. Gruff Provençal against the old lady's sparkling and clear Gascon....

"I must be going."

"And bring your chair up with you. You can't leave it there cluttering up the door. The neighbours will complain."

She was wearing carpet slippers and shuffled off up the stairs without another word.

Littlejohn passed a thousand-franc note to Madame Bonjour.

"This will pay the fare to the funeral, I hope, Madame Bonjour. We may meet again if you're coming to St. Marcellin. You must call and ask for us at the *Hôtel Pascal.* Perhaps we'll still be there...."

"I shall be surprised. St. Marcellin's not much of a place to spend a holiday in. You must be short of somewhere to go. But thank you for the money, monsieur. It will be a rather expensive journey, because the children will be disappointed if I don't bring them each a little something back, and they won't be satisfied with a toffee-stick, as we were when we were little, I can assure you. Good day, sir, and madame."

"Let me help you up with the chair."

Littlejohn carried the chair up two flights of stairs and put it down in front of the door indicated by Madame Bonjour. Behind the door Fonsine's voice was raised at one of her offspring. Then slaps and wailings.

On the way down, Littlejohn found the whole staircase blocked by a huge gendarme who was ascending. The policeman looked at him suspiciously, grunted, and drew in his breath and hugged the wall to let the Chief Inspector pass.

It was like struggling with a feather bed and in the middle of the scrimmage, the officer blew a great blast of alcohol over Littlejohn. ... He must have been Fonsine's husband, for he halted on the floor above and as he opened the door, his wife started to nag him.

"You're half an hour late. ... Dinner's been ready. ... Here am I. ... You don't care how hard I work."

The words floated intermittently down the well of the stairs until the door banged and cut them off.

Chapter Fourteen
The Listener at the Door

Littlejohn felt there was one thing he could do in Digne which it was not safe to do in St. Marcellin. He must telephone to Spencer Lovell in London for information. The Post Office on the Boulevard Gassendi was only a stone's throw from Madame Bonjour's home.

It did not take long to get through to London, but it cost a lot. The name of Spencer Lovell, Minister of Commerce, seemed to open many doors. Half an hour after registering his call, Littlejohn was speaking to Lovell himself.

"I expected to hear from you, Littlejohn."

"Nothing has happened until quite recently. Now, everything seems to be taking shape at once, sir."

"Was it murder or an accident?"

"I rang you to ask one or two questions which might help me to answer yours. Did you ever hear your brother speak of a Captain Sylvestre Barge?"

"No. Can't say I did. Why?"

"Or do the names Mengali or Latour, one a doctor, the other a Colonel in the French Army, strike any chord of memory?"

"Latour... Colonel Latour, did you say? I knew of him. As a matter of fact, he died a few days before my brother. Chris was almost at his death-bed."

"Do you know the circumstances?"

"Rather. It was I who put Chris in touch with Latour. It seems the Colonel came here with the Free French. He went back to France at the time of the liberation. He'd been badly wounded in an air-raid on London and was a shattered wreck when he returned home to France. A few days before Chris met his death, the British Embassy in Paris rang me up ... Can you hear?"

"Yes, sir. Please continue."

"It seems the Embassy had been asked if they could find a Christopher Lovell in England. Latour was on his deathbed and couldn't die comfortably unless he saw my brother. He had something or other he wished to tell him. Something to do with the war, I guess. Anyway, Paris rang me up and asked if Christopher Lovell was a relative of mine. I said he was my brother. That set things in motion. ... Chris and Elise went to France right away. Latour's home was at Mélun, I believe. I heard later that he'd died. I never saw Chris again after he left for Mélun. He must have gone right on to the Riviera and then to St. Marcellin. Is what I tell you of any use, Littlejohn?"

"Of great use, sir. I'm sure now, that your brother's accident was engineered."

"Are you, by gad! Who did it? Let me know and I'll ... "

"I can't tell you, sir. It may be any one of three people."

"Who are they? Tell me their names."

"I can't do that yet, sir. Especially over the telephone. I shall call in the French police as soon as I'm sure of my case. Meanwhile ... "

"Write to me at once. Send for me as soon as you have some definite information."

Littlejohn left the telephone-box with the old feeling he always had when, at last, the case was beginning to unfold itself and the end of the road seemed in sight, however far distant.

"You look pleased about something, Tom."

A wave of gratitude for his wife's company, encouragement and untiring patience surged over him. He kissed her lightly on the cheek in front of all the passers-by. An old gentleman in a panama and cream alpaca suit smiled upon them and, kissing the tips of his own bunched fingers, he wafted the kiss skywards, and smiled at them again.

Digne seemed brighter and the way back to St. Marcellin less hot and tedious. They ate a late lunch picnicking in the valley of the Bléone.

"I'm so glad Marie packed us some lunch, Tom. I couldn't have eaten a thing in Digne... Whilst you were telephoning, I looked up one of the hotel menus in the Boulevard. Do you know what the speciality is in Digne? Thrush pie!"

"It *would* be!"

"Yes... Thrush pie with truffles... How utterly abominable! When are we going home, Tom? I don't like it here."

"Only another day or two, dear."

They got back to St. Marcellin at the same old time. The heat of the day just breaking, the priest asleep in his garden, his face under the same grubby handkerchief, the cool splash of the fountain, the shadows of the trees beginning to lengthen across the parched road... And, of course, Marie Alivon with the menu for dinner. Hors d'œuvre of crawfish, fresh trout from the Verdon, strawberries in red wine. And to drink, a Clairette de Mouans, sent by a cousin of the Alivons from his vineyard somewhere or other.

"Thank goodness, there's no *pâté de grives truffé,* Marie. In England we love thrushes for their singing, not in pies."

Mrs. Littlejohn hadn't got over the menu at Digne.

"Monsieur and Madame have been to Digne, then?"

It seemed impossible to keep a secret in St. Marcellin! One way or another, it always came out and found its way to the château.

"Yes... We heard that the valley of the Bléone was well worth seeing and, as we were then so near Digne, we visited the town. We were not very impressed... We had our picnic on the banks of the Bléone. It was very charming there."

"Perhaps madame would like a bath before dinner, to take the dust of the journey away. Then, later, we may be able to heat enough water for monsieur."

"If it won't be too much trouble."

"Of course not. My brother will look after it. He is here. He came home early to do the books. He enters them up once a week and pays the bills for me. I was never much good at book-keeping."

She left the room to pass on their orders and again Littlejohn became aware of a faint gust of French pipe tobacco. He spoke in English to his wife.

"Alivon has been listening behind the door again. It's surprising how the château set-up seems to keep abreast of all that we do. I wonder if César has guessed what we were doing in Digne."

As if in answer to his name, Alivon appeared with the bath on his head, his face not visible, but the smoke from the pipe he still held in his mouth, trickling from under his grotesque headgear.

"Monsieur... 'dame..." came the greeting from the bath, and then the feet beneath found their way accurately through the door of the dining-room and up the stairs.

Mrs. Littlejohn retired early with a book and Littlejohn played bowls again with his friends, which included the mayor this time. Monsieur Savini was all smiles and compliments, as they sat drinking after the game.

"We don't have the pleasure of madame's company, sir. All the same, we hope to see her to-morrow evening. I am invited to dinner at the château... It should be quite a party... Monsieur le Marquis, his friend Monsieur de Barge, you and madame, the curé, myself, and, I understand, to keep your wife company, Madame Ferté de Bormes, a friend of Monsieur le Marquis, is coming from Peyrolles... I am looking forward very much to it. You will also see our friend César acting as a waiter. Claudius is getting on in years and can't cope with a large party any more. So César lends a hand."

Littlejohn had been watching Alivon, who didn't quite seem himself. Instead of, as usual, filling the glasses as the men emptied them, he stood by the zinc counter lost in thought and they had to thump on the tables to attract his attention.

"César... César... More wine... You're neglecting us. One would think you had fallen in love."

"So César often goes to the château in the evenings when the Marquis gives a dinner?"

"Eh? You were saying, Mister Littlejohn...?"

Savini also seemed lost in thought. Littlejohn repeated his question.

"Now and then. They don't entertain much at the château nowadays, sir. Money is scarce, you see, and also since the death of Madame la Marquise, mother of Monsieur Arnaud, there have been no women there to take a hand. I wonder why Monsieur Arnaud never married... In spite of the state of the château and his own finances, he would be a good catch. But it's said he loved and lost someone and, although he seeks feminine company now and then, his thoughts never turn to marriage."

One by one the customers departed, and finally Littlejohn was left alone with Savini. He took the mayor to the door to see him off. Another hot, starry night, with frogs croaking in their hundreds and in the far distance, the noise of a train whistling and rattling on its way on the main line from Grenoble to Marseilles. Almost as soon as the mayor had said good night and gone, a dark form came from behind the hotel and crossed the road. There was no mistaking the long, loping stride. It was César Alivon. He opened the gate of the presbytery and vanished in the curé's garden. A small light shining through the trees showed that the abbé was at home.

Indoors, Marie Alivon was washing glasses and putting them on the shelves behind the bar.

"A nice night, madame."

"Yes, monsieur. It is like this for weeks at this part of year. It is a nice time to stay in Provence."

"We are dining with Monsieur le Marquis to-morrow evening, so we won't trouble you for a meal."

"My brother told me. He will be there, too, helping Claudius at table. Claudius is ageing and is not so nimble as he used to be. He needs assistance when there are guests at the château."

"Does César often help him, then?"

"Only when there is a dinner-party. They are few enough these days."

"Was he attending at table the night Mr. and Mrs. Lovell were there? The night they met their accident?"

Marie looked at him with a timid, puzzled air.

"I don't understand."

"I was with the Marquis last night and he mentioned that the Lovells had dined at the château the night they met their death. I wondered if César saw them there."

"Oh, if Monsieur le Marquis told you, I can speak. Since the sad accident, my brother has not wished to mention it.

It upset us all...You see, my brother attended at table that night. There was a little party there. Monsieur Lovell and his wife, Monsieur de Barge, the curé. With the misfortune coming so quickly afterwards, it gave him a shock. He was stunned for a long time. He knew Monsieur Lovell and his wife very well. Working at the château as César does, he gets to know all the friends of the family. I think he liked Monsieur Lovell."

"I see. It must have upset him very much, as you say."

"Do you want anything more, sir? I am just going to put out the lights and retire."

"No, thank you, madame. I'm just off myself...Good night...."

"Your bath is ready...My brother has taken up the water and you will find three cans of it at your bedroom door."

His wife was still reading when he fell asleep. After what seemed a few minutes, but which was really half an hour, she gently shook him.

"Someone's crossed the road and entered the hotel from the back. I heard him."

"Him?"

"The steps were too heavy for a woman."

"It is probably César returning from the presbytery. I saw him going across. Perhaps he's been to confession."

He felt so tired that he went off again in the middle of talking to his wife and he slept like a log until she shook him again.

"Somebody else crossing the road, Letty?"

"No...It's daylight; about five o'clock...Someone has gone off in a car from behind the hotel again. Sorry to wake you, but I thought it might be important."

"I feel guilty using you as a watchdog whilst I lie snoring here! Which direction did the car go?"

"Manosque. Who could it be?"

"Perhaps they had another guest last night, although we saw nothing of him, did we? Have the Alivons a car?"

"I saw an old Citroën in the shed in the yard."

"I wonder if it's César on another of his mysterious jaunts. We'll see when we get up."

As they took breakfast on the balcony of their room at just after nine, the tumbledown car returned, with Alivon driving and without even looking up at them, César turned into the yard behind the inn, parked the vehicle, and went indoors with his usual solemn, unhasting tread. He must have eaten a quick meal, for before the Littlejohns had finished their second cup of coffee, César was out again, this time on his way to work, still without hurry. Presumably he walked to the château. His double-barrelled shotgun was over the crook of his arm. Nothing strange about that, as he was a part-time gamekeeper as well as other things. In fact, general factotum to Monsieur le Marquis.

Littlejohn and his wife spent the morning writing letters. The Chief Inspector concentrated on giving a long but reserved report on his work hitherto to Spenser Lovell. This finished, they told Marie Alivon they would be back for lunch at one, and motored over to Mirabeau to post their mail. Littlejohn was not running the risk of his letter to the Minister falling in the hands of Léonidas.

From noon, things grew busier in the village. It was Saturday and a few motorists kept passing through on excursions into the interior and at the *Restaurant Pascal* a few strangers dropped in to dine.

The church, too, was in a state of great ferment. The curé was occupied with a number of young boys and girls about to take First Communion very shortly and their parents, dressed in their best and looking stiff and solemn in it, were making arrangements and bossing their offspring around. The women were particularly active and their husbands hung about, wondering why they had been brought there and thirstily eyeing the inn.

The Abbé Chambeyron appeared at the church entrance with his young charges and seeing Littlejohn smoking at the door of the inn and lazily watching what was going on, waved a hand at him and indicated that he would like to speak to him. Littlejohn crossed the road. The eyes of all the people round the church door turned on him and some of the men who had seen Littlejohn in the *Hôtel Pascal,*even spoke to him or saluted him. Then, they whispered to their wives and explained who he was.

The curé gently pushed the children before him.

"Excuse me, my little ones, I wish to speak to this gentleman."

The abbé took Littlejohn in church, closed the door, and faced him. He looked to have been awake all night. Dark pouched rings under his bloodshot eyes. His lips moved nervously and his breath was like great sighs.

"I wanted to see you, Inspector. I am worried about César Alivon. I fear he might do you an injury. Late last night, he called here. He is always a calm man, never angry, never showing his emotions. Last night, however, he seemed to be under some great strain and, although he did not say it in so many words, I gathered that he was angry with you... extremely angry... for prying into his family affairs."

Littlejohn gently patted the agitated priest on the arm.

"Don't worry, Monsieur l'Abbé. It is always so when the police try to lay bare private matters. What have I been doing to César?"

The sacristan, busy cleaning the sacred images with a feather duster, passed them and looked daggers at Littlejohn.

"... He asked me first of all, why I had sent you to Digne. I replied that I had never mentioned Digne to you. César said I had been seen talking to you earnestly on Thursday night, and first thing next morning you were off to Digne. I fear Colomb, there, talks far too much and gossips about you. He dislikes you, I think, because he says through you, his wife has left him. Between you and me, it is better that way and she will be happier. He beats and starves her when she is at home."

"But César Alivon, father...."

"He said you were spying on Monsieur le Marquis and that you had gone to Digne either to consult the official files or else to talk to Eulalie Bonjour about happenings at the château long ago... happenings which concerned an unfortunate member of the Alivon family. I have never seen César so angry. I thought I must warn you. He may take up the matter with you and even prove violent. I would not like..."

"You told him you had not mentioned Eulalie to me?"

"Yes. But I remembered the letter you so kindly stamped and posted for me. I told him of that, and he said that now he understood. What did he mean?"

"He knew I had obtained Eulalie's address from your letter, father. Anything else?"

"He asked then what we had said, and I simply replied that his name or that of his family had not passed our lips. I had merely told you that Eulalie and her late sister had once been in service at the château."

"Did you know that very early this morning, César went off in his car and returned just after nine? My guess is, that he went to Digne to see Eulalie."

"I did not know, Monsieur Littlejohn, but that must be what he intended to do. He said as he left me... 'We shall see, then'... That is all César said."

"I will take care, father. Thank you for warning me. And now, may I ask you a question?"

The priest looked at him with terrified eyes and then at the door, behind which the voices of the waiting parents and children were mingled in a great impatience.

"What connection had César Alivon with the deaths of Christopher Lovell and his wife?"

Father Chambeyron looked all round him, like a badly frightened animal choosing a direction in which to bolt.

"The children are waiting for me. Their parents will be annoyed at this delay. I beg you, forgive me. I must go."

Beads of sweat stood on the poor priest's forehead.

"I quite understand, sir. César Alivon is a good Catholic, is he not?"

"One of the most faithful of my little flock."

"I see. I will not ask you anything more, father, and I regret if I have embarrassed you."

The priest opened the door and let in a stream of eager people. They ignored Littlejohn this time in their haste to get on with their business. Some of the little girls were even in their First Communion gowns, like little brides, and a few of the boys wore white brassards on their arms.

There were more cars outside the *Hôtel Pascal*. Passers-by eating lunch or else having drinks. The sun was beating down on the road and the heat made Littlejohn gasp. He was just thrusting aside the bead curtain when a commotion occurred.

A very ancient Rolls-Royce appeared, driven at high speed from the direction of the château. Littlejohn was about to call for his wife to come and see the gallant veteran from home, but the alarm on the face of the driver put all such thoughts from his mind. At the wheel sat the young fellow with the calf-lick of hair, whom Alivon had enlisted the night before to help him empty the bath. Presumably, César's assistant.... The car halted at the mayor's house and the driver hurried inside. The mayor followed him out again in a hurry, and the gendarme, Mora, came on their heels. Next, the youth with the calf-lick ran to Dr. Mengali's surgery but emerged without him. He spoke hurriedly with Savini and then, as if by an afterthought, ran into the presbytery and brought out the priest.

Before the car could start with its load again, Littlejohn was across the road and speaking to the mayor.

"What is the matter, Monsieur Savini?"

The mayor hesitated.

"There has been an accident at the château. We must go at once. It is very grave. Mengali is out at a confinement, too. His servant is going to find him. It's very awkward."

Through Littlejohn's mind there flashed, all in an instant, the thoughts of César Alivon's anger, his visit to Digne, his departure that morning with his gun across his arm. He had learned the truth about something and...

"It is César Alivon, monsieur. There has been an accident. César is badly injured. In fact, monsieur, Marius here says they fear he is dead."

"Make room for me in the car, if you please, Monsieur le Maire."

"But this is a matter for the French police. Mora will be in charge until the officers from Manosque or Digne arrive...."

"I quite agree, sir, but I'll come with you, all the same.... Have you advised Manosque or Digne?"

"Not yet. We will ring up from the château...."

"Very well. I'll come with you."

Littlejohn pushed his way into the car and Marius drove away with them.

"This is all very irregular, Mister Littlejohn. I don't know what Monsieur le Marquis will say."

"I don't care a damn what the Marquis says, Mister Mayor. This time I'm going to make sure there *has* been an accident, and neither you nor the Marquis is going to stop me."

The priest, gently holding in his large hand the case containing all that was necessary for the Last Offices, sat with his eyes closed, saying his prayers in a whisper.

Chapter Fifteen
The Shooting-Box

They entered the grounds of the château by the great gates, now familiar to Littlejohn, and drove along the main drive to the front door. There, Marius, the boy with the calf-lick, halted, got out of the car, and made as if to enter the house. Littlejohn laid a hand on his arm.

"Where is the body?"

"In the shooting-box at the west wall, sir."

"Can you drive there?"

"Part of the way, sir, but I must first report to Monsieur le Marquis."

"Never mind the Marquis.... Drive on."

"But... It is as much as my job's worth."

"All the same, drive on."

The Mayor gave Littlejohn an almost frightened look and the gendarme made as if to say something, and then remained silent. The priest was still saying his prayers.

Marius diffidently climbed in the car again and they set off across a minor road which led behind the château. As they gathered speed, Littlejohn, looking back, saw the Marquis himself and de Barge appear at the front door, run down the steps together, and then, without hats or coats, hasten after them at a brisk pace.

"Who found César, Marius?"

"I did, sir."

The young man had to keep his eyes ahead to steer along the tumbledown road, and therefore did not see the eyes of the mayor, which flashed and blinked as he tried to make up his mind whether or not to order him to be silent.

"Was he dead?"

"Yes, sir."

The young man said it in a sobbing whisper and his chin fell on his chest.

"You have seen him before, this morning?"

"Yes, sir. We met at the big gates on our ways to work. César went in the house to receive his orders, as usual, from Monsieur le Marquis. I went on to fell one of the trees in the west wood. It was struck by lightning last autumn and is now dangerous."

"You didn't see César again after you left him at the house?"

"Yes, sir. He passed me on his way to the shooting-box. He said Monsieur le Marquis had told him to look the building over. It was falling down and the master wished to know if it could be repaired without much expense."

"What time would that be?"

"About ten-thirty, sir. We usually have a drink of wine in the middle of the morning, and we drank together. César said it was about time."

The car halted as the road petered out. Beyond lay about fifty yards of rough grass and then the trees started again. They got out of the car. Littlejohn spoke to Savini.

"You and Mora had perhaps better wait until the Marquis catches you up.... Marius and Monsieur l'Abbé and I will go on...."

"But–"

"Stay and wait for them and tell them where we are. ..."

Littlejohn said it in a tone which would take no refusal. The gendarme looked at the mayor and they both shrugged.

"Very well. But I think, Mister Littlejohn—"

The Chief Inspector had gone ahead, however, hustling his two companions with him.

"Now Marius... How long after your drink together did you find César?"

"An hour later. We arranged to meet for lunch at the shooting-box. I went there a little after noon. Then it was I found César."

"Dead?"

"Yes, sir. He was sitting on one of the wooden chairs in the pavilion, with his gun between his legs. I fear, monsieur, he had shot himself."

Marius and the priest crossed themselves simultaneously.

"You ran for help?"

"Yes. To the château. Monsieur le Marquis told me to get out the car and go at once for the doctor, the police, the mayor, and the priest. I went right away."

"Leaving the body. ..."

"Of course, sir."

"Was the Marquis at the hall when you called?"

"Yes, sir. He and Monsieur de Barge were in the library writing."

"What do you think of this, Monsieur le Curé?"

"Eh?"

The priest seemed lost in meditation and had been briskly keeping up with the long strides of his companions, his soutane flapping round his big feet.

"I do not know what to think.... I am distressed that César died alone and by his own hand.... He seemed very depressed, even distraught, when I saw him going to work this morning. I wonder…"

"You wonder what, Monsieur le Curé?"

"Nothing, nothing."

Again the fearful look which Littlejohn was getting to know so well.

The three of them had by now reached the forest. Pines, small oaks, brambles and hazels, all mixed up together and forming a thick barrier all around them. Now and then, the thickets vanished, giving place to a small space where ash, beeches and limes appeared. Then the neglected jungle of St. Marcelin took over again.

Finally, a clearing where the trees thinned out. An odd oak or two, some laurels, and then a terrace covered in long, neglected grass. This formed a sort of rough lawn in front of the shooting-box itself, a single, round, brick edifice, with a smaller room on the second storey, giving it the appearance of a two-tier cake. It was sturdily built, and facing the little group as they approached it, was a small open door with two windows on each side, curving with the general structure of the place. The bricks were broken and neglected, the tiles of the roof smashed and missing in places, the timber of the windows and door rotting. The back of the pavilion gave straight on to the wall which surrounded the estate.

Rising from the grass about ten or a dozen yards from where it took over from the forest, was a granite column about the height of a man. It stood solitary and neglected, but, as they passed it, Littlejohn paused to examine it and was just able to make out some words chiselled on the stone, almost worn away.

Bernard de St. Marcellin
13 mars, 1939
R.I.P.

This was the spot where Bernard de St. Marcellin had fallen years ago!

The two men accompanying Littlejohn crossed themselves again as they entered the old building. The place was a wreck. The ceiling had fallen in, revealing the timbers beneath the plaster. Dust everywhere. Opposite the front door, the small exit through which Captain Barge had told Littlejohn the murderer of Bernard had made his escape. The single room was perfectly round and, in its heyday, must have been pretty. Even now, the delicate decorations were visible on the dirt-covered plaster of the walls. The loft above was reached by a ladder.

The place must have been used as a store-room, for there were hurdles and old barbed wire, rakes, spades, and other odds and ends stacked round the walls. The middle of the room held a plain, round wooden table and a couple of large chairs, roughly thrown together by some native carpenter. Sitting on one of these was César Alivon, or what was left of him. His gun was between his knees and a discharge from the barrel had blown away half of his face and head. The shot had obviously been fired at point-blank range and had scorched much of the remaining flesh and beard of the face.

The priest caught his breath and began to say his prayers again in a sobbing voice, this time on his knees. Marius, too overcome to remain with the body, staggered out of doors, buried his face in his hands, and burst into noisy wailing. Across the lawn hurried the quartet which included the Marquis and de Barge.

Littlejohn quickly examined the positions of the body and the gun. The latter had apparently been fired by Alivon by the simple process of untying one shoelace of his large hobnailed boot, passing the loose ends over the trigger, tying them, and discharging the gun by a jerk of the boot, with the stock firmly on the ground and the barrel resting against his temple. The Chief Inspector examined the way in which the lace had been re-tied. A large, inexpertly made knot of the variety which he vaguely remembered from his Scouting days as a 'granny'. It hung loosely together, however, and as Littlejohn depressed the boot through which the rest of the lace passed, the knot merely drew tighter without putting much pressure on the trigger....

"You seem to have taken charge, my dear Inspector!"

The Marquis stood in the doorway, looking far from good-tempered. Mouth twisted, nostrils dilated, he cast a quick glance round the room, stood before the body of Alivon, and clicked his tongue against his teeth in a melancholy way. That was all.

"I told him, Monsieur le Marquis..."

"Be quiet, Savini. Not before the dead. Leave this to me."

Littlejohn turned quickly on the Marquis.

"As nobody seemed interested enough to investigate and watch by the dead, I came here at once without your permission. I advise you to telephone the police right away."

"All in good time, Inspector. Our good Mora will attend to that. Meanwhile, we will lock the pavilion and depart. If Monsieur l'Abbé wishes to stay, I shall lock him in. Meanwhile, Inspector, I ought to tell you to get off the premises. You are trespassing on my property. However, I don't wish to seem lacking in hospitality to such a distinguished friend....You will, I therefore trust, accompany us to the château...?"

Littlejohn could have said many things, but now it paid best to take it all with good grace. He shrugged his shoulders and made for the door.

"Far be it from me to intrude, Monsieur le Marquis."

"I would advise you, Monsieur l'Abbé, to come back with us. We can do nothing here and the police may be annoyed if anything has been disturbed. They may even resent your being left alone with the body. Come along."

"Very well, Monsieur le Marquis."

The callousness of leaving an old and faithful servant alone, shattered in death, needed a lot of stomaching, but Littlejohn followed the rest into the open air, and St. Marcellin locked the door behind them. They continued in silence for a time and then St. Marcellin let the rest walk a couple of paces ahead and drew Littlejohn back by the arm.

"I'm sorry for my outburst, Inspector. We are all upset. I saw César earlier in the day when he came for his daily orders. He was not himself. He even spoke of having made a big mistake. Of having committed a great sin.... I don't know what he meant, but it must have turned his brain. This is obviously a case of suicide, don't you think?"

"I haven't been allowed to form an opinion, sir. I haven't examined the scene of the tragedy. That is, as you say, sir, a matter for your own police."

"That's a sensible fellow! You will only be snubbed by the official police if you try to interfere. Just leave it to them. They are very efficient, as you know."

They reached the car which would not hold them all.

"You will call at the house for some refreshment, Littlejohn?"

"No, thanks, Monsieur le Marquis. My wife will wonder where I am."

"Ah, yes. The charming Mrs. Littlejohn. We will all meet later then. I hope this tragedy will not prevent your joining us for a farewell meal another evening. You will be leaving us when ...?"

"I don't know, sir. Very soon."

"Till we meet again, then."

Marius drove Littlejohn and the priest back to the village, leaving the mayor and the policeman behind.

"The Marquis tells me César talked of having committed a great sin, Monsieur l'Abbé.... What could it be?"

The priest wrung his great hands and his teeth chattered.

"I beg you, sir.... "

"Very well, I won't press the point. You are going to break the sad news to Madame Alivon?"

"Yes. It is my duty."

The village was in a state of great confusion. The population, swollen by the influx from the country of families interested in First Communions, had somehow learned the bad news, and knots of people were standing in the streets talking over the tragedy. The car was surrounded when it arrived and the priest was questioned by villagers who wept, moaned and made strange noises of grief. Monsieur Chambeyron gently brushed them all aside and went in to see Marie Alivon.

"She will not weep," someone told them. Inside the inn, a group of men silently sitting in the bar without drinks of any kind, were expressing sympathy by their mute presences. Now and then, one would whisper to another. Leclerc, the garage owner, was among them. He sidled up to Littlejohn as the Chief Inspector entered to find his wife.

"You are sure it was an accident, sir?"

The crafty, long face now bore no sign of humour. Leclerc was worried.

"I don't know. Why?"

"César was my friend. We were leaders of the Resistance here during the war. It was a shotgun and not...?"

"Not what?"

Leclerc looked at the glowing end of his cigarette. "In the war, many weapons were dropped here by 'plane and by allied troops passing through. Automatic weapons, grenades, booby-traps. ... It was done by a shotgun?"

"You had better ask Mora. It isn't my case, you know."

Mrs. Littlejohn was with Marie Alivon, who seemed to have fled to her for comfort. The priest had now joined them and seemed baffled because Marie preferred talking to the English woman instead of saying prayers. She kept repeating what a good man her brother had been and telling incidents in his past life. Littlejohn expressed his sympathy.

"He was a good man, monsieur. Whatever anyone says, he would not take his own life. Whatever anyone tells me, I will never believe it."

The curé stood first on one foot and then on the other. He was puzzled by the way Marie Alivon was taking it. As a rule, in such circumstances, women wept or went into hysterics and convulsions. This woman persisted in recounting tender memories of her brother, as though he had merely gone on a journey and would be back one day. Mrs. Littlejohn finally recommended the priest to go and attend to his neglected flock, who now seemed totally without a shepherd, and were wondering whether or not to go back to their homes in the distant hills and valleys of the parish.

"She will realize what has happened soon, and I'll send for you."

The abbé backed out of the room to rejoin his parishioners, who received him with joy and a lot of chattering.

"Did your brother make his own cartridges, Madame Alivon?"

Marie Alivon looked at him with her still serene grey eyes, and replied as though it had no bearing on the present tragedy.

"Yes, sir. Would you like to see?"

They were sitting in the Alivons' quarters behind the dining-room and Marie rose, opened an old walnut cupboard, and thence brought out a large, rough, wooden box. Littlejohn raised the lid. Gun-cleaning tackle, rags, oil in one section and, in the other, a large tin of smokeless powder, wads, caps for sealing the cartridges, percussion caps, tools for the job.

"He liked best to fill his own. It was much cheaper and he said he knew then that they were good and well-made...."

Littlejohn had opened another tin, this time of shot. He poured some out in his hand. Number 5's. The same load he used himself at home when he went to shoot with his uncle in the marshes of the north. Mixed among the small shot, a proportion of large ones, in about a ratio of one in ten.

"Duck shot?"

Marie smiled.

"My brother liked to put about three duck shots in each cartridge. There are a lot of fowl on the estate and whilst the small shot is good for the rabbits and pests like weasels, the ducks, he used to say, needed a harder knock. To save loading two kinds, he added one or two duck shots to make one cartridge do both jobs. He was a good man....A good shot."

Littlejohn put the box and its contents away.

"Will you excuse me, if I go for a run on my own in the car? You two will comfort one another better without me."

He felt he must go to Digne again and make certain what Alivon had been at earlier in the day. He found the run in the Durance valley hot and tedious, but it must be done. He left St. Marcellin quietly, gathered speed when he reached the main road, and reached Digne at six. As he drove from the village, the dismal tolling of the cracked bell followed him a long way to remind him of Alivon, whose body they had left alone in the pavilion by the château wall.

In the Boulevard Gassendi, Digne, Madame Bonjour was, luckily, sitting at her door, with the twins playing on the sidewalk in front of her. She was taking the air before the glow of sunlight vanished behind the overhanging hills, and watching the passers-by. Littlejohn approached her casually.

"Good evening, Madame Bonjour."

She looked surprised, but was still smiling.

"Good evening, sir. Are you in Digne again?"

"Yes. I had an errand.... I'm just on my way back now."

"I shall be in St. Marcellin on Tuesday, as I told you before. I must pay my respects to the dead.... I had a visit from César Alivon early this morning. It was very nice of him to come all this way to express his condolences about Madeleine and invite me to stay as their guest after the funeral."

Littlejohn didn't mention César's death. He had seen enough distress for one day and, besides, he would have to make a lot of embarrassing explanations.

"Funnily... he spoke of the very matter you and I were talking about yesterday, sir. He said it was so long since Céleste died, that the wound had healed and he would like to know before he died who really was the father of Blanche. He was jocular about it, monsieur. He said he wondered if her departed and unknown father was an aristocrat, or a soldier, or a mere peasant.... We laughed together, and I said I could make a good guess. We were amused when I mentioned Claudius."

So, Alivon had been to Digne exactly for that, and had got to know what he wanted from this merry, irresponsible old lady. César had put on an act to secure the details which, although he laughed for his own purposes, must have been a shattering blow.

But why had Alivon killed himself and not Claudius when he got back home? He had spoken of some sin or other to the Marquis. Was it the sin of having killed the wrong man in days gone by? Had Alivon been the one who shot Bernard de St. Marcellin whilst he was fighting a duel? If so, who had told him that Bernard was the cause of Céleste's ruin and death?

"A pleasant evening, monsieur? But growing cold, so I must get indoors. Digne is sad, isn't it, in the last rays of the sun? The Gascon nights were so much happier and full of laughter and merry talk."

He bade the old lady *au revoir,* and to the children he gave fifty francs apiece, which upset them because they couldn't wait for morning when the shops would open and the money could be spent.

Littlejohn got back to St. Marcellin at about nine o'clock. The inn was closed. On the door a black-edged card: *Closed temporarily owing to bereavement.* The habitual topers were suffering, for there was no other place of refreshment in the village and their wives would not allow them to broach the family wines for mere drinking's sake.

Marie Alivon had retired to bed. She had insisted on leaving an excellent cold meal for the Littlejohns, and Mrs. Littlejohn met her husband at the door.

"Marie broke down at last and was quite beside herself with grief. The priest has been with her, and Blanche has been a great comfort. I think she's asleep now.... Oh, by the way, I forgot. There's a man waiting for you in the Alivons' room. He's been there about an hour. He must have the patience of Job. He said he'd sit by the fire and wait till you got back. He wouldn't say what he wanted."

Littlejohn hurried to the back room and opened the door. A man was sitting in a chair in front of the fire, his short legs crossed. A plump man with delicate white hands and a broad, high brow from which a streak of baldness stretched to the crown of his fine head. Pink, chubby cheeks, a firm chin, and a small dark moustache. He was serenely reading a book and he raised a pair of clear grey eyes to Littlejohn's face as he entered, and smiled at him. Whoever he was, Littlejohn liked him from the start.

"Chief Inspector Littlejohn?"

"Yes, sir. You wish to see me?"

To the Chief Inspector, he looked like the Alivons' lawyer. He wore a dark suit of a rather old-fashioned cut, spotless linen, and there was an air of elegance about his appearance and general manner which marked him down as a professional man.

"I called to make your acquaintance, Littlejohn, and I'm very pleased to meet you. My name is Audibert... Inspector of the Sûreté at Marseilles. I arrived here at seven o'clock. Too late to begin work, but I heard a sketchy account of what happened to-day from Pietri, the Inspector from Manosque. It seems he was not sent for until late, too, and didn't get in St. Marcellin until dusk. It is very important that I should see you."

He laid down his book, took off his spectacles, rose, and held out his hand, which Littlejohn shook warmly.

"Thank you, Inspector Audibert. I'm glad to meet you, too."

"A little while ago, my good friend Dorange, of the Nice Sûreté, telephoned me about you. I shall regard it as a great honour if you will work with me on this case. It is no ordinary investigation."

"I agree. Instead of a series of accidents, it might easily turn out to be a series of murders."

"I know little about the affair at present, but there have been too many fatalities in St. Marcellin recently and Manosque asked for our help. They fear the local police might be intimidated by the gentry at the château. And, I might also add, your presence here has made them uneasy, as well. They must fear international complications."

Audibert chuckled.

"I am a man of Provence myself and I know the way of things in these parts. They all hang together in a pall of secrecy and fear. You will take a glass of wine with me after you have eaten, and you must tell me what you have discovered. Then we can co-operate. It will be a great pleasure, I assure you."

The pair of them sat talking together until long past midnight and when Littlejohn retired, he felt much happier. He wasn't on his own any longer!

Chapter Sixteen
Audibert Intervenes

Littlejohn and Audibert set out for the château good and early next morning. Even at seven o'clock the village had settled down to Sunday routine. A group of women leaving church after Mass got mixed up with a flock of goats which an old man was driving down the road, and the gander which seemed to spend its time leading four geese up and down the village street, hissed bellicosely and went for Littlejohn as he passed....

The heat of the day had started as they drove to the château. Thin mists hung over the fields here and there, but on the warm land which grew the finest olives, the air was clear and everything stood out stark in the landscape.

Audibert was as spick and span as ever. His linen spotless, his shoes shining like jet, clean shaved and smelling slightly of *eau de Cologne.* He saw Littlejohn looking at his shoes.

"I always clean my own shoes. Servants don't know how to look after leather. I would rather wear them soiled than entrust them to anyone else. Not even my wife."

He had already told Littlejohn about his wife and seven children and the villa on the outskirts of Marseilles.

They drove through the familiar great gateway and rang the bell of the front door of the château. Claudius answered and let them in. He seemed older and more furtive than ever. Littlejohn gave him a good look-over in view of the added interest which had arisen in connection with the paternity of Blanche. He was more cut-out for a farmhand than a personal servant and had only become butler presumably because the Marquis couldn't afford to pay a properly trained man.

Claudius led them to the library, which had now been turned into a temporary police headquarters. There, Inspector Pietri, of the Manosque police, was holding court. Two gendarmes lounged just behind the door, Pietri was sitting at the Marquis' desk in a large bergère chair from which the stuffing was leaking, and before him, a tall, elderly, gangling peasant was taking a full bastinado of abuse.

"But I tell you, Inspector, it wasn't me. I don't know a thing about it."

Pietri looked up as Audibert and Littlejohn entered. There were introductions and the peasant stood neglected, chewing at nothing with his toothless gums, muttering to himself in indignation at being accused of something he said he hadn't done.

Pietri pointed to him.

"It was dusk when we arrived on the scene last night and we couldn't examine the grounds around the shooting-box. So I posted two men there overnight to see that nothing was interfered with. Then, this oaf, this fool, lets his sheep and cattle in the park, and when at dawn the men on guard look round the place, they find themselves among a flock of silly sheep and stampeding cows, and all the scene of the crime trampled to pieces...."

"But I didn't do it. I admit I've five cows, twelve goats, and about fifty sheep.... I admit they were in the field next to the park. I rent it from Monsieur le Marquis. The sheep were down for marking and dipping before I took them into the hills."

"Well? Get on with your excuses."

"But I didn't break down the fence. Some tramp must have done it. It was in order yesterday morning as I penned the sheep. I always keep an eye on it, because I know if my animals ever stray in the park, I shall get my notice to quit. It's in the lease that I keep them out."

"But they got in through the gate.... You must have left it open."

"I swear I didn't. I always keep an eye on it."

"... because if you didn't you'd get notice to quit.... Go on, don't say it again. I know it all by heart. The gate was open and I can't see who else could have done it but you."

Pietri was a tall, well-set-up officer, with a hatchet face and a long inquisitive nose. He was a good mimic, too, and ironically imitated every expression and gesture of the peasant he was grilling and driving into a state of complete bewilderment.

Littlejohn looked at Audibert and he saw they were thinking the same thing.

"If I were you, Inspector Pietri, I wouldn't worry too much. The cattle and sheep trampling down all traces of the criminal are quite in keeping with events at St. Marcellin. It fits in the case, and I'm sure Inspector Audibert agrees."

"Absolutely."

The shepherd looked from one to the other.

"Can I go then ...? I've my cows to milk and the goats."

"And the sheep, and the hens," said Pietri in the same voice as the peasant and with the same flapping gestures. "Yes, be off with you, but don't go and hide in the hills. Stay on your farm in case we want you."

"But the sheep?"

"But the sheep.... Go and do as you're told."

"Yes, Inspector.... Can I tell my wife it's on your orders? You see, she might think I'm dodging work."

"Get out."

Pietri seemed to have done a day's work already. He had before him several dossiers in which he rummaged and over which he bent his long, foraging nose.

"The report on the body of Alivon is here, Inspector Audibert. It looks like a clear case of suicide."

"But it might be murder, eh?"

"We can never be certain, can we, in matters like this?"

"Where is the Marquis?"

"In bed. So is Monsieur de Barge. They don't, as a rule, get up till around nine and I thought they'd be better there till we want them again."

"As I told you, Inspector Littlejohn will be co-operating with us. He is interested in the deaths of the Englishman and his wife in a motor smash here last February."

"I was concerned in it. The Manosque police handled it. It seemed to be a pure accident."

"Like the one which happened to Alivon with his gun."

Pietri jumped and looked hard at Littlejohn as he spoke.

"You mean ...?"

"Three deaths; all accidents. And all to people who were becoming a nuisance to Monsieur le Marquis."

Audibert sat on another chair and lit a small cigarette, as neat and elegant as himself.

"Who else is here on the job?"

"Judge Bouchard from Digne is coming later as examining magistrate. He thinks it will merely be a matter of form, but from what you say, it looks like being a bit more complicated. I'd like to see his face when we suggest it might be murder."

"Who did the autopsy? I know Mengali made the first examination, but in view of what I said last night, which is confirmed by Inspector Littlejohn, you sent to Marseilles ...? Who is coming?"

"Dr Parpalède, the medico-legal expert."

"That's good. He is our best man, Littlejohn."

"When he comes, let us know. We'll be somewhere around. And now we'll leave you to your files."

Audibert strolled into the hall with Littlejohn, and turned up his nose at the sight of so much ruin and decay. He fingered the dusty tapestries and then wiped his fingers on his spotless white handkerchief.

"A pity. You want to see anyone, Littlejohn?"

"A word with Claudius wouldn't be out of place."

"How to get him, short of shouting the place down? The bell-pulls have all fallen down."

He went to the front door, opened it, and rang the bell there. From somewhere in the distance they could hear the shuffling steps of Claudius, who eventually appeared from a door at the end of the corridor.

"Monsieur rang?"

"Yes. Inspector Littlejohn wishes to talk with you. You will answer his questions truthfully. Understood?"

"Yes, sir. Perhaps it will be better in the dining-room, sir...."

Claudius opened a door and bowed them in with a graceless movement.

Another large room, hung with dusty tapestries and old family portraits which damp had disfigured. In the centre, a long, heavy, oak table, large enough to seat about a score, with heavy, carved, oak chairs to match, set around it. Here, too, there was evidence of selling-off of valuable pieces. Patches on the walls where pictures had been removed, plaster broken on the fine ceiling where the chandelier had been roughly torn out, no carpet on the floor, which was of uneven parquet.

"You wished to ask me, sir … ?"

"Yes. Let's come straight to the point. Claudius … You are the father of Blanche Alivon?"

Claudius reeled back a pace. His ruddy cheeks grew purple with either blood pressure or shame, and he put out a large hand as though to fend off some evil.

"The truth, please."

"Who has told you that, sir?"

His shifty eyes turned to the door, which was ajar, and he hurriedly closed it after looking down the corridor outside. Littlejohn remembered that Madame Claudius was a jealous woman and her husband feared her.

"I know the truth, Claudius. … You seduced Céleste Alivon and someone gave César to understand that it was Monsieur Bernard instead. … Is that true?"

"It is so long ago, sir."

Audibert tapped Claudius on the chest with his firm, white hand.

"Is it true? Speak. Or … "

"It is true, messieurs. … It happened long ago. I was always bitterly sorry about it, but how was I to know that Céleste … ?"

"Never mind that, Claudius. Sit down."

Littlejohn pulled out one of the heavy chairs for the butler and himself sat on the edge of the table above him.

"Do you know who told Alivon that Monsieur Bernard was responsible for Céleste's misfortunes?"

Claudius licked his dry blue lips and looked at the door, as though ready to bolt.

"I don't think anybody told him directly. He overheard something."

"Tell me all about it."

"It was so long ago."

"You're not trying to tell me that an event so vital to your own safety has slipped from your mind.... You knew that if he'd discovered your share in his sister's downfall, César Alivon would have killed you."

"He was a hard man, sir. There was no pity in him, although he regularly went to church."

Audibert removed another small cigarette from his mouth and then tapped Claudius gently on the top of the head.

"Tell the Inspector. Tell him.... Or..."

There must have been some deep hidden significance in the 'Or' of Audibert, for Claudius hastened to do as he was told.

"It happened on the first day of the betrothal ceremonies of Monsieur Bernard and Mademoiselle de Barge. If I may say so, the family money was not so plentiful even then, and the servants had been dismissed. César had to serve at table with me when there were a lot of guests. On the first night of the betrothal party twenty-two guests sat down at this table, sir. César and Ginette, one of the maids, assisted me. It was after the dinner that César came into the kitchen and told me that he had found out who was responsible for Céleste's... Céleste's..."

Audibert smiled.

"You must have been scared, my good Claudius. Did you think César was entering to kill *you*?"

"I must admit my knees knocked until he told me it was Monsieur Bernard. César never rested about Céleste. He always swore that when he found out... I was tempted many times to pack my bags and go far enough way, but nobody wanted butlers in those days and how could I explain it to my wife? It would have meant going back to farming, too. I was a farm worker before Monsieur le Marquis said I would look well as a house servant."

"Well?"

"I asked César who had told him. He said that whilst serving brandy to some guests in the library, he had passed the small gun-room where Monsieur Arnaud was showing a gun to Monsieur Charles de Barge, and he had heard Monsieur Arnaud say quite distinctly, 'I am worried about something. Bernard is the father of Blanche Alivon and with Céleste dead and Bernard going to be married, I feel we ought to do something for the child. I must speak to him…' Words to that effect, sir. It's so long ago, I don't exactly remember, but something like that. César was like a madman. He took off his uniform and gloves and for the rest of the night I had all the work to do myself.… Next day, the duel was fought and Monsieur Bernard died. So that put an end to any thoughts of revenge César might have harboured.… Is there anything more, sir? Monsieur le Marquis will be wanting me.… "

"One thing more, Claudius.… The duel.… Do you know anything about it? Presumably you were here, there and everywhere about the house. Do you happen to know how it came about?"

"Not exactly, sir. But I was in the library seeing to things… the fires, the brandy, and so on… when the actual challenge took place. Personally, neither of the two gentlemen, Monsieur Bernard or the Englishman, seemed even to have thought of a duel until Monsieur Arnaud and Monsieur Charles de Barge began to quarrel themselves."

"What do you mean?"

"Monsieur Arnaud made an insulting remark about Mademoiselle Elise. He was, I know, very bitter about the engagement, for he loved her himself. Her cousin, Monsieur Charles, took exception to it, and soon they came to blows. In the skirmish, tempers grew frayed and Monsieur Bernard and the Englishman became involved. Challenges started to fly about the room. They had all been drinking and it was in the course of high words that Monsieur Lovell was accused of being in love with Mademoiselle Elise himself. He admitted it and said she also loved him. I really do think that had not Monsieur Arnaud and Monsieur Charles persisted in challenging one another, the matter would have been amicably settled between the other two. They were both great gentlemen and peaceable. Two duels were arranged. The one between Monsieur Arnaud and Monsieur Charles was not fought, because of Monsieur Bernard's death, which caused such a commotion that personal quarrels were forgotten."

Littlejohn nodded. It was all coming out now.

"How did you know Monsieur Arnaud loved Mademoiselle Elise, Claudius?"

Claudius coughed, looked sheepishly at them both, and spoke huskily.

"As a servant, one gets to know things, monsieur. I was his valet, you see, among my other numerous jobs. And I have ... ahem ... seen letters he has written to her pleading his cause."

They did not press the matter. Claudius was evidently a snooper.

"Did Alivon help you at table on the night the Englishman and his wife dined here? The night of the motor accident?"

"Yes, sir."

"The curé was also here?"

"Yes, sir."

"And was César with you until the Englishman and his wife departed?"

"No, sir. He served at table with me until the end of dinner and then went home right away. He said he did not feel well. There was a lot of tidying up to do, but he asked to be excused. What could one do?"

"Right, Claudius. That will be all for the present, unless Inspector Audibert wishes to ask anything."

Audibert turned from studying a large mildewed portrait of a man in military dress which hung over the marble mantelpiece.

"I have nothing more to ask, but something to say. You will not tell Monsieur le Marquis that we have questioned you.... You understand?"

"Certainly, sir. I will not say a word."

Littlejohn halted him on his way to the door.

"There *is* something else, Claudius.... Alivon called here on his way to work to receive instructions from the Marquis. Did he see the Marquis?"

"Yes, sir. They were together in the library for quite a long time. I met César on his way out. He must have been rebuked for something. He was in a very excited state. He was almost running, which was unusual for him."

"Was de Barge about at the same time?"

"He, too, was in the library, but near the window, writing, I think. I went in before César arrived, to ask for my own instructions. They were both in the library, writing."

"Did you see either of them go out after César left?"

"No, sir. I was busy talking to my wife about lunch. There should also have been a dinner to-night, but that will not be held, I suppose, on account of César."

"I don't know, Claudius. What other servants are there here nowadays?"

"In addition to me and my wife, Marius, who does odd jobs about the place, and Yvette, a maid-of-all-work."

"Was she likely to see anyone going out after César?"

"She was with my wife and me talking about the day's duties."

"It would be easy to get to the shooting-box where César was found, unobserved?'

"Oh, yes, sir. You see, the wood almost comes up to the house on the north gable. There is a door there and anyone wishing to get in the woods unobserved could easily do so. I hope, sir, that nobody…"

"That's all right, Claudius. You may go now. And remember what you promised Inspector Audibert."

"I am not to say you have been talking with me.…"

He stumbled from the room, dimly trying to think of all he had said, and wondering if it would in any way incriminate him, particularly if Madame Claudius got to know.

They rejoined Pietri, who had now set his files in order and was ready to do another tour of the grounds.

"Not that it will do any good. The livestock which somebody let in overnight, have trampled all over the place. Impossible to find footprints or anything else.…"

"You have questioned all the staff?"

"Yes, Monsieur Littlejohn."

"Marius.… He saw nobody about after he and Alivon had their drink and parted?"

"No. He can't help us at all."

"The body has been removed?"

"Yes. Dr. Parpalède and Mengali are at work on it. I don't expect much from their report."

"You examined the body before it was moved?"

"Yes. It was possible for it to be suicide, judging from the position. We emptied the pockets, but there was little in them to help. He also had his lunch with him.… It's in the knapsack there.…"

On the table was the pathetic little bundle which Alivon had taken, as usual, to work with him. Half a bottle of red wine, a roll of bread, a large sausage, and a piece of cheese. All the food was wrapped in paper. Littlejohn opened and examined it. The slice of cheese was intact, but a considerable part of the bread roll had been eaten. The same with the sausage, half only of which remained.

Littlejohn turned to Audibert.

"Funny.... He must have eaten part of his lunch before it happened. Did you ask Marius, Pietri, if they had some food together...?"

Pietri smiled. He'd thought of that.

"Yes. They only drank. Alivon died between twelve and one, according to the doctors. He and Marius usually ate their food about noon. Marius was a bit late. He said the job took longer than he expected and he wanted to finish it."

"So Alivon started his lunch. A queer thing for a man to do when he was planning to blow his own head off. One would think hunger didn't matter."

"I thought the same, sir. This is not an easy case...."

A small car had drawn up at the front door and out stepped Mengali and a tall, heavy man with a dark, close-clipped moustache and ruddy cheeks. Dr. Parpalède.... He looked more like a prosperous farmer or an innkeeper than one of the most eminent medico-legal experts in France. Beside him, Mengali looked like a fussy little puppy running with his master.

Footsteps in the passage, and they expected the two doctors to appear. Instead, it was the Marquis. He took in the scene with a bitter look.

"All the vultures are here, I see. And you've taken full possession of the library.... Well, well... I can't do with you here. I've work to do. You must take your police records elsewhere. There are plenty of rooms, but I can't promise you the elegance of this one or even a fire."

Audibert turned from looking through the window.

"I would have thought you wished to co-operate with the police, Monsieur le Marquis. After all, the death of one of your old retainers is concerned."

"I don't want to know what you think, whoever you are...."

"Inspector Audibert, of the Marseilles Sûreté, at your service."

"So they've called in the sleuths, have they? On a case of suicide."

"It is not suicide. It was murder, Monsieur le Marquis. And now, if you please, we will stop bandying words and get on with the investigation. I believe Monsieur de Barge is still here?"

"Yes."

"He is not to leave until I say he can."

"He will leave when he wishes."

"In that case, Monsieur le Marquis, I shall have to arrest him. Pietri, see to it, please."

"Wait. What is all this nonsense?"

"Murder. I gather you will be responsible for Monsieur de Barge's remaining as your guest for a little longer?"

"Very well.... But I shall complain to the authorities about your impertinence, Adelbert."

"The name is Audibert, and I am not afraid of any complaint you may care to make, sir.... I think Inspector Littlejohn wishes to ask you something, judging from the look in his eye."

The Marquis tried to appear surprised.

"Littlejohn.... Well, well. Is he also with the vultures?"

"The French police have asked for his co-operation. And now, may I ask you . .?"

"What is it, Littlejohn?"

"If you don't mind, Monsieur le Marquis, I'd like you to show me again the skull you produced the other day from the cupboard there."

For the first time St. Marcellin lost a little of his aplomb. Then he was himself again.

"How dare you! It was not a showpiece, but brought to convince you of the truth of my account of the death of my brother years ago. I thought I had given you sufficient proof."

"Not of identity, sir. The medical experts are on the premises and I want them to check the evidence. ... "

"I refuse to have the remains of my brother disturbed again. ... That is final."

Littlejohn turned and made for the cupboard in which St. Marcellin had placed the skull after showing it to him. The box was still there when he opened the door.

"I forbid you. ... I ... "

"The key, monsieur. ... Otherwise, I shall break the box."

"Break it then, at your own peril. ... You shall pay for this desecration."

There was an old paper-knife on the desk and it took no time for the Chief Inspector to prise open the lock. The skull was still there in the silken interior.

St. Marcellin quickly moved to take the box and, with an angry gesture, thrust Littlejohn aside. The scuffle didn't last long. Littlejohn held him firmly until the gendarmes by the door could intervene and leave him to get on with his task.

"Is Dr. Parpalède out there?"

"Yes, sir. He and Dr. Mengali are discussing something in the dining-room."

"Ask him kindly to step in here."

"You'll pay for this.... I'll kill you, Littlejohn."

"Not another murder, *please,* Monsieur le Marquis!"

Dr. Parpalède entered with Mengali on his heels. The local man looked petrified at the sight of the Marquis in the easy grip of a couple of policemen.

"They've not arrested you, Monsieur le Marquis...?"

"Don't be a fool, Mengali."

Introductions and compliments again. Parpalède had heard of Littlejohn. He'd been to Scotland Yard several times and sent his very kind regards to a number of colleagues, whom he mentioned by name to Littlejohn and asked him to jot down in his notebook. He also said he would soon be in England again, and invited Littlejohn to meet him there one day. There might have been no business in hand at all. Audibert was delighted. It suited his sense of humour. The Marquis was almost going mad. "What is this nonsense? A cocktail party, eh?"

Littlejohn showed Parpalède the skull. The famous expert handled it like an antique dealer examining a rare find.

"It is about a hundred and fifty years old. Where did you get it?"

Littlejohn explained.

"I see. The natural owner of this fine specimen certainly met a violent death. But then, it was nothing fresh in these parts. It was the hobby of the local gentry... Death by violence. Those who did not die in the wars came back to fight duels, or else to assassinate one another out of greed or passion.... I have no doubt Monsieur le Marquis has disturbed one of his ancestors to produce this. It is certainly not the skull of his brother, who died less than twenty years ago. The position of the wound in the skull and the soft lead in the cavity indicate, shall we say, an act of precision. He was probably murdered."

The Marquis did not even attempt to deny it. He tore himself from the restraining arms of the gendarmes and stamped to the door without another word. Professor Parpalède called him back.

"May I keep this, Monsieur le Marquis? I could make good use of it. Skulls are expensive and there are many very poor students in my classes at Marseilles."

The Marquis de St. Marcellin slammed the door behind him without a reply.

Chapter Seventeen
Silence is Broken

Audibert and Littlejohn walked back to the village from the château.

"It will blow away the cobwebs, Littlejohn, and we can talk."

The cobwebs and the blowing were mere figures of speech. The sun shone mercilessly down on them, the flies pestered them relentlessly, and they ended carrying their coats and smoking heavily to keep the insects away. Now and then, they paused under the shade of one of the large trees on the roadside to rest and cool off. It was only when, at last, they sat in the shade of the *Hôtel Pascal* with a glass of cold beer each, that they were properly able to compare notes and assess the work yet to be done in the case.

Audibert admitted that Littlejohn had done most of the investigation before he arrived or the French police were called in.

The whole affair had apparently started when someone had allowed Alivon to overhear it said that Bernard de St. Marcellin was the father of Blanche and the cause of her mother's suicide. This information had been quite false, as Madame Bonjour had borne out by her statement. Claudius had confirmed that Arnaud had been responsible for misinforming Alivon, and Arnaud was the heir to the estates if Bernard died. The first shot in his locker had been to foment the duel. If Bernard died, he got the estates; if Lovell died, Mademoiselle de Barge could scarcely marry Bernard, which would increase Arnaud's chances.

"Alivon, believing that Bernard was the cause of Céleste's downfall, sought the first chance of killing him. He learned of the duel; the rest we know."

"And then, *mon ami*?"

"The surviving parties to the duel must have known that Lovell didn't even hit his adversary. They knew someone else had shot Bernard with a rifle. But their hands were tied. They couldn't very well call in the police on a murder investigation. Otherwise, they would have all been arrested and disgraced for taking part in a duel, which, whoever killed Bernard, had proved fatal. They decided to hush it up by behaving in the prearranged way they'd decided in the event of one of the parties to the duel being killed.... Lovell, you recollect, knew nothing of this. He fled at once, without learning that he wasn't guilty, but some unknown marksman..."

"And the whole matter passed off as they wished, Littlejohn. Mengali, completely under the power of the château people, co-operated, I suppose. How he persuaded the police surgeon from Digne to support him, I cannot guess.... We will soon know."

Audibert made a brief note in small, neat handwriting in a little notebook he carried in his vest pocket.

"Proceed, my dear Chief Inspector."

"The war intervened. Then, when Arnaud thought everything had been forgotten, Colonel Latour died. The Colonel must always have had on his conscience the fact that Lovell had been tricked into thinking he had killed

Bernard. Even if it was in fair fight, as Lovell thought, it was bad enough. Latour sent for Lovell and told him the whole story on his deathbed. Lovell and his wife came straight to St. Marcellin for a showdown.... I have already traced his movements from his wife's parents and others."

"He came here and faced Arnaud with the truth?"

"It seems so. Arnaud must somehow have remained friendly, but again, Alivon got to work. He was by repute a ruthless man and when he discovered—someone may have told him or he may have overheard a discussion—when he discovered that the case of Bernard's death was going to be reopened and the truth sought, he took fright. Remember, he was a chauffeur and presumably a motor mechanic as well, before he became a gamekeeper.... He tampered with the Lovells' car. There was an accident and the Lovells died. That, Alivon thought, put him out of danger again."

"But the damage César had done to the car would surely have been discovered at the enquiry?"

"That's a point we've yet to clear up, Audibert."

Marie Alivon entered to ask if they needed more beer. She had insisted, in spite of the tragedy, on doing her usual duties. She was deadly pale, but carried on with her old serenity, greatly to the admiration of the Littlejohns.

"Yes, Marie. Two more, please. By the way, was Leclerc at the garage, a particular friend of your late brother?"

Marie hesitated.

"Yes, monsieur. I did not like it, and I told my brother so, but, of course, it was not my business to interfere. Leclerc is the head of the Communist cell in St. Marcellin. The cells are everywhere. They grew very much during the war, you see. The underground was often run by the Communist cell, as well, and César got associated with them then."

"I see. Leclerc will be very upset about the accident...."

"Yes, sir.... I'll bring the beer."

The two detectives raised their eyebrows at each other.

"That explains a lot."

Audibert made another neat note in his tiny book.

"And then Inspector Littlejohn, from Scotland Yard, arrived, and between the silence of the château and the silence of the Communist cell, he had hard work in finding anything out at all about the so-called accident to the Lovells."

"Exactly. The Marquis had Savini in his power, politically, I presume. The local villagers and farmers, if they knew anything, hung together, either covering the Marquis or obeying the instructions of Leclerc and his Communist organization. The curé may have heard a lot in the confessional-box and was, therefore, almost hysterical when I tried to get anything out of him. Alivon, by the way, was a devout Catholic, they tell me. He must, therefore, unless he had a very elastic conscience, not have been an actual member of the Communist Party."

"The wind sometimes blows this way and that, Littlejohn. This neighbourhood is a vast secret society.... I know; I am a native...."

"Leclerc, working late in his garage, must have heard the crash. He may even have known what was afoot. If he didn't, he was soon informed. He either put the defect right in the smashed car, or else obliterated it."

"There was the case of the baker, Hénoch Rossi, too. He began to talk too much. By then, Alivon was madly afraid. He spent a lot of time listening at keyholes to find out what I knew. Rossi got drunk and began to talk about the night of the motor smash. He was in his bakery at the time and knew a few details of the case. For example, it had been made out the car was travelling from Manosque, instead of the château. That was to keep the limelight from the Marquis, I presume. When Rossi looked like being indiscreet, someone—I guess it was poor César, now completely in the toils—closed the door of the furnace room and almost resulted in Rossi's death from the charcoal fumes. Somebody, and I think it was the Marquis, got Rossi out of the way. They wanted no more murders and no more chattering tongues whilst I was in St. Marcellin."

Marie Alivon returned with the beer and announced that lunch would be ready in five minutes. Cold Bresse chicken and mountain strawberries from Taneron.... Audibert gave her a grateful look.

Outside, the village seemed dead. The heat was intense, and it was as if everyone had gone to bed out of the way of it. All the same, you got the impression of being watched from behind the closed shutters which lined the street, and news seemed to travel secretly as it often does in a prison. The little dying community of St. Marcellin appeared to be holding its breath, waiting for the climax of the great tragedy which had unfolded itself in its midst over many years.

The windows of the *Pascal* were wide open, but there was not a breath of air moving. And yet, the scents of lavender, lucerne and wood smoke entered and made the room sweet with their presence.

Audibert broke the silence.

"And then ... Alivon?"

"Yes. César seemed to overhear all that I said. He heard us tell Marie we had been to Digne. He at once wanted to know why. He questioned the priest and discovered I'd got the name and address of an old servant who was at the château when his sister Céleste died. He went to Digne and questioned Madame Bonjour. He found out that he had been tricked about the paternity of Blanche. My guess is, he immediately went to the Marquis and faced him with the whole affair. He must have threatened to tell the full story either to me or your own police. That wouldn't do at all.... Alivon, in turn, was murdered. Murder tricked-out cleverly to look like suicide, but just one slip was made. The mechanism whereby César pulled the trigger was bungled. It didn't work."

Audibert flung up his hands.

"Poor Pietri.... He won't have seen that, I'm sure...."

"He couldn't have done. I tightened the shoelace when first I saw the body, and when Pietri arrived it looked quite a genuine arrangement...."

"You indicate some doubt about the culprit. It is surely the Marquis?"

"I don't know, Audibert. The case isn't watertight. Do you think it is?"

"It needs a confession to finish it, if that is what you mean. We will get that out of the Marquis. It will be difficult, but—"

There was a steely glint in the calm eyes of the little, neat Frenchman, which boded no good for the Marquis, whatever his local power might be.

"You'll lunch with us, of course, Audibert?"

"I shall be delighted after I have washed, and cleaned my shoes.... Please excuse me."

After lunch Audibert opened his little book again.

"There is work to do."

Together, the two Inspectors crossed the road to Leclerc's garage. The owner of the place was under a large tumbledown car of ancient vintage, his long legs, clad in dark blue overalls, projecting from between the wheels and his efforts indicated by groans and sighs as he wrenched savagely at some hidden part of the machinery. The noises ceased as Leclerc saw the two pairs of feet appear near the car, and his long, crafty face eventually appeared, topped by a dirty beret. He smiled, winked, and then slid out and stood upright.

Once in a position from which he could properly sum-up his visitors, Leclerc didn't look so pleased or comfortable. The fag in the corner of his mouth dropped at a greater angle and he turned the spanner he was holding over and over in his fingers in his nervousness.

"I am Inspector Audibert, of the Marseilles police. You know my friend here?"

"Yes, Inspector."

Leclerc licked his narrow lips and braced himself for whatever shock was coming.

"He wishes to ask you some questions. You will answer them truthfully, or..."

Leclerc was not so easily intimidated as Claudius had been. After all, he was the head of a Communist cell and, in his own tinpot way, he imagined he had, in a fashion, the power to set in motion forces which would bring down the government itself if he cared to use them! He gave Audibert a defiant look.

"Or *what*?"

"Or we will make our way to Digne together, and hear your answers there."

Leclerc was a pale man, but he turned paler and his manner grew quite ingratiating. Sometimes, he'd heard, interviews at the police headquarters lasted for days on end, and you finally didn't know what you'd said and what you hadn't.

"Of course, if I can help in any way."

He wished he hadn't offered when he heard Littlejohn's voice.

"What did you do to the Lovells' car the night you found it… the night they were killed?"

"Me, sir? Nothing. I don't know… "

Audibert tapped him on the front of his filthy overall.

"The truth."

Leclerc licked his dry lips again and his eyes roved all over the place.

"I heard the crash, sir, and I naturally went to see what had happened. The car was just a mass of old metal. It had hit a tree hard, and crumpled up."

"Then, what did *you* do?"

"I saw there were two people in it.… One of them, the woman, was quite dead.… It looked as if she'd broken her skull on the windscreen. The man died as I got there.… The steering-wheel had crushed his body.… I tried to get at them, but till help came, I couldn't."

"Meanwhile, someone else arrived. Who was it?"

"César Alivon, sir. He, too, had heard the crash from where he stood at the door of his inn."

"And together, you effected a repair of some kind. What was it?"

"I don't know what you mean."

Audibert took Littlejohn by the arm and made as if to lead him away.

"This stupid fellow doesn't know what he did.… We will take him to Digne later and jog his memory."

"Here… Don't go.… I… I… "

Leclerc's cockiness had vanished and he lit a cigarette with trembling fingers to hide his fright.

"You know what it is, gentlemen.… When one is a good mechanic and loves one's work, one instinctively puts little defects right.… It comes naturally. I had my lamp with me and I was shining it under the car with a view to trying to move it to get at the dead man, when I suddenly saw—"

"Yes?"

"The steering had become disconnected."

"So, you just instinctively put it right. Well, well."

"That's right."

"Quite a job."

"No, sir. Not to a good mechanic."

"I see. How did you know to look at the steering? Did Alivon tell you?"

"He said to me, 'Looks as if the steering might have gone phut.' And I says, 'Yes.' And I looks, and there it *had* gone phut."

"So you just put it right. And then at the enquiry you said nothing about it, although that was what caused the accident?"

Leclerc shrugged his shoulders.

"One forgets, messieurs. There was so much disorder and upset."

"And, after all, César was a pal of yours and a member of your party."

"He was my friend, but he wasn't a party member."

"I understand. You'll be seeing us again, Leclerc, so don't run away.…"

They left him, crawling back under the car, as though in its dim shadow he found some form of comfort or courage.

Audibert consulted his little book. He seemed to have thoroughly absorbed the spirit of Littlejohn's case and went with him officially opening all the doors which had hitherto been locked.

Docteur Hilaire Mengali.
Ancien Interne, Hôpital N.D.
de Bon Secours, Montpellier.

Audibert rang the bell which hung beside the enamel plate setting out Mengali's qualifications. The doctor himself appeared.

"Come in, gentlemen."

He took them to a barely furnished consulting-room. A cheap desk, an armchair, two glass cases of medicines and instruments, one wall covered in books, two more chairs, an examination couch.

The little, bearded doctor thought they'd come for a report on the body of César Alivon. Instead, Audibert began as before.

"Inspector Littlejohn wishes to ask you some questions about the past tragedies of St. Marcellin."

Littlejohn thought of a terrified hare seeking a place in which to bolt. Mengali mopped his forehead as the sweat sprang out and then wiped his lips which showed red through his beard.

"It is so long ago."

"Not too long, doctor. It is about the duel in which Monsieur Bernard met his death. He wasn't killed by the bullet from Mr. Lovell's pistol, was he? He was shot by a rifle bullet from some unknown assailant."

"I cannot tell you. It was a professional matter and..."

Audibert emerged again. This time he spoke gently to the doctor.

"Don't make it necessary for us to take the enquiry to Digne and you with it, my friend. We understand your reticence. One word or two from you, in confidence, will make everything right. Well?"

"What you say is true, Inspector Littlejohn. There was an enquiry, of course. The burial certificate was given by the examining magistrate from Digne."

"On your medical report?"

"That of myself and Doctor Toselli."

"Did Dr. Toselli also know about the rifle bullet?"

"He examined the body."

Audibert intervened again.

"Who asked them to send Toselli?"

"I think it was Colonel Latour."

"In order to hush-up the whole affair?"

"I don't know what you mean, Inspector Audibert."

"Yes, you do. Toselli was discharged from the service for his drunken habits not long after the death of Monsieur Bernard. Was he intoxicated when you and he examined the body?"

"He was a little unsteady, I must admit."

"And he took your word for it. Colonel Latour probably asked for his services because he knew Toselli didn't know whether he was coming or going.... We understand the embarrassment of such a death when a duel was being fought, but you shouldn't have connived at the verdict, doctor."

"The circumstances were ... "

"I agree.... They could have made the future a little uncertain for you, to say the least.... Have you anything more to tell us, doctor?"

"What else is there? I have always been a model of rectitude in my professional work. I hope you will not make this public. After all, I have been family physician to the St. Marcellins for a long time."

"Too long, if you ask me, my friend. Good afternoon."

The sunshine outside dazzled the two police officers as they emerged; the interior of the doctor's house was so dark. They stood for a moment in the heat, which made everything around unbearable to the touch. Walls, doors, everything solid, seemed to be scorched by fire.

"What would you like now, Littlejohn? Or have you had enough?"

There was still one port of call which Littlejohn had avoided. It hardly seemed fair, but it had to be done.

"The presbytery," he said.

Audibert seemed to understand.

"I sympathize with you. More so, since I, too, am a Catholic. You, I take it, are of the Church of England or one of the score of diverse denominations for which your country is so notorious.... Let us get it over."

They found the priest indoors. He had been praying by the body of César Alivon, which was now in the small town-hall under the guard of a gendarme or two. Marie had just relieved him and was herself watching by her brother's remains.

The Abbé Chambeyron was sitting exhausted in the large chair beside the empty grate of his dining-room. The face he raised to them now seemed strangely composed, although his eyes looked bright with a kind of fever.

"Excuse us disturbing you, Monsieur le Curé, but we want to ask you a question or two."

The priest did not seem unduly troubled. All the excitement of recent days had left him. The three of them sat there in the silence, broken only by the footsteps of the old housekeeper doing something in the room above, the steady ticking of the old clock, and the flies humming about the place in different keys, like a symphony from a minute orchestra.

"César killed Monsieur Bernard, didn't he, Monsieur l'Abbé?"

"Yes. He saw me late on the night before he died. He said if he found that he had murdered Monsieur Bernard for a sin he did not do, he would come to you after he had made sure, confess everything, and take his punishment. I have known he carried a great burden of guilt, but as a priest, I could not..."

"We understand, Monsieur le Curé. He also caused the death of Mr. Lovell and his wife? He disconnected, or tampered with the steering of their car and brought about the accident?"

"He also said he would tell you that. I can speak now, because he would have wished me to do so. He died penitent and forgiven. It seems he was afraid Mr. Lovell would reopen the case of the duel, discover the murder, and a police investigation would result in his being questioned and perhaps his guilt found out. He said he was seized with panic, because he didn't wish disgrace to fall on his sister and Mademoiselle Blanche. He loved Blanche as if she were his own daughter."

Poor César! Littlejohn remembered Blanche's way of showing her gratitude to her uncle and returning his love. She had left for Manosque, as usual, that morning. There was a young fellow, it seemed, at the office, who was paying her unusual attention, and she had to meet him for lunch.... Mrs. Littlejohn had been quite unable to persuade her that her Aunt Marie needed her more.

"Did César tell you anything more when he talked with you, sir?"

"He told me quite a lot. It seems it all began with his overhearing a conversation between Monsieur Arnaud and Monsieur Charles de Barge."

"Excuse me, Monsieur le Curé.... Let us get this quite clear. *Who* said *what*? In other words, who spoke the words which set César on the wrong and tragic road to murder?"

Audibert, sitting with closed eyes and with his fingertips together, listening to the conversation, opened one eye and nodded encouragingly at Littlejohn.

"Yes, Monsieur le Curé. Let us have it," he said.

"According to César, it was something like this. He came upon Monsieur Arnaud and Monsieur Charles talking in the gun-room and overheard the word 'Céleste'. He remained outside the door and listened."

"Excuse me again.... Why was César in the vicinity of the gun-room? Why wasn't he looking after the rest of the guests in the *salon*?"

"He said they had rung from the gun-room for service."

"I see. Please go on, monsieur."

"It was Charles who spoke first. It seems he was asking Monsieur Arnaud to use his good offices to obtain some benefit for Blanche Alivon. Monsieur Bernard was about to be betrothed, he said, and as they both knew, Blanche was Bernard's illegitimate child and would need a proper upbringing, as her mother was dead. Monsieur Arnaud said he would speak to Monsieur Bernard."

Littlejohn leaned forward and looked the priest in the eyes.

"That is not what Claudius told us. He said it was Arnaud who was speaking, and César overheard *him*, returned to the pantry in a rage, and told Claudius."

"Claudius must have been muddled. After all, *he* was the father, and it is only natural that he should be terrified and not listen properly. In any event, what does it matter now?"

"Were you at the château when the party gathered in the spring of 1939 for the betrothal of Bernard de St. Marcellin and Elise de Barge?"

"Yes."

"You were in the room, then, when the quarrel occurred which caused the duel?"

"Yes."

"How did it arise, Monsieur le Curé?"

The priest passed his hand across his tired face and tried to concentrate.

"It was a long time ago.... However, I will try.... Monsieur Arnaud began it, I think. It happened suddenly as we were all smoking and talking and taking brandy. The ladies were absent.... Monsieur Arnaud had drunk too much. He was, I know, also in love with Mademoiselle de Barge and he took the betrothal badly. He mentioned Blanche to Monsieur Bernard in front of all the others. Monsieur Charles de Barge was obviously embarrassed and tried to stop him. Monsieur Charles said he had only spoken on hearsay and without proof. It ended in a quarrel between Arnaud and Charles, and Arnaud challenged Charles. Monsieur Lovell took it all seriously and asked Monsieur Bernard for an explanation, saying that Bernard was unfit to marry a lovely girl like Mademoiselle Elise.... They were all a little drunk and I did my best to make peace. But Bernard ended by accusing Monsieur Lovell of himself being in love with Mademoiselle Elise, and Monsieur Lovell admitted it and was challenged by Monsieur Bernard. The duel was arranged at which Bernard was killed."

Littlejohn sat back with a sigh.

"That's better. Claudius had got that part all mixed up, too. Now I think I see it all."

Audibert opened his eyes again and smiled a sleepy smile.

"That's right," he said. "So do I."

And they left the good priest in such a fog of misunderstanding that he fell on his knees and asked for guidance amid the heavy air of impending tragedy.

Chapter Eighteen
The Delayed Invitation

After the cool presbytery, the village street was like an oven. The bus for Manosque had just left and seemed to have cleared the place of people. There wasn't a soul about; the shutters of most of the houses were closed and the only living things in sight were two dogs, lying flat in the shade of the trees, their tongues hanging out, and the gander, which seemed to make a hobby of hunting for Littlejohn and going for him, followed by four geese.

A smell of warm decay emerged from the ruined windows of the empty, deserted houses in the side street near the mayor's house and mingled with the odours of drains and wood smoke which hung about on the hot air.

Littlejohn and Audibert returned to the *Pascal* and ordered beer, which they sat and drank in the bar, the coolest spot they could find.

The telephone rang.

"A call for you, Monsieur Littlejohn."

"Who is it, Marie?"

"Monsieur le Marquis."

Arnaud sounded in a better temper. In fact, he apologized for his bad behaviour of earlier in the day.

"This business is getting on all our nerves, Littlejohn. One thing after another. And now, Alivon. He's been a faithful servant of our family all his life. You understand, don't you?"

"Of course, Monsieur le Marquis."

"Good. I hope, then, you and Mrs. Littlejohn will come to dinner this evening. Naturally, we all forgot about our appointment last night. It wouldn't have been right to go on with it in view of the catastrophe. Even now, it will be a quiet meal.... I would like to ask Audibert, too. A nice fellow and I was rather rude to him.... That is all right, then?"

"For myself, sir, yes, and I'm sure Inspector Audibert will be honoured, too. I must ask you to excuse Mrs. Littlejohn, though. She is looking after Madame Alivon. Naturally, Marie is very upset, and seems to have found comfort in my wife's presence here."

A pause. Littlejohn could almost hear the Marquis thinking it out.

"Very well. I'm sorry. It will mean asking a lady friend of mine not to come. I'd invited her for company for your wife.... So, it will be all men.... You will request Audibert on my behalf, then?"

"Yes, sir, thank you."

"At seven this evening."

Littlejohn returned to Audibert and passed on the invitation and, as they discussed it over their drinks, they learned who were to be their fellow guests at the château. First, the curé. Through the open window, they heard the telephone ring in the presbytery.... Then, at the town-hall for the mayor. Finally, at Dr. Mengali's.... And even as Mengali was speaking, the priest left his house, strode across the road, and entered the inn.

"Could you give me a lift in your car to the château and back to-night, messieurs? I understand you are invited, and Monsieur le Marquis suggested..."

They picked up the priest at a quarter to seven. It was not a very convivial party. Audibert drove with a distracted air and Littlejohn, sitting beside him, caught his melancholy mood and didn't come to himself until they pulled up at the château steps. It was dusk and the lights were on in the kitchens in the basement. Madame Claudius was visible bending over the fire, and Claudius in his shirt sleeves was sitting at a table with Marius, the handyman, eating soup.

The door was open and the Marquis himself stood in the dimly lighted doorway waiting for them.

"Good evening, gentlemen.... Good evening, Monsieur le Curé."

He took their hats and led them down the corridor, which, once the light had been passed, was almost in darkness. He gave Littlejohn a friendly pat on the shoulder.

"In here."

A room Littlejohn hadn't seen before, and obviously the gun-room spoken of by Claudius. It was illuminated by a tarnished metal chandelier. Glass cases on two sides; all empty. The guns had obviously gone the way of everything else, to the saleroom. No curtains at the window, beyond which were visible the dark branches of a large twisted tree of the type beloved by Arthur Rackham. The mayor and Mengali were already there, looking uncomfortable, for they didn't quite know what to make of the gathering. Greetings were exchanged.

"Excuse me.... I must find something to drink, if there's anything left worth drinking...."

The Marquis went into the corridor and called loudly for Claudius. The butler arrived, settling himself in his coat, his mouth half full. He was followed by Charles de Barge, who looked ill at ease and nodded briefly to them all.

"Claudius ... *apéritifs.*"

"There's only brandy and whisky, Monsieur le Marquis, and not much of those."

"But I told you ... "

Claudius shrugged his shoulders.

"There was nobody to send, monsieur. ... Dinner for seven ... and only two hours to do it in."

St. Marcellin bit his lip.

"Bring what we've got, then. ... You'll excuse me, gentlemen. We're all sixes and sevens here nowadays."

Claudius brought in two half-empty bottles, found some glasses, and carefully shared out what he'd got.

"Drink, gentlemen. ... Your very good health. I can't promise that this will be much of a party, but I insist on entertaining you all once, at least, whilst you're all in St. Marcellin together."

Mengali, the priest and the mayor sipped their drinks with worried looks. They didn't know what to make of it all. Savini, usually very garrulous, tried to make conversation.

"You will be able to teach your friends to play bowls in the French fashion when you return, Mister Littlejohn. The Chief Inspector is almost a champion at the game now, gentlemen."

Nobody took any interest. They all wondered what the Marquis was doing. He had hurried from the room and now they could hear him upbraiding Claudius in the corridor again.

"I don't care if it *is* the last six bottles. ... Get it up, at once. *Vin rosé,* indeed! This isn't a girls' school. ... "

The Marquis returned.

"Would anyone like a cigar?"

Nobody answered, but they all shook their heads respectfully.

"It's perhaps as well.... They're some my father left and I could hardly call them in the prime of condition."

Mengali edged himself beside Littlejohn.

"What's all this about, Inspector? Have *you* arranged it?"

"No, doctor. Your guess is as good as mine...."

De Barge had drunk all his brandy and was gingerly pouring himself another glass from the almost empty bottle.

Claudius appeared, followed by Marius. They both wore white gloves. Those of Marius were too small and he was struggling to get his fingers in them. Finally, he gave it up as a bad job and put them in his pocket.

"It's no use," he whispered to Claudius, who pretended not to hear.

"Dinner is served."

The Marquis led them down the dark corridor again. The supply of electricity in St. Marcellin was good, but at the château the bulbs had old-fashioned filaments and only half illuminated the place.

"You'll excuse the frugal meal, gentlemen. To-day has been an upsetting one. Luckily we had some pigeons in the dovecote. Please be seated."

It was the room Littlejohn had seen earlier in the day. The heavy old chairs, with seats and backs of cracked leather, leaking horsehair, set round the heavy table. A single wire descended from where the chandelier had been removed and a large bulb, with a cheap parchment shade, illuminated the table with a harsh white light. Littlejohn sat on the right of the Marquis and Audibert on the left, with Mengali facing the mayor and de Barge opposite the priest.

Claudius and Marius served the pigeons *en casserole,* with small potatoes and beans, all excellently cooked. Father

Chambeyron joined his hands and started to say grace. Even before he had finished, the Marquis was calling for the wine.

"The last of our own vineyards.... The last of the good old days.... The year my father died.... A good wine, gentlemen. I shall be glad of your opinion."

Marius was evidently new at the job, which Alivon had hitherto done. He did his best to imitate Claudius, but spilled the wine and even dropped gravy down the priest's cassock. The curé tried to hide the mistake and furtively mopped up the mess, eyeing the Marquis apprehensively, lest Marius be rebuked.

There was little or no conversation. Everybody seemed to be expecting something.

"Don't look so scared, Marius. Everyone knows you aren't a trained servant. Alivon should have been here, but is lying in the village morgue.... Poor César."

The Marquis tore at his pigeon with his fork as he spoke. His voice was strained. He seemed to be sorting out the way to get something off his mind.

"I gather, Chief Inspector, that you are of the opinion that poor César didn't commit suicide."

There was a hush. Mengali paused with a forkful of vegetables half-way to his mouth and these slowly fell back on his plate.

"In that case, you must admit that whoever murdered him is eating with us at this table.... Are you not enjoying the pigeons, Mister Mayor? I remember.... You always admired the dovecote.... It is empty now.... Like this château."

Littlejohn thought he detected a trace of a sob in St. Marcellin's voice, but the Marquis was already filling his glass with the excellent white wine of better days.

"A little more wine, Inspector Audibert? This is somewhat of a farewell party for us all. Littlejohn and his charming wife will soon be on their way to their pleasant London again, and you, Audibert, returning to Marseilles.

But not before you have finished the case, I'm sure. Littlejohn has done most of the work. I think you agree, Audibert. In fact, had he never arrived in St. Marcellin, all this trouble and suspicion would have been avoided. I demand that he shall throw a little light on the whole affair. He doubtless intends to do so before the night is out. Otherwise, he would have brought his charming wife with him. He owes it to us, criminals and police alike, to clear the air before we leave the table. That will have to be our evening's entertainment, I'm afraid. We have nothing else. The billiards table has been sold, the best brandy and port has all been drunk, and the cigars are decayed, like this house. As for conversation, it can hardly be described as scintillating."

He drank another glass of wine, finished off the rest of his fowl, and pushed the bottle across to de Barge.

"Another glass, my dear Charles."

The rest of them had stopped eating.

"Clear the table, Claudius, and open some more wine. Then, bring in the fruit and nuts."

"There's a peach flan, Monsieur le Marquis.... And the cheese..."

"Why didn't you say so, Claudius? It seems Madame Claudius has conjured food from an empty larder...."

They ate the sweets with as little appetite as before. It was only when the table was cleared of all except a jumble of wine bottles that the Marquis found his tongue again.

"I take it, Littlejohn, you will soon be saying good-bye to us?"

"Yes, sir."

"Your task here is finished?"

"I've finished the work I came to do."

"And that was...?"

"To find the answer to the mystery of the death of Mr. and Mrs. Lovell. Was it an accident or a deliberate plan to kill them? I am satisfied that it was deliberately done. It is now my duty to report the matter to Mr. Lovell's brother. The rest is his business."

"And, I suppose, that of the French police. Otherwise, to what do we owe the pleasure of Inspector Audibert's visit?"

Littlejohn filled and lit his pipe. The rest of the guests were silent, hanging on his words. It was like a scene at a gaming-table where all the other players withdraw and leave the play for high stakes to two expert gamblers.

"And that is that, Littlejohn."

"Except that my main enquiry has been like throwing a stone in a pond. The first splash has widened into many ripples which interest me. I would like to ask a question before I go...."

The surrounding faces had grown haggard, except that of Audibert, who was smiling and smoking one of his elegant little cigarettes. The curé was gripping the edge of the table to keep his nerves steady.

"I wonder if you and Monsieur de Barge would throw your minds back to the gun-room on the night before the death of Monsieur Bernard. You had just rung the bell for Alivon, who was doing duty as a footman. As he was about to enter the room, one of you said to the other, among other things, 'Bernard is the father of Blanche, the daughter of Céleste Alivon.' Which one of you said that?"

Charles de Barge was on his feet.

"This is ridiculous! As though we could remember! It is years ago and much has happened."

"Sit down, Charles! Can't you be civil to our guest? We must try to remember. Which of us said it?"

He poured himself another glass of wine.

"You're not drinking, gentlemen. Claudius..."

Claudius, a scared expression on his face, slowly moved to the table and sorted out one of the bottles which wasn't empty. He stood over Littlejohn, who, in turn, turned his face up to him with an affable smile.

"Claudius says it was Monsieur Arnaud who made the statement...."

The butler jumped and the wine dribbled from the bottle down his coat.

There was a brief silence. Somewhere in the house a clock struck nine in heavy ominous notes.

"I... I... It was César who told me that. I did not hear it. I assure you, Monsieur le Marquis..."

"Don't make excuses, Claudius. Serve the wine."

The curé cast a beseeching look at Littlejohn, who, in turn, lit his pipe again. He looked over at de Barge and saw that the sweat glistened on his forehead.

"A glass of wine, Charles...? And, by the way, what have you to say to that, my dear Charles? Did *I* tell *you* about the paternity of Blanche, or did *you* tell *me*?"

"I don't remember."

De Barge drank off the wine in one gulp.

Littlejohn was sitting with his fists under his chin, his elbows on the table.

"On the other hand, Monsieur le Curé tells me that César told him that Monsieur de Barge made the statement.... I'd like to know who really did make it before I go. It is most interesting...."

Another silence. It seemed to exasperate the Marquis, who was now half drunk. He thumped the table and made the glasses rattle.

"Why did you say I said it, Claudius?"

The butler stepped back a pace. His face was now as white as his gloves. Marius stood by the door taking it all in with wide eyes.

"Well?"

"It must have been a mistake, Monsieur le Marquis. It was so long ago."

The Marquis sprang to his feet and seized the butler by the throat. Weight for weight, Arnaud wouldn't have stood a chance in a struggle, but Claudius was disciplined and afraid.

"The truth.... Who bribed you to lie about it?"

St. Marcellin shook the man until his teeth rattled.

"Tell me. Or, by God, I'll kill you."

The rest, with the exception of Littlejohn and Audibert, were on their feet, standing in a ring round the two main actors, ready to interfere, if needs be, but otherwise interested, like spectators at a street fight.

"I swear nobody bribed me, sir. It was only that... that..."

Littlejohn finished the sentence.

"Only that he didn't want somebody to tell his wife who the real father of Blanche was."

St. Marcellin flung the man away from him and then followed him and stood chest to chest with him, his fist in the air.

"Who threatened to tell Madame Claudius...? Tell me, or..."

"It was Monsieur Charles."

It was de Barge's turn now to fling himself upon Claudius.

"You lying swine! I never..."

And then St. Marcellin flung himself upon de Barge! This time the guests intervened, the priest thrust his powerful arm round Charles, and Savini and Mengali gingerly held Arnaud by an arm apiece.

St. Marcellin shook himself and laughed nervously.

"This is ridiculous! Let us sit down, gentlemen, and at least be civilized. No good will be done by violence."

They broke up and took their chairs again.

"It's a lie. Claudius has made it all up to appear clever.... I demand an apology."

De Barge mopped his brow with a table napkin and took another glass of wine.

"Rubbish! You know you said it, my dear Charles. Why deny it? We also have the testimony of Monsieur le Curé. Why should our good Abbé Chambeyron lie about it?"

The priest looked as if for two pins he'd begin to say his prayers then and there.

"Well.... Where does it all lead to? Even if I did say it, which I deny, are we going to sit here arguing and quarrelling for the rest of the night? Because, if we are, I'm going to bed."

"You will remain just where you are until I say you may go."

Although Audibert said it quietly, they all jumped. It was as if one of the pieces of furniture had suddenly found tongue and issued orders.

The Marquis leaned over to Littlejohn and affectionately placed a hand on his shoulder.

"And now you've had the answer to your question, you can leave Provence with an easy mind, Inspector, can't you?"

"Yes, Monsieur le Marquis.... But what of the ripples in the pond I mentioned earlier? This is just another example, only this time the stone was the comment made by Monsieur de Barge about Blanche's paternity. That was the cause of it all. My case, my investigation into the death of Mr. and

Mrs. Lovell was merely a ripple from that. And the rest is Inspector Audibert's business."

Audibert shrugged his shoulders. He was peeling a peach and looked very contented.

"Finish the story, my friend.... I am as entertained as the rest."

The rest didn't seem very entertained. They all looked as if they expected a ghost to walk in the room.

"May we go, sir?"

Claudius looked ready to collapse.

"Yes, be off with you. Take the empty bottles and bring some more."

"There aren't any more, Monsieur le Marquis...."

St. Marcellin paused.

"Get out, then!"

Claudius and Marius didn't need telling twice. They departed almost at the double.

"Your health, gentlemen, in the last of this wine.... Our cellars are empty and to-morrow it will be *vin ordinaire* from Marie Alivon. You were saying, Littlejohn...?"

"On the strength of what he heard from Monsieur de Barge, Alivon, who had been nursing vengeance against his sister's betrayer, took advantage of the duel, and shot Monsieur Bernard dead with a rifle. The parties to the duel had to hush it up. Otherwise, would they not themselves be arrested for indulging in duelling? Dr. Mengali and a drunken colleague from Digne certified the death, and the rest swore, as prearranged, that it had been a shooting accident..."

Mengali didn't say a word. He just sat there, half drunk himself, and two large alcoholic tears of self-pity formed and slowly trickled down his face and vanished in his beard.

"... Lovell fled, thinking he'd killed Bernard, his good friend. None of the other parties dared say anything. Two men in the party hoped to benefit from it all. They had been responsible for Alivon's conduct, because, obviously, the false statement about Bernard was prearranged."

St. Marcellin gently tapped Littlejohn on the shoulder.

"The only blame that lies at my door is that I didn't contradict Charles when he made the statement. I was drunk."

"Liar! You were as sober as I was."

"Oh, do shut up, Charles. Do let us settle all this like civilized beings. Perhaps we were both drunk. You were saying, Littlejohn ... ?"

"I insist on being heard! You can't arrest me for a mistake. I thought Bernard and not Claudius was the father of Blanche ... "

Charles was half drunk and frenzied, too, but Littlejohn silenced him.

"Who told you it was Claudius? Even Alivon didn't know until lately and, when he found out, he was shattered. He'd killed the wrong man, his old master, and he was going to expiate by confession to the police. For that threat, someone killed him. The morning he died he spoke to the Marquis about it. Monsieur de Barge was in the room and heard it all."

"You seem to have learned quite a lot, my good Littlejohn."

"In spite of you, Monsieur le Marquis. You gave orders through your lackey, the mayor. ... "

"I protest! I ... "

"Silence, Savini! It's all true, you know."

"But, Monsieur le Marquis ... "

"I said, silence! ... Continue, Littlejohn."

The mayor shuffled in his chair and cast startled glances round the room, like one in a nightmare wondering if he's awake or asleep.

"Monsieur Sylvestre Barge was right, but it was the dying Colonel Latour who told Lovell how Bernard met his death. He had it on his conscience. Lovell came to Provence right away for an explanation. First, he called at Cap Ferrat and telephoned from there that he wished to see you, Monsieur le Marquis. You, in turn, hastily sent for Monsieur Charles to see if he knew what it was all about. He came here and, after a discussion, he telephoned for the Lovells. Lovell and his wife dined here, just as we are doing now..."

"Hardly, my dear Littlejohn. There were ladies present. There was no drunkenness and no accusations. We told Lovell the truth and settled matters amicably. He and Elise had not eaten for hours. They dined and went away, intent on staying in Digne for the night and reporting the old crime to the police next day.... As you know, they never reached Digne.... The accident..."

"The murder, you mean. Alivon lost his head when he heard what they proposed to do. The police might never have solved the murder of your brother, but César didn't stop to argue. He tampered with the steering of their car and, at the first big curve in the road, they crashed into a tree. Leclerc, at the village garage, either repaired or obliterated the parts which had been tinkered with, and the case again was closed as an accident. Furthermore, the records told nothing of the Lovells' visit here. They spoke of their driving in the direction of the château. That, I presume, to avoid awkward enquiries.... The village baker, who knew something of the events at the accident, almost lost his life through talking to me in his cups. César locked him in his furnace-room among the fumes.... You, Monsieur le

Marquis, presumably spirited Hénoch away to keep him out of further mischief."

"I admit it. I shipped him off out of harm's way. But Alivon is dead now and, even if we admit he interfered with the car, he is past paying for his misdeeds."

"Yes. But the guilty one is he who started all this chain of disasters, the one who first threw the stone in the pond."

"Here.... You can't blame me for a mistake."

"It was no mistake, Monsieur de Barge. You and the Marquis were involved in the murder of Monsieur Bernard. If Lovell had brought in the police, you'd both have been incriminated, even if the murderer was never laid by the heels. You both hushed up the crime.... You know what that means.... Prison and disgrace for the pair of you. It was stupid, if I may say so, Monsieur le Marquis, of you to try to put me off by exhibiting an old skull as proof of your brother's death in a duel. You might have known I would have it verified."

"It was foolish, I admit.... As for my brother's death ... The courts will understand our dilemma. The sentence will be a light one."

"Not for the crimes the pair of you have committed, sir."

"The pair of us.... Really, Littlejohn, you must be careful. You must explain yourself.... This is fantastic."

He seized a bottle of wine and served everyone except de Barge and himself, for the wine ran out before then.

"Go on, Littlejohn.... More fantasy ... more fairytales.... I admit I said this wasn't going to be a good party, but it has exceeded my wildest expectations.... More, more, Littlejohn!"

He stood grasping the back of his chair. The cold white light from the solitary bulb above the table shone down on them all, giving them the ghastly expressions of ghosts at a feast.

"Monsieur Bernard, murdered by Alivon on the strength of a deliberate falsehood specially uttered to incite him; the Lovells, also murdered by Alivon, to keep them quiet; Rossi almost gassed for the same reason. Then, Alivon learned the truth. He was spying on me on your behalf, Monsieur le Marquis, and he learned too much. He found out who the real father of Blanche was and how he'd been cheated. He then proposed to tell the police, just as Lovell had done. So, Alivon was murdered."

"Really.... It was as plain a case of suicide as I ever knew."

"No, Monsieur le Marquis. After his threats, he was followed to the shooting-box, the very place whence he had killed Bernard with his rifle and escaped by the back door. There, someone shot him with his own gun and made it all look like suicide. But the cunning mechanism whereby he was supposed to have pulled the trigger of his gun, as he sat at the table with the barrels to his head, was bungled.... The idea of the shoelace round the trigger was most ingenious, but whoever did it wore gloves and didn't tie a proper knot. It was too slack ever to pull the trigger and when I tried it, it gave way in my hand. It was a cleverly arranged murder."

Charles de Barge rose to his feet, trembling like a leaf, his burning eyes fixed on the Marquis.

"So that was where you went.... You were going to the lodge, following Alivon to kill him.... you said you were going to see Claudius, and all the time..."

"*What did you say?*"

St. Marcellin rose and made for de Barge. He now seemed cold sober and, as he approached, de Barge moved round the table out of Arnaud's way. Mengali and the curé rose, as if to interfere.

Audibert raised a hand.

"Leave them. Sit down."

The two one-time friends faced each other at the end of the table with the anxious faces of the rest turned to them.

"*What did you say?*"

St. Marcellin raised his fist and struck de Barge full in the mouth. The blood spurted from his split lip, but Charles did not heed it. Instead, he looked round like a hunted animal and tried to run for the door. The Marquis pounced on him and hauled him back under the light. The curé rose again to intervene.

"Leave them."

"But, Inspector Audibert..."

"All of you, leave them."

Audibert said it in a voice like the crack of a whip and they all sat back horrified.

De Barge was on his knees, with St. Marcellin towering over him.

"You killed César.... It was you who went out, saying you must pack your bag, and you sneaked across the back and through the coppice to the shooting-box.... You knew *I* would never kill Alivon. And you know why.... Because of Marie, his sister. Tell them, Monsieur le Curé. I haven't the heart."

The priest shrugged his shoulders. Things had got beyond him. He was quite out of his depth.

"Monsieur le Marquis has always loved Marie Alivon. He swore he would never marry anyone but her. His family forbade it, and Marie married someone else. When her husband died, it was too late."

"Yes... Too late. All the money of the family gone.... This place a ruin.... And Marie convinced that peasants ought not to marry into the gentry, as it was against the will of God."

St. Marcellin almost sobbed again and then he remembered de Barge, still struggling in his grip, and he struck him across the face again.

"You killed César. ... Confess."

He raised his fist in the air.

De Barge rolled his eyes like someone dying and struggled to release himself.

"Confess. ... Say it."

"I confess."

But St. Marcellin wasn't satisfied. He raised his fist again.

"Tell us all what you did. ... Go on. ... Alivon called here and told me, in the library, with you sitting on the window-seat, pretending to write to your uncle about returning. ... He told me that he had found out who the real father of Blanche was. ... Didn't he? You heard him ... ? Tell them all. ... "

"I heard him."

De Barge's nose was bleeding and he wiped away the blood with the back of his hand.

"He said, didn't he, that he would have to think what to do? He said the years had taken away his hatred of Céleste's betrayer, and Claudius was now an old man. That he would either write a confession and kill himself, or go to the police, tell them all, and give himself up. He was tired of murder and hatred and sin. The mention of killing himself gave you an idea. ... Didn't it ... ? Say it out loud."

"Yes."

"Say it."

"It gave me the idea of killing him and making it look like ... "

De Barge began to crawl on the carpet, trying to get away, like a wounded animal. St. Marcellin dragged him to his feet.

"You knew you'd be involved for hiding the first crime, but you didn't do what I did. I told Alivon that I would go to the police with him and together we would try to see the thing through. He then swore not to kill himself. I told him I would do all I could for Marie's sake.... Did I do that, or not? Speak, or ... "

"You said that."

"And yet you followed him and killed him. How?"

"I went to the shooting-box."

"Speak up."

"I went to the shooting-box. He was just starting his lunch. I said, I, too, would go with him and you to the police. He turned to put down his food bag and I picked up his gun, which was lying across the table.... "

Then he fell on his knees.

"Mercy.... Don't hit me again.... Don't."

"You dirty coward.... You worm."

St. Marceilin seized him by the coat collar.

"Say to them all, 'I'm a dirty worm and coward'."

This time the curé intervened, strode across the room, and with his powerful arms lifted St. Marceilin and carried him back to his chair.

"I have been silent long enough. Sit there and control yourself. You disgrace your manhood.... Have you no compassion ... no mercy?"

Arnaud helped himself to a drink—the dregs from several bottles—and drank it with a grimace.

Audibert raised de Barge to his feet, wiped away the blood from his face with a white handkerchief, and sat him down, too, in a chair.

"Compose yourself, monsieur. Compose yourself, and then you will both come with me to Digne."

"Digne ... ? You don't want me, too?"

St. Marceilin looked quite surprised. He thought that he'd somehow acquitted himself.

"You, too, monsieur. As Inspector Littlejohn will tell you, you have condoned all these things by remaining passive. Is that not so, Littlejohn?"

The emotional scene had disgusted Littlejohn. He was anxious to end it all, get back to the quietness of the *Hôtel Pascal,* and watch his wife pack their bags ready for home. He laid down his pipe and spoke quickly.

"De Barge not only arranged the lie which Alivon overheard; he also fomented a duel. He showed some skill in the provocation, I'm told by both Claudius and Monsieur le Curé. It ended in Bernard and Lovell fighting. De Barge hoped one would be killed. It didn't matter which. It would prevent Elise marrying either. He loved his cousin and wanted her for himself. His family, too, would have liked the marriage. He didn't reckon with Elise, though. She turned away to support Lovell, and they were married.... De Barge was due to fight Monsieur Arnaud himself. Two duels were arranged. Did he apologize to avoid it, Monsieur le Marquis?"

"What do *you* think? He said there had been enough trouble already."

"When I arrived, you, Monsieur le Marquis, were afraid I might find out enough to re-open the case. You had shielded Alivon after his murder of Lovell and his wife. You now went one farther. You used your local influence to close all doors against me. The mayor, the doctor... even Monsieur le Curé.... They all remained silent on your account."

"I could not speak... I am a priest.... Alivon was one of my flock.... He had confessed many things."

Tears were running down the priest's face.

"The other two had no such excuse. They, and even Mora, the policeman, were afraid of the power of the château."

The doctor and the mayor said nothing, but bit their lips. Mengali was wondering how he would come off for his share in the matter of the duel.

"I suppose you did it all for Marie Alivon, Monsieur le Marquis. Or did you?"

"What is the meaning of that insinuation, Littlejohn?"

The Marquis looked more interested than annoyed.

"After all, Monsieur le Marquis, there is this place to keep going."

With a wave of his hand, Littlejohn indicated the château.

"It would not do to kill the goose that laid the golden eggs. Monsieur Charles de Barge is now, I understand, in sole charge of the banking-house of de Barge & Co., of Lyons. He has doubtless provided you with a considerable overdraft.... Also, before he became heir to his uncle's business and fortune, there were rumours in the village that you, too, sought the hand of Mademoiselle Elise."

The Marquis tottered to his feet again and slapped Littlejohn on the back.

"I compliment you, Littlejohn! Who but an Englishman would have thought of the financial... the shopkeeper's aspect of the case? Quite true. Charles is a very complacent mortgagee, aren't you, Charles? If he and I had gone to gaol for our share in hushing-up crimes, others would have taken over Charles's powers and discovered what a rotten loan the St. Marcellin mortgages were. This place would have been sold up, and the last of the noble line of St. Marcellin would have been thrown on the street."

The Marquis took another drink and made a wry face at it.

"I love this place.... It is shabby and tumbledown, but it is my home. Well... we shall be sold up in any case, now. The vultures will gather whilst I languish in gaol at Marseilles. When I'm free again it will be gone. A nursing-home... A sanatorium for wealthy trade-unionists.... Who knows...? Is there nothing more to drink...? No...? Not even a drop of Aunt Hauteclaire's gentian cordial?"

He flung his glass in the fireplace where it smashed into a hundred pieces.

"You mentioned my wishing to marry Elise, Littlejohn. We all wanted Elise, didn't we...? Charles here, Bernard, myself, scores of suitors.... And she didn't want any of us. And now she's dead and gone, Littlejohn, just because she preferred the Englishman. As for me... Marie Alivon wouldn't have me for love, so I turned where there was money. Cynical, you say? But not more of a mockery than most marriages, you must surely admit.... Perhaps, however, I shall come to a happy end, after all. Marie Alivon might pity me when I return from gaol, and I may even become the landlord of the *Hôtel Pascal*.... It would bring a lot of business. Monsieur le Marquis de St. Marcellin et de Brômes-St. Eusèbe, landlord of the *Restaurant Pascal*.... It would attract a lot of clients from the Riviera.... Well, Inspector Audibert.... Let us go. On our way to Digne."

Arnaud de St. Marcellin went to gaol for twelve months. Marie Alivon visits him there and perhaps something will come of it when he returns to the village, where a company has bought the château and is turning it into a thermal establishment.

Charles de Barge was sentenced to fifteen years penal servitude. He got a good lawyer and they spun a tale about César's threatening him during a squabble at the shooting-box. The preliminary enquiry and the trial dragged on interminably.... De Barge's time is now fully occupied in preparing his appeal. He works twice as hard as his lawyers and his cell is overflowing with legal books and documents.

The Littlejohns entertained the official French investigators to dinner before they left for home. When she heard their Christian names, Mrs. Littlejohn said her guests sounded as fabulous as the Knights of the Round Table.

Fulgence Bouchard, Clovis Audibert, Dagobert Pietri, Jérôme Dorange.... And, of course, plain Thomas Littlejohn!

Marie Alivon served excellent roast goose for the meal, and when, next morning, the gander in charge of only *three* geese this time, again rushed to attack him, Littlejohn fled with stirrings of conscience and remorse!

Death Sends for the Doctor

George Bellairs

Chapter One
The Puzzle of Abbot's Caldicott

A murder was committed at Abbot's Caldicott last Friday.

Superintendent Littlejohn turned over the dirty piece of paper between his finger and thumb. The message was pencilled in uneven capitals on a scrap roughly torn from the top of what might have been a magazine. The envelope was just as disreputable. Cheap, soiled, properly stamped, with the cancellation a mere smudge—the kind of angry, inky mess they make in the sorting-office when the stamp hasn't been properly spoiled at the first go. The address was in illiterate printing as well.

SUPT. LITTLEJOHN
SCOTLAND YARD
LONDON

Whoever had written it was right up to date. Littlejohn had only been promoted three days and now he was sitting at his desk in front of a litter of congratulations from his colleagues and friends. He reached for the reference book.

ABBOT'S CALDICOTT. (Soke of Dofford, Fenshire.) Pop. 3400. London 104; Abbot's Dofford 4; Norwich 31; Cold Staunton 4; Peterborough 34; Kegworth Ducis 7... Lic. Hours. w.d. 11–3, 5–10; S. 12–2, 7–10...

"Give me the Soke of Dofford police, please..."

At the other end of the line, the Chief Constable of the Soke listened, answered briefly, turned purple, and then hung up.

"Scotland Yard have had one of those blasted things as well. What the hell does Plumtree think he's doin'? Get him on the phone right away."

Sergeant Plumtree was drinking a cup of tea and smoking a cigarette when the telephone rang in his little police station in Upper Square, Caldicott. Before picking up the instrument, he docked his fag, pushed away his cup, sprang to attention, smoothed his tunic, and looked guilty, as though the caller were about to materialise and denounce him.

"Yes... Caldicott police..."

Plumtree was a large, fat, pneumatic-looking officer who, with the help of six constables, kept order in Caldicott. He had a bald, orange-shaped head, a large ginger moustache, a bulbous nose, a nice wife and four children, and he had been awarded a medal for gallantry in air raids during the war. Now he didn't look very brave.

"But I've combed the town, sir. I assure you nobody's been murdered. No, sir; I 'aven't called the roll, but if there'd been a murder, I'd have been the first to know... Somebody would 'ave reported it."

Plumtree spoke in the posh voice he used when addressing his superiors and smacked the top of his head as though punishing or stimulating his brain for slowness. He always knew exactly what to say and how to deal with a situation after the event. He called it *afterwit,* and it was his great cross in life.

"Yes, sir. The only person reported to us as out of town is Dr. Beharrell. He's been visitin' his mother on her deathbed and his assistant's doin' the work..."

There were loud and angry noises from the telephone.

"I'm sorry, sir, but you asked and I thought... Very good, sir. I'm doin' my best... I said, I'm doin' my best, sir..."

He hung up the instrument and then, in a sudden gust of rage, apostrophised it and went to the extent of shaking his huge fist at it.

"Unreasonable old devil, that's wot you are! Silly old fool! Clever Dick! Johnny Know-all! Slow, am I? I'll ruddy-well show you. 'ubbard! *H*ubbard!!"

The last word sounded all over the square and there was a response of heavy feet to it. A young, thin, aquiline and melancholy constable wearing a startled expression appeared at the door.

"You've taken your time over it, 'ubbard! Why can't you come when you're called?"

Hubbard's lips moved as Plumtree's afterwit began to function.

"I'd got my boots off..."

"Don't chat back at me. Get your 'elmet on."

The constable made a measured exit and returned wearing his official headgear. He looked mildly at the sergeant, waiting for an explanation or another rocket.

"That was the Chief ringin' up. It seems he's just 'eard from Scotland Yard, and they've also got one of those bloomin' bits of paper saying there was a murder 'ere last Friday..."

"You don't say, sergeant!"

"And wot might that remark mean? That what I say isn't true? Or that you've gone deaf all of a sudden? Pull yourself together, 'ubbard, and for Pete's sake, don't stand there with your mouth open. The Chief's 'oppin' mad and wants immediate results."

They both stood silently brooding on where the results were coming from.

"Let's get cracking then. Although what we're goin' to do about it beats me. We can't very well go round all the shops and houses and ask 'Has there been a murder 'ere lately?' And we can't start diggin' for bodies, because we've no bloomin' idea where to dig or who to dig for. All we can do is keep our eyes and ears open, and *hope*... Better take a stroll over to the housin' estate, and I'll take the town."

"What about Clowne?"

"What about him? You can ask him if he's heard anythin' unusual, can't you? Sometimes I despair of you, 'ubbard. Try to use the few brains you've got..."

Sid Clowne was the bobby who occupied the police house on the new estate where the bulk of the ratepayers of Caldicott were herded in their little red brick houses. This was the most likely hunting-ground for missing or murdered persons.

"Go on, then, and get weavin'..."

Hubbard, who, according to his colleagues, had only two speeds, damned slow and stop, turned and left without another word.

Plumtree put on his helmet, took up his stick of office, and walked solemnly out of doors.

Upper Square was the oldest part of Caldicott. It was a complete quadrangle of old grey buildings, entered from the town below by Sheep Street, which gently rose from the Kegworth Ducis road, passed through a double line of shops, widened out to become the square, and then contracted and continued thence as the Cold Staunton—Peterborough highway.

The sergeant breathed deeply and looked about him. A nice spring morning. Languid smoke rose straight upwards from the chimneys of the square and the sun, shining over the roof of the Guildhall, cast the shadows of the double avenue of trees across the houses of the west side. A blackbird was singing loudly in the sycamore a few yards from the door of the police station. Plumtree looked up at it, recognised it, and nodded at it approvingly. It had a white feather in its tail, was officially known as Whitey, and had held pugnacious and noisy possession of its present perch for three years. Plumtree was very interested in birds...

The Guildhall clock struck nine. The bell of St. Hilary's, which stood at the top of the square, had done the same five minutes before, and now Plumtree could hear the 9.10 to Norwich leaving the station beyond the town, promptly, according to railway time. There was always bother about the time in Caldicott. Some said it was the damp, others sheer stupidity on the part of the inhabitants. The Caldicott Archers were reputed to have arrived at the Battle of Flodden ten minutes too late to enjoy the fun...Plumtree took out his own watch, a silver turnip inherited from his grandfather and which he boasted never gained or lost a second a day...Nine-sixteen...

Plumtree was sure the whole business was a hoax. A murder, indeed! This was Tuesday, and the notes had said last Friday. Not a word since. No bodies, no alarms, nobody reported missing. It was his theory that some Communist, member of the I.R.A., madman, mischievous schoolboy or enemy of the state was trying to destroy the morale of Abbot's Caldicott, and that the best thing to do was to treat the whole thing with contempt. But the Chief Constable...

The sergeant turned right and entered the Guildhall next door. The corporation pigeons, disturbed by his heavy tread, halted in their cooing and their festooning the building with droppings like white bunting, and took leisurely to the air. The place was almost deserted. Nothing much went on there before ten o'clock when some of the councillors started to hang about and the local justices arrived for the petty sessions. It was far too large for the needs of the small town, many rooms were closed, and there was an odour of dust and dry rot always there. But it had a history of its own and was a showplace for visitors.

In the days of the medieval wool trade, Abbot's Caldicott had been a busy and prosperous little metropolis. It was then that the Guildhall and the large church of St. Hilary had been erected, as well as most of the other buildings in the Upper Square where the wealthy merchants lived. Then, fortunes had declined... In 1928, the population of Caldicott had fallen below 1,000 and the dying little town had been scheduled to lose its borough status. It had been saved by three godsends. The establishment, almost simultaneously, of an R.A.F. depot, Cropper's Chemicals, Ltd., manufacturing a patent cleaner called *Whodunit,* and Samuel's Stockings (Caldicott), Ltd., with a large new weaving shed. The population had risen rapidly, a housing estate had grown up like a bed of mushrooms, and prosperity had returned with a bang. Now, the powers-that-be had decided to close the R.A.F. station for reasons known only to themselves, and *Whodunit* had gone bust. So Caldicott was starting to die all over again.

"Mornin', sergeant."

Fred Mold, who combined the duties of municipal caretaker, mayor's valet, and professional cobbler, emerged from his den, half office and half bucket and brush store, and greeted Plumtree. A little wizened man with a stiff leg from the first war.

"Mornin', Fred. Everythin' all right?"

"Yes. Why?"

"Just wondered."

What more could the sergeant say? Suppose he said, "you've not heard of any murders round here, have you?" Fred would think he'd gone off his chump. It was very awkward.

Plumtree sauntered into the open air again, and Mold followed his huge form with his spiteful little eyes until it disappeared. Then he returned to his football-pool form, clicking his tongue against his teeth.

"Plumtree's gettin' past it, or else a bit above himself."

On the other side of the Guildhall, the *Red Lion,* an old posting-house. George Hope, the landlord, small, hen-pecked, and gone to seed, was just sweeping out and about to push a heap of sawdust, fag-ends and spent matches down the grid in front of the pub. When he saw Plumtree, he paused, smiled sheepishly, and went indoors for a shovel. Poor George. Plumtree felt sorry for him. He'd married a French woman who put little tables and parasols out in front of the *Red Lion* in summer to make it look continental, and made George do the chores whilst she preened herself among the customers.

The great church of St. Hilary, with its vicarage attached, dominated the top of the square. From the school behind it came the sound of shrill sweet voices:

His chariots of wrath the deep thunder clouds form, And dark is His path on the wings of the storm...

Plumtree went hot and cold. It reminded him of what was likely to happen if he didn't report something to the Chief Constable soon.

Across the square, Eccles, the postman, was delivering letters. He slipped some envelopes in the letter-box of Dr. Beharrell, who practised in a large grey house, with a fine doorway at the top of four stone steps and high sash windows, opposite the police station. Morning surgery began at ten, and already a few patients were starting to trickle through the open door of the waiting-room...

One minute, the square was just as usual, quiet, serene, dignified, dominated by the bronze soldier of the first-war memorial, charging with his bayonet in the direction of Sheep Street. The next minute, the whole place had sprung to life. A large pantechnicon, which almost completely blocked the entrance to the square, arrived and, after lumbering here and there like a huge frightened animal, came to rest. The driver thrust his head out of the cab, shouted at the postman, who shouted back and pointed with his thumb. Then the van drew up at the house of Dr. Beharrell.

JEREMIAH NUTT, SONS AND NEPHEW, LTD.
PETERBOROUGH
REMOVALS

FULLY INSURED. ESTIMATES FREE
BY ROAD, RAIL OR SEA.

Huge yellow letters on a black ground. The contraption seemed to fill the square.

On a flap hinged to the back of the van and supported by heavy chains, sat three men like wrestlers, their legs swinging, their expressions strong and pug-like, their short pipes all going. They were almost replicas of one another and of an elderly man who dismounted from the driving cab. He was, in turn, followed by a little wiry man, quite unlike the others, who reminded you of the runt in a litter and, compared with the rest, resembled it as well. He wore a suit made for somebody larger than himself. It was easy to recognise the dramatis personæ so boldly described on the pantechnicon.

At a signal from their parent, the three brothers peeled off their jackets, rolled up their shirt sleeves, revealing huge hairy arms, put on green baize aprons, and indicated to Nutt, senior, that they were ready. The nephew then followed suit more diffidently, disclosing sickly white arms with knobs on his elbows, and he started to beat them together as though the cold struck to his marrow.

Plumtree watching, remembered what it was all about. The aged mother of Dr. Beharrell had just died, he had been away to deal with her estate, and now he was sending some of the family furniture to his own spacious house.

Meanwhile, across the way, Dr. Beharrell's housekeeper, a scraggy peasant-like woman, was upbraiding the removal men. They had obviously arrived too soon and she wasn't ready for them. She was joined by a young man with a mop of red hair and big ears, who was the doctor's assistant. He, too, seemed in a rare temper and even looked ready to try conclusions with the lot of them. This might have been interesting, for the young doctor had the physique of a Rugby full-back. Mr. Nutt, senior, opened negotiations with dignity and restraint. He was small and fat, with a good-tempered red face, and looked like a benevolent clean-shaven Father Christmas. Meeting resistance, he ordered the runt of the party to start the engine in a threat to drive away and never come back. Agreement was thereupon quickly reached, the signal was given, and the team began their job.

Plumtree stood there fascinated by it all. A small crowd had gathered, and the seats which surrounded the charging bronze soldier rapidly filled up with old men.

First, the nephew scrambled inside the van like a monkey and flung out a shower of packing, old sacks, and wads used to protect the contents from injury. Then, the wrestlers began in procession to enter the vehicle and solemnly bear into the house the more precious parts of the load. All under the eagle eye of the old man, who looked ready to box the ears of any member who bungled a trick. Small fussy tables, lustre ornaments under glass globes, a stag's head, a musical box, four huge Chinese ornaments, a cello and a trombone, a brass standard lamp, a bead firescreen, a marble clock. The strong men were transformed into ballet dancers in their efforts to be careful with the delicate parts of the cargo. Now and then, the nephew, sorting-out in the interior of the van, emerged to help with this or that, showing so much strength and enthusiasm, that he upset the balance of the load and had to be checked by his uncle.

The spectators gasped, murmured, and cheered, as one after another the valuable contents saw the light of day like prizes from a lucky packet. The church clock struck eleven as the small stuff was finished, whereupon, with the consent of Nutt *père,* the performers adjourned for refreshment to the *Red Lion,* where the landlady received them with cordiality and admiration, continually eyeing the rippling muscles of the mighty bare arms with voluptuous pleasure.

Ten minutes later, they started again. This time the weight-lifters really showed what they could do. A huge mahogany sideboard with a carved eagle with glass eyes perched on the back, a large double-pedestal dining-table and twelve Regency chairs to go with it, a harpsichord, an out-sized Chippendale wardrobe, an enormous oak chest with 1687 plainly visible on the front panel...They all emerged from the van where the nephew was sorting them out, and vanished indoors with the greatest of ease. Then followed packing cases which held valuable china…or so the spectators said. All the while, the senior Nutt did nothing but smoke his pipe, watch the procedure and rumble admonitions, cautions, or advice.

Whilst all this was going on, the doctor's housekeeper could be seen through the front windows, rushing madly here and there, ordering the wrestlers where to put their loads, and rebuking them for technical faults. Now and then, the steady inflow of furniture was impeded by a patient from the surgery who got mixed up with the removal and was battered by a sideboard or borne into the interior behind a large wardrobe.

Sergeant Plumtree had retired to his office, the window of which faced the present battleground. He stood there like a pillar of salt watching the strong men at work. 'It's all in the knack', he kept saying, as though excusing himself for his own feelings of impotence. He had forgotten the dirty piece of paper warning him about a murder last Friday. He felt convinced that he was performing a genuine constabulary duty in seeing that all the proceedings at the home of Dr. Beharrell were carried out in a proper law-abiding manner.

At one o'clock it was all over and the nephew, whose name was Crumpet, restored the packing and old sacks to the van and solemnly closed it. The men then took off their green aprons, rolled down their sleeves, put on their coats, and presented themselves to their parent properly attired for lunch. Each carried a fibre case which held a gargantuan meal. They again crossed to the *Red Lion.*

At ten minutes past one, there was a fearful scream from the home of Dr. Beharrell. It disturbed the municipal pigeons in the silent square and they took to the air, wheeled once round the houses, and alighted again. Then,

Mrs. Trott, the housekeeper, appeared at the door waving her arms and shouting incoherently. Sergeant Plumtree had just bitten in two, a huge sandwich which his missus had packed for his lunch, and he emerged from the police station with his jaws locked in brown bread and brawn. He was met by the trio of wrestlers, led by their father and followed by Crumpet, all of them masticating their own enormous rations.

"Wot the ... ?"

They all ran across the square, the removal party looking apprehensive, thinking of broken Crown Derby, Ming and Dresden. Mrs. Trott flailed them into the house indiscriminately, pushed her way through them, and led them to a room on the first floor. It might have been the doctor's own bedroom and was simply furnished in a calm, orderly way. The walls were ivory white, with here and there an engraving hanging on a nail. A double mahogany four-poster bed with a dark red quilt, a large Chippendale chest, two small period chairs, and little else. A bright room, illuminated by three sash windows, with heavy red curtains hanging from old-fashioned poles and brass rings.

The first thing the party encountered was the large antique wardrobe, which, on Mrs. Trott's instructions, the removal men had carried there and placed between the bed and the window to be properly manoeuvred into position later. The next thing was the door in the wall.

Mrs. Trott was going to have her say and explain everything before she let the rest of the group pass her. She stood in the space between the newly arrived wardrobe and the rest of the room. Her eyes were wide with fear and her jaw trembled in a spasm of terror. She pointed at the wall opposite the door by which they had just entered.

"I've been here for fifteen years and I never knew that door there would open. I thought it was blocked up."

It was an ordinary door, painted white, gone soiled, and stood open. Beyond was a black void.

"I started to arrange the furniture and I thought I'd try to shift the wardrobe. I always thought it was a fixture, but when I pushed it, it moved, and there was the door behind it."

The wardrobe itself was also of plain wood, with panelled doors. The kind of thing known as "built-in" and fixed, as a rule, for all time.

Sergeant Plumtree was getting impatient.

"Well, that's nothin' fresh. It's an old 'ouse and these places always 'ave queer hidey-holes here and there. It used to be a bank in the old days. Perhaps..."

In reply Mrs. Trott stood aside and let the party pass.

Mr. Nutt, senior, was first, and he looked in the void beyond the door, seemed unperturbed, cleared his throat, and whistled and nodded. His eldest son peeped over his shoulder, turned pale, reeled back, and had to hold the wall to keep on his feet.

Plumtree's turn next. He took out a pocket-torch and switched it on. Then he peered gingerly through the dark hole into the interior, blew through his moustache, drew himself to his full height, and raised a huge paw in a benedictive manner.

"Nothin's to be touched. Nothin'... I 'ereby take charge in the name o' the Law."

A murder was committed at Abbot's Caldicott last Friday.

The sergeant almost heaved a sigh of relief.

By the light of his torch, he could make out a small platform beyond the secret door, whence a plain wooden staircase descended into a black pit.

The body of Dr. Beharrell was sitting comfortably on the small platform, cold and stiff.

Mrs. Trott uttered a second scream and fell unconscious on the parquet, and the youngest Nutt, the giant of the family, hurried out to find the bathroom, for he was going to vomit.

Love George Bellairs? Join the Readers' Club

Get your next George Bellairs Mystery for FREE

If you sign up today, this is what you'll get:

1. A free classic Bellairs mystery, *Corpses in Enderby*;
2. Details of Bellairs' new publications and the opportunity to get copies in advance of publication; and
3. The chance to win exclusive prizes in regular competitions.

Interested? It takes less than a minute to sign up, just go to www.georgebellairs.com and your ebook will be sent to you.

Printed in Great Britain
by Amazon

11098270R00171